"When I saw you I fell in love, and you smiled because you knew."

— Arrigo Boito

PLAYLIST

- Kings & Queens – Ava Max
- Patience – Huns N' Roses
- After The Landslide – Matt Simons
- Brother (feat. Gavin DeGraw) - NEEDTOBREATHE, Gavin DeGraw
- Forever Young – Acoustic Version – Kaiak
- Iris – Natalie Taylor
- Never Enough – Loren Allred
- Wicked Game – Acoustic; Live – Stone Sour
- Pieces – Rob Thomas
- Come On Get Higher – Matt Nathanson
- Read My Mind – The Killers
- Radioactive – Live London Sessions – Imagine Dragons
- I Will Wait – Live From Annexet – Mumford & Sons
- Summer of '69 – MTV Unplugged – Bryan Adams
- Everlong – Acoustic Version – Foo Fighters

- Stay With Me – Sam Smith
- Precious Love – James Morrison

http://bit.ly/AENGPlaylist

AUTHOR'S NOTE

I've heard people say if you've met one child on the Autism Spectrum, you've met one child on the Autism Spectrum. As the mother of a twelve-year-old son on the Spectrum, I can say that this is true from personal experience. As with any child, each child with Autism has their own strengths and abilities. The character of Tommy is based on my son. He may not behave the same as a child, you know, or how you imagine a child with Autism would, but I promise you, there is a child out there incredibly similar to this character.

I hope you enjoy Always Earned, Never Given.

XO,
    Bella

1

ANNABELLE
BEFORE

I can't believe I'm here. Center stage at Lincoln Center, taking my final bow of the night, having just danced *Giselle* for a sneak preview for the ballet company's most prominent patrons. I've worked my entire life to achieve my dream of being a principal dancer, and tonight those dreams are coming true.

The strong grip on my hand by my partner, Mikael, forces me to move, as he leads me to the front of the stage for our final bow. The spotlight blinds me, and the heat of the stage lights keep my exhausted muscles warm. The bouquet of roses is heavy in my hands, their scent overpowering my senses.

I can't believe this is happening. I did it.

I achieved a dream tonight.

My smile stretches across my face, pride taking over.

As we step back, the heavy red velvet stage curtains close, and Mikael's arms wrap around me. I've known him for years. He's a good-looking man. Blonde hair, blue eyes, and a lean dancer's build all combine to create a beautiful package and a magnetic dancer. "You were incredible tonight, Annabelle." I'm lifted off my feet and spun around.

"You were wonderful tonight too. I can't believe tomorrow is opening night," I squeal as my feet touch the ground. When we turn to walk offstage, our dance master, Mr. Archer, is there waiting.

"Annabelle, I need to speak with you. Please come with me." The tiny lines around his mouth highlight his frown.

Shit. This isn't good. He must have caught the mistake in our performance.

"Arch, if you're going to give her shit for the pas de deux, it's on me, not Belle. I was a beat off. She tried to compensate." Mikael can be sweet and caring when he wants to be, but he usually wants to get in my pants as a reward.

"This does not involve you, Mikael. Annabelle, I need to speak with you." He looks pointedly at Mikael then back to me. "Alone."

When Mr. Archer walks toward my dressing room, I follow. I started out as part of the corps de ballet with him when I was seventeen. He saw something in me then and pushed me to give more than I knew was possible that year. By the time I turned eighteen, I was a demi-soloist and was promoted to soloist only a few months later. Dancing *Giselle* is my first time as a principal, and I cannot wait for my parents to see me tomorrow night. I can't wait to show them that all my work has paid off. That I did it. That it was all worth it.

When we enter my dressing room, my smile grows as I pass by my name posted on the door.

Holy shit.

I have my own dressing room.

I doubt that will ever get old.

Mr. Archer points to the chair in front of the brightly lit vanity. "Please, Annabelle, take a seat." His voice has taken on a tone I'm unfamiliar with, and suddenly, I'm feeling the fluttering of panic.

When I hesitate to sit, he gives me the look. The one that says, *"Do not argue, just do as you're told."* I gently sit down. "What's going on, Arch? I know the pas de deux was a beat off, but—"

He interrupts me, "Annabelle, I got a call during the second act. Your parents were in a car accident in Pennsylvania."

"What? When? How?" A million questions fly through my mind as the room begins to spin.

Arch walks over to me, placing an arm on my shoulder and squeezing. "Annabelle, I'm sorry to be the one to tell you this." His voice sounds distant. Fuzzy.

"Then don't." I shrug his arm off and stand up. The room seems to tilt on its axis until I lean on the vanity in front of me and lock eyes with Arch through the reflection in the mirror. "When ... when did you get the call?"

"Annabelle, you need to sit back down. I wasn't finished." He tries to grip my shoulders, but I turn away.

My hands are shaking. I try interlocking my fingers to control it.

Refusing to look at him, I raise my clasped hands in front of my face and ask again, "When did you get the call?"

"Right after the curtain went up on the second act. We didn't want to bother you with the information until the performance was over. It wouldn't have changed the outcome."

I'm a dancer. I have a pain threshold three times higher than the average person. I dance seven hours a day on my legs. They are my tools. My strength. And they just gave out beneath me.

Arch is unable to move fast enough to catch me as I fall to my knees.

I can't breathe as the sobs get caught in my throat.

He lowers himself down in front of me. "Annabelle, I'm sorry, but your parents are gone."

"Where's my brother?" I can't bring myself to look at this man yet. This man who let me dance the last hour and a half without telling me my parents were gone. Who allowed my brother to stay alone?

Who's with him? Is he scared?

I refuse to let my tears flow freely.

Not yet. No, I have things to do. I need to find Tommy.

Archer shakes his head. "They didn't mention anyone else. The hospital was looking for you. That was all I was told. Tell me what you need, and we'll get it for you."

"I need to get to Philly."

~

I didn't even go back to my apartment. Just changed into sweatpants, a long-sleeved Guns 'N' Roses t-shirt, and my Uggs and walked out the door. Ginny, the admin for the ballet company, meets me in the hall. She wraps her seventy-five-year-old arms around me and gives me her best squeeze. "Annabelle, I have a town car waiting out front for you. There are no direct flights to Philadelphia International from New York. So I've arranged to have you driven. I've also called the hospital and given them your contact information. Now, stay strong and let us know if there's anything we can do for you, honey."

Going through the motions, I limply hug Ginny back

and tap her arms to get her to let go of me. "Thank you, Ginny. I'll call when I can."

Then I'm out the front door of Lincoln Center, not knowing if I'll ever dance on this stage again.

∼

*T*wo hours later, I'm running through the front doors of the hospital in my hometown of Kroydon Hills, Pennsylvania. I spoke to a nurse during the ride from New York. My brother, Tommy, is in the pediatric ICU. He has a severe concussion, a broken arm, and cracked ribs.

Running across the old, yellowing linoleum floor, I get to the security desk and ask them where I need to go.

This hospital is like a maze. Go down the hall, make a left, take the elevator to the third floor, make another left. The steel double doors I'm greeted by are locked, and I have to press the intercom and ask to be buzzed in.

Once inside, I'm met by a kind nurse in Mickey Mouse scrubs who escorts me to Tommy's room, and for the second time tonight, I fear my knees are going to give out on me. He looks so small in the bed, wrapped tightly in a white blanket that I have no doubt will be too itchy for him when he wakes up. He has a tube coming out of his nose and more tubes attached to his uncasted arm. His beautiful green eyes are closed, and his head is shaved and bandaged up on the right side of his body. "Is he . . . Is he going to be okay?" The tears burn behind my eyes, pushing to be let free. But I absolutely refuse to allow myself to lose control now.

The nurse, who barely looks older than me, steps closer. "He will be. It looks worse than it is. We had to sedate him to calm him down, but he should be waking up soon."

I slowly move to the side of the hospital bed and tentatively run my fingers over what's left of his hair. "He has autism. Did you know that?"

He'll hate this. He'll hate this room and having so many things touching him.

"We had an idea but couldn't be sure. Ms. Hart, do you have anyone I can call for you? Any family we can have come to stay with you?"

I shake my head no, never looking away from Tommy. I didn't realize I lost my battle with my tears until I see one hit his bruised cheek. "No. We don't have any extended family. It's just us." Dad used to say it didn't matter that we didn't have a big family. As long as we had four Harts, we had more than everyone else.

All you need is heart and soul.

I look back to the nurse. "Was his dinosaur brought in with him?"

"Let me check for you. I'll be right back."

Dropping my big purse on the floor, I pull the vinyl lounge chair next to Tommy's bed and sink down into the squeaky fabric. I've spent more time with my little brother on Skype chats than any other way during his short little life. Mom found out she was pregnant the year after I moved to New York for dance school. I thought about coming home, about skipping that year and trying out again the following year, but she wouldn't let me do it. She told me we'd have holidays and summers and that New York was only a two-hour drive away. She was right, and we made the best of it and offset the rest with a ton of Skyping.

My little brother marches to the beat of his own drummer, and that drummer is a dinosaur.

When the nurse reenters the room with a plastic bag

containing Tommy's sneakers, clothes, and his stuffed *Toy Story* Rex, I breathe a sigh of relief.

I know this stuffed animal will help Tommy deal with the trauma of the day.

What I don't know is how *I'm* going to deal with it.

2

DECLAN
TWO YEARS LATER

"Could I take a selfie with you, Declan?" the pretty waitress asks as she drops the check on the table in front of me.

I lean in without touching her and smile for her selfie while my sister, Nattie, tries hard not to laugh. We're used to this. We come from this. Our mother is a retired model, and our father played professional football before he started coaching. We've had media coaching for years, and yet, it's not really something I've ever become comfortable with.

Used to it—yes. Comfortable with it—no.

When I was drafted last spring to the Philadelphia Kings, I wasn't exactly thrilled. Every football player dreams about being a first-round draft pick. Hell, most just dream of being drafted in general. But I was drafted by my own father, complicating things.

Joe Sinclair is in his second year as the head coach for the Kings. His first season didn't go so well when both his starting and backup quarterbacks suffered career-ending injuries. He needed a quarterback he could count on, so he took me.

My dad's a fucking awesome coach, but nobody thought it was a good move, me included. But you don't get to choose which team drafts you.

The first headline I saw was "Declan Sinclair Drafted By Daddy."

Every sportscaster in Philadelphia has been talking about it for months.

Will I live up to the hype?

Did my dad show the ultimate case of nepotism?

Can I help the Kings have the winning season this year that eluded them last year?

Not to mention that the owner of the team died last year while he was in bed with a very pretty twenty-five-year-old model, while his very pretty twenty-five-year-old former Olympic figure skater wife was pregnant with his eighth kid. The team has been tabloid fodder since.

The upside of being drafted to Philly is that I live in the same city as one of my siblings for the first time since I left for Notre Dame five years ago. My sister, Nattie, and I have a standing Tuesday morning breakfast date. She's a freshman at the local university, living off campus with her boyfriend, Brady, and two friends.

When the friendly waitress walks away, Nattie throws a piece of bacon at my head. "Have you heard from Cooper?" Cooper is my little brother and her twin. He's currently killing it in Navy bootcamp.

"Not since last week. You?" I pick the bacon up and put it back on her plate. Can't eat that shit during the season.

"Me either," she frowns.

My phone rings, and I groan. I'd normally ignore a call when I'm with my sister, but I can't. "It's Dad," I tell her before answering. "Hello?"

"Declan, why do you sound like that? Are you still in bed?"

Tuesdays are our only day off during the season. I may sleep a little later, but not nine in the morning late. "I'm at breakfast with Nattie, Dad. What's up?"

"Hi, Daddy," Natalie calls, smiling from across the table.

"I need you to meet me at the office today at ten."

I check my watch. "That's in thirty minutes, Dad. What's going on? Why the last-minute meeting?"

We're eight games into the season with eight more to go. We've won six of those eight games, but our back end is loaded with division rivals. The pressure is mounting, and my game is dissected second by second every day. At least the nationally televised assholes only do it during pre- and post-game shows. Last night, the local sports show spent half the program discussing whether I was worth the salary they're paying me or whether I'm a vanity project for an ambitious father. It doesn't help that one of my teammates and I have a rocky history, perfect for the tabloids, and that we lost on Sunday. I'm guessing this has something to do with the need for a meeting today.

"Nothing to be worried about. I need you to meet with the GM and me. Ten o'clock, Dec. Don't be late." He clears his throat before adding, "and bring me a coffee."

The phone clicks off, and I close my eyes. Tuesdays are sacred.

No practices.

No weightlifting.

No meetings.

Coach's rules.

I pocket my phone and finish my water. "Looks like I'm meeting with Dad."

I may not be thrilled to be meeting with my father and Max Kingston, our GM. However, I still make a pit stop at Starbucks to grab my Dad the vanilla coffee he's too embarrassed to admit he likes and a plain one for Max. I stick to water. Coffee has never been my thing.

My sister consumes enough for the whole family.

Dad's assistant is on the phone at her desk. She puts a finger up, asking me to wait a moment and then hangs up the phone.

"Good morning, Emery. I'm here to see Coach."

She looks over the tip of her black glasses up at me, smiling. "Hey there, Dec. Coach and Max are waiting for you. You can head in."

I hand her the third coffee cup from the carrier. "For you."

"Aww, Dec. Thank you. Now move it. You don't want to keep Coach and Max waiting."

"It's more like I want to get in and out, so I can enjoy my day off." I wink and cross to Dad's door. No use letting her know I'm dreading this meeting.

Emery shakes her head and purses her lips in an attempt not to not smile. "Just go in, Dec. He knows you're here."

I knock once and open the door. Dad and Max are laughing at something when I enter but stop abruptly to look at me. Dad clears his throat. "Thanks for coming in today, Dec."

I hand him his coffee and offer the other to Max, who raises his eyebrows as if to say, "*For me?*"

"Well, it's not mine. I don't drink that shit." I hold it out until he takes it from me.

Max laughs. He's a good guy and the youngest GM in the league. His family has owned the Kings for over fifty years. When his father died last year, ownership of the team was left to his siblings and him. He took me out to dinner, when I first flew in for rookie camp in the spring. We had a lot more in common than either of us expected. I don't think either of us was looking for a new friendship to develop, just a GM–quarterback understanding, but now, I'd call him a friend. He and his brother Becket, the in-house counsel for the organization, have been great since I moved to the city.

I don't think it hurts that we're winning games either.

"Alright, Declan. Have a seat." Dad nods toward the chairs on the other side of his massive mahogany desk as he takes the seat behind it. He looks to Max, who's standing by the window overlooking the stadium.

Max moves to lean against Dad's desk, facing me. "Listen, Dec. You're already aware that you're our franchise quarterback. I told you when we brought you on board that this team is being built around you, and you have our full support. I think your contract backs that up. It's been a hell of a season so far. That being said, I know you like to keep your private life private, but . . ." He trails off, giving me time to process the blow that's about to come.

My spine straightens as a dull ache begins to form at the base of my skull.

Max leans back, gripping the desk behind him. "Look, part of being a franchise player is being the face of the franchise. I know you got the 'Stay in line and don't get any bad press' lecture your first week in rookie camp, but we need you to start getting some good press. They're still hammering the nepotism thing home. They're still bringing up the hot-head shit from your first Heisman run. They've been waiting to catch a glimpse of you and Curt

Kenny in some kind of altercation and haven't stopped talking about your issues with each other while you were both at Notre Dame. We need to start to counteract all that. If they aren't talking about you, they're talking about my father's death and the mess he left. I'm doing my part to clean that up, and now it's your turn. We aren't giving them anything else to talk about, and that needs to change."

I start to tap my thumb against my thigh. "We've won six games and lost two. Why the hell can't they talk about that? I did the fishbowl thing with the first Heisman run. Didn't work out too well for me. I avoid it on purpose now. I want them to be focused on my game, not where I go to dinner."

My dad leans forward and steeples his hands on his desk. "Declan, I wish this were debatable, but it's not. Part of proving your worth to this team is how you appear in the media. You need to let them get to know you. Give them something else to focus on. You don't have a choice."

Max pulls his phone from his pocket and swipes through a few screens. "My sister, Scarlet, can meet with you today."

The throbbing in my head intensifies at the thought of meeting with his sister, aka the Ice Queen. "Why am I meeting with your sister?"

Max glances at me, not looking amused. "She's the head of PR, Declan. She's going to go over everything we need in detail. But it starts this weekend. The team has purchased a table for Senator Cabot's fundraiser at the Union League. It's this Saturday night. We need you to attend."

Dad decides he needs to pile on to this shit sandwich of a conversation. "And you need to bring a date."

I take a deep breath in and slowly exhale through my nose in an attempt to contain the annoyance bubbling below the surface. "I don't have a date. I haven't exactly made time for a woman in my life since I got to town."

Dad places both palms flat on his desk as he leans forward. "Find a date, Declan. Preferably one you don't have to pay. But if you do, get her to sign an NDA first."

I bite my damn tongue and remind myself that I'm not talking to my father but to my coach. "Yes, Coach. Meeting with Scarlet and a fundraiser at the Union League Saturday night. Got it." I stand, asking Max, "When am I meeting Scarlet?"

He checks his phone, types something quickly, then looks up. "She's in her office now. She says to come up as soon as you're done here."

I nod, then turn to say goodbye to my father, who at least has the decency to look like he feels bad. He knows I like to keep my personal life private. The press was all over me during my first run at the Heisman, and it was a nightmare. I was labeled a hothead because of a fight I got into with a guy who now plays tight end for the Kings. "Declan, you were a first-round draft pick. You had to know you wouldn't be able to fly under the radar for long. Time's up."

Shoving my hands into my pockets, I force my feet to stay still while my father continues. "Quite frankly, you're lucky we gave you until now before we asked more from you. We wanted to give you time to find your bearings on the team. You've got Max to thank for that. I was ready to start counter-attacking the narrative months ago."

As calmly as I can, I push, "Thank you," from my lips and wait to be dismissed.

Lucky for me, his phone rings just then. Max turns to me as Dad sits back down. "Guess we're done here." We both head for the door. "Don't let Scarlet intimidate you. She's a bit of a ballbuster."

"Yeah? Does she want to go to the Union League with me Saturday night?" I shove my hands in my jeans as we walk along the hallway.

"Nice try. She's already going. My family goes each year. Before my father died last year, he was a huge supporter of local politics. It's not that bad, Declan. We just need a few photo ops. An in-depth interview. Something to get the press to stop talking about the fact your father drafted you and my father died fucking a wannabe celebrity while his pregnant wife, who happens to be younger than most of my siblings, was sitting at home." Max pinches the bridge of his nose. "Drafting you was the right move. You were the best quarterback. But we've got to change the damn narrative now."

We take the elevator up to the next floor. When the doors open, Max grins. "This is your stop. See ya Saturday."

∼

An hour later, I've lost the fight with the tension headache that's been building all morning, and I'm ready for this meeting to be over.

"I'll have an outline of everything we discussed sent over to you today, Dec. Take a deep breath. My team will get you through this."

Scarlet reaches out and grips my hand with a stronger handshake than most men.

"Thanks, Scarlet. I appreciate your help. See you later."

I wait until I get into my truck to pull my phone out of my pocket and call my sister. She answers after one ring.

"Hey, hey, big brother. Miss me already?" she chuckles.

"Not much. What are you up to, kid?"

I hear paper moving in the background. "I'm just

sketching something I'm working on for my art class. What's up?"

Looking out over the mostly empty parking lot of the stadium, I breathe deeply before answering. "I need a favor."

"Anything for you. You know that." We'll see if she still feels that way after she hears the favor.

"I need you to give me Annabelle's phone number." There. That wasn't so hard.

Nattie squeals into the phone like she did when Mom gave her backstage passes to see One Direction a few years ago. "It's about damn time, Dec! Took you long enough." Annabelle owns the dance studio where Nat teaches. She's a few years older than Nattie, but Annabelle and her brother Tommy are close with Nattie and her friends, and my dad treats them like family.

"Cool it, kid. I just need her number to ask her for a favor. No need for the excitement." Even as I tell her that, I know it's a lie. This girl has made my head spin every time I've seen her since the day last spring when I landed in Philly. My brother, Cooper, picked me up at the airport and drove me to Dad's house. Cooper, Nattie, and their friends were barbecuing in the back yard, and there, on a teak chaise lounge, sat Annabelle Hart. Light purple plaid bikini, caramel-colored hair held back with a matching purple headband, emerald-green eyes, and the prettiest smile I'd ever seen.

I hear Nattie pout through the phone. "Whatever. You can lie to yourself if you want, but I don't buy it. What's the favor?"

"Nat." I grind my teeth. I've kept my cool throughout this shit show of a day. I'm not about to lose it on my sister, no matter how close I am right now.

"Nope. Not getting it unless you spill the deets. What's the favor, Dec?"

I close my eyes and rest my head against the headrest. "I'm being forced to go to an event this weekend and was informed that I need a media-appropriate date. I don't know anyone in this town. I thought maybe Annabelle would do me a solid and go with me."

Hands clapping echo through the line. "Perfect. Okay then. I'll text you her number." I hear a door shut, and what sounds like her hand covering the phone before whispered words are exchanged and . . . What the hell? Was that a moan?

"Nattie . . ." I wait for her to answer.

Nothing.

Speaking louder this time, I try again, "Natalie!"

"Oops. Sorry, Dec. Brady just got home. I've got to go. I'll text you later." The call ends, and I try not to think about what would have had my sister making that noise.

After a quick glance down at the card Scarlet gave me, I'm plugging an address into the GPS.

I guess it's time to get a tux.

3

ANNABELLE

The whirring sound and strong scent of coffee beans being ground in the coffee maker I set last night wakes me up moments before the chime of my alarm clock does. It was a full moon last night. That always means a rough morning the next day in our house. One of the many things no one ever warned me about when I became my brother's guardian was that the full moon can affect people's sleep cycle, Tommy's in particular. I thought maybe he'd outgrow it, but at ten years old, it doesn't look like that's happening any time soon. My little werewolf was up half the night last night, and while he never lacks energy, I'm going to be dragging ass today.

I stumble blindly into the bathroom and make the mistake of looking in the mirror. The dark circles under my eyes should at least warn people to not mess with me. Reaching into the shower, I turn the water to scalding before stepping under the hot spray and hanging my head.

Lathering shampoo into my hair, my mind begins to drift.

Always Earned, Never Given

Sometimes, I wonder what my life would have been like...

It's been two years since I came home to Philadelphia.

Two years of being a sister and a mother to my little brother.

Two years of creating a new life for us.

Two years ago today...

Tommy doesn't realize what today is. His concept of dates is questionable.

We do a lot of countdown calendars in our house.

Countdowns to Christmas or birthdays.

Weekly countdowns until special football games or fun outings and adventures we're looking forward to.

He talks about our parents a lot less now than he did in those early days after the accident. Today, I'm a little jealous of his ability to not remember dates. My shoulders shake as I lose my battle with my emotions. My tears are washed away by the hot water beating down on my face. This is my safe space, the only place I ever let myself cry.

I would never want Tommy to see or hear my weakness.

He deserves so much more.

But damn, some days still suck.

Twenty minutes later, I've successfully compartmentalized. "Come on, munchkin. We've got to get moving or we're going to be late for school." I place his peanut butter toast on the counter, hoping we've got time for him to eat it in the kitchen and not the car.

The sound of heavy footsteps is slightly muffled by the thick carpeting my mother had installed down the center of the staircase. When my parents died, the mortgage on this house had been paid off. Living here gives me one bill I don't have to worry about and keeps Tommy in a familiar place. "I'm coming, Belles. I had to get Rex."

"Make sure you hold on to the banister!" I yell up to him. His body may be growing by the day, but his coordination is not.

His chubby face pops into the kitchen moments later. A *Toy Story* backpack embroidered with his name is on one shoulder and his stuffed dinosaur, Rex, is in his arms. Wavy brown hair sits in a mess on top of his head, and his deeply dimpled smile is contagious.

He plunks himself down at the kitchen table before happily announcing, "I'm hungry, Belles. Pancakes today?"

Lack of sleep doesn't affect this kid the way it does me. I place the paper plate with two pieces of toast smothered in peanut butter and sliced banana onto the table next to a glass of milk. "Nope. No time for pancakes today. I promise we'll have some this weekend."

I ruffle his damp hair before checking my giant canvas tote bag to make sure I have everything I need for my day in there. I always carry a change of clothes for Tommy in a dinosaur bag that fits into the side pocket. I have a black waterproof bag inside my big bag with trail mix and goldfish crackers inside, along with two bottles of water and two juice boxes. My ballet essentials bags go inside my tote too, carrying things like extra toe pads, dividers, tape, water spray, a brush, barrettes, bobby pins, rubber bands, a sewing kit, and extra pink ribbons for pointe shoes. My spare chargers and cords slip into the other side pocket, and I'm ready to go. My friends call it my "Mary Poppins bag" because I basically carry my entire life around in this thing. They swear one day, penguins will pop out of it.

Marie Kondo's got nothing on me.

I click the lid on my travel coffee mug into place and grab the keys to my car.

"Alright, you ready to rock and roll?" I ask my brother.

"Ready." Tommy stands and reaches for his coat. He stops and smiles at me.

I kiss the top of his head. "Love you, munchkin."

~

After I drop Tommy off at school, I head to Hart & Soul, the dance studio I opened when I moved home. My favorite acoustic Guns N' Roses song is blasting through my speakers, and I'm trying to sing along in an attempt to not let myself sink into the cloud of self-pity that's surrounding me today. I was at the top of my profession two years ago. Everything I had worked for had brought me to that moment. But instead of celebrating it, it's ingrained in me as the worst moment of my life.

Not a day goes by that I don't wish things were different. I'd have given it all up for another day with my parents.

Dad and I shared a love of rock music. He played drums in a band all through high school and college. He pushed it to the side when he joined the state troopers but made sure it was our thing. We'd listen to music together for hours, picking cool versions of different songs that I could use for ballet.

You'd be surprised how amazing an acoustic version of a rock song can be for a ballet or lyrical dance.

Just as Axel Rose starts singing about needing a little patience, my phone rings through the Bluetooth in my car. I click the button on my steering wheel. "Hello?"

"Annabelle, hey." There's a pause. "It's Declan Sinclair."

I'd know that voice anywhere. That voice has no idea that the body it belongs to stars in my favorite fantasies.

"Hi, Declan," I answer, a little anxious about what he might want.

There's another pause before he speaks again, "Is this a bad time?"

"No," I answer quickly, trying to pull myself together. "I'm just heading into the dance studio. Is everything okay?"

"I actually have a favor to ask. I'm sorry to bother you with this, but I have to go to a fundraiser for a local senator Saturday night. The team sprung it on me yesterday and then told me I needed to bring a date. I don't know anyone in the city, and they don't really want me calling an escort service," he rambles.

You've got to be kidding. I stop him. "Declan, can I give you a little piece of advice on asking a girl out on a date, even if it's just a friend you need a favor from?"

"Annabelle, I didn't mean—"

I cut him off. "Do. Not. Tell her she is one step above a hooker." I did not get enough sleep to deal with this today.

"I'm sorry, Belle. That came out wrong," Declan groans. Frustration and I think embarrassment lace his tone.

I take pity on him. "I'll need to see if I can get one of the girls to stay with my brother."

"You mean you'll go?" he asks, hope lacing his sexy voice.

I pull into the small parking lot behind Hart & Soul and throw my car in park. "If," I emphasize the word, "I can get someone to watch Tommy, I'll go. Who's the Senator?"

"I think they said it's Senator Cabot."

"You do realize that's Sabrina's dad, right? And that she's dating your future stepbrother slash sister's roommate. I think they'll be there too." I feel better for a hot minute until I start to think through the implications of leaving Tommy for an entire night. Someone else would have to put him to bed, which could complicate things.

I lift my hot tumbler of coffee to my mouth and blow on

it. "Seriously though, Dec, I've never left Tommy with someone else needing to put him to bed before. I don't know how this is going to go, and I may have to leave a few minutes in if I get a call."

The more I start to think this through, the more this night sounds like a disaster waiting to happen.

"Annabelle, if we can have a few pictures taken of us as we walk in, I'm pretty sure I'll have satisfied the GM and my dad. I'll owe you one. Let me know if you want me to talk to Nat for you." The relief in his voice echoes throughout the speakers of my car.

"Thanks, but she'll be at the studio tonight to teach a few classes. I'll talk to her then. What's the dress code?"

There's another long silence.

"Hello . . . Declan? Are you still there?"

"Yeah, shit. I'm trying to find the email that's got the details, and the trainer is calling my name. Can I call you back? Or I can text you the info later today."

"Yeah. Go. I'll call Sabrina."

"Thanks, Belle. We'll talk later." The call ends, and I slam my door shut, momentarily shaken. He called me Belle . . . and I liked it. Only my closest friends call me Belle. What the hell is wrong with me? I do not have time to catch feelings for the uber gorgeous Declan Sinclair. It doesn't matter how his velvety smooth voice affects me, or what my name sounds like on his lips. My mind starts to wander to what those lips would feel like on my skin, and that same skin warms at the thought.

When I step into the studio, I turn on the lights and shake myself out of my daydream.

Tommy and the studio.

That's all I've got room for in my life.

4

ANNABELLE

I love dancing. I love all types of dancing.

I love the way the perfect leap in a ballet can bring a tear to your eye.

I love to hear the perfectly tinny sound ten people tapping in sync can make.

I love to feel the beautiful sensuality of a burlesque routine.

I love to see the power and control in a seductive lap dance.

I love it all.

I've even learned to love teaching. Not as much as performing, but there's something rewarding about watching students I've taught dance a routine I've choreographed. Although a bigger piece of me than I'm willing to admit feels like it died with my parents when I had to give up my first dream, I'm learning to embrace my new one. Giving up the dream was better than trying to chase down the magic I was lucky enough to capture once. At least I can say I went out on top.

I needed to make a choice, and I chose a new dream.

A different dream I could learn to love.

A dream that keeps my brother safe.

A dream that gave birth to Hart & Soul Academy of Dance.

One day, maybe I'll capture that magic again. But I'm not holding my breath.

What doesn't feel magical is bookkeeping. Balancing a checkbook sucks, and taxes are the devil. They need to be done, but I hate them. One of these days, I'll spring for an office manager or bookkeeper, but unfortunately for me, that day is not today.

The studio is doing well enough, but I'm still pinching every penny. My parents had life insurance policies, but they barely covered their funerals. There's no mortgage on the house we live in, which gives me a little breathing room, but the taxes are expensive. There's a trust for my brother, but it covers his private school and not much else. Unfortunately, I'm constantly trying to come up with creative accounting to cover his social skills classes, his ABA therapy, and any of his extra activities.

All this means I'll be pinching my pennies for a little while longer.

The bells over the front door chime, letting me know someone has just entered the building. A quick glance at the security screen hanging on the wall shows me it's Nattie walking through the studio. I've got another twenty minutes before our toddlers' ballet class starts. Parents should be bringing their baby ballerinas in shortly. But for now, we're completely alone.

"Natalie Grace Sinclair," I yell through the open office door. "Get your butt back here. I've got a bone to pick with you."

The young woman who walks through my door has

grown so much in the year that I've known her. She was eighteen when she stopped in my studio last fall, searching for something. I don't think even she was sure what that something was. Maybe it was a way back to the love she used to have for ballet. Maybe it was to figure out who she wanted to be. She found part of what she was searching for in my studio. But she wasn't the only one who got something out of our relationship. She also provided me with something I didn't know I desperately needed. She brought Tommy and me into her circle of friends, giving me a closer group of friends than I'd ever had in my life. She made us part of her family. They treat us like one of their own, and I'll love her forever for giving us that.

Today, however, I'm going to kick her little ass.

Metaphorically speaking.

After I'd had a little time to process my phone call with Declan, I called Sabrina to discuss the dress code for the fundraiser and Nat was with her.

So, Nattie's probably got an idea of what's coming.

The tiny blonde pops her head in my door. She hates being compared to Tinker Bell, but she's seriously only five foot two on a good day and constantly surrounded by football giants, making her appear even tinier. With her blonde hair piled high in her ballet bun and her leotard and skirt on, she's the picture of a mischievous fairy. Luckily for me, I've got our Tink beat by about five inches, but she's got me beat by a solid cup size.

You win some, you lose some.

"What's got your panties in a twist, Belles?"

I close my MacBook and give her my best evil queen glare. "Nattie, what the hell? You didn't think to tell me you gave Declan my number? Or, I don't know, . . . give me some kind of warning that he was going to call?"

She walks into my office and throws her dance bag on the dove gray couch that sits against the wall before dropping dramatically down next to it. "What's the big deal? It's just Declan. I was supposed to text it to him yesterday, but Brady came home, and it . . ." She glances away, a blush tinging her cheeks.

"Nattie . . . focus. I'm trying to yell at you."

"Yeah, well, you're doing a crap job of it." She hops up off the couch like a jumping bean and crosses to the door. "I've got to stretch before the baby ballerinas get here. What time is Tommy getting dropped off from social skills? Brady said he'd stop by to do his homework with him."

And how am I supposed to be mad at her after that? "He should be here within the hour. Speaking of . . . Any chance you want to watch Tommy for me Saturday night?"

"Of course. After your call with Sabrina, Brady and I were talking about it, and I want Tommy to spend the night at our house. We're gonna give him one hell of a sleepover."

Tommy has never spent the night at someone else's house before. At least not since I've moved home. But he loves Nat and Brady.

Shit.

Sometimes I hate adulting.

Making decisions sucks.

Nattie smiles and spins through the door and down the hall before I even have a chance to respond.

My phone vibrates on my desk as the bell over the door jingles again. Picking it up, I see a group text from my girls, Nattie included.

Group Chat:

Nattie: Looks like Belles & Declan will be joining Brina and Murph at the fundraiser!
Chloe: Belles has a date with Declan? How come I'm just hearing about this?
Annabelle: Because it only happened today. And it's not a date. Just a favor.
Nattie: You keep telling yourself that.
Sabrina: What are you wearing?
Annabelle: Not sure yet. I've got a few options.
Nattie: Let's meet at your house tomorrow night and pick!
Chloe: Perfect!
Sabrina: Sounds good to me!
Annabelle: Who said you guys get a say?
Nattie: I do. You need to rock my big brother's world!
Annabelle: It. Is. Not. A. Date.
Nattie: Sure, it's not.

I give up and throw my phone face down on my desk. Truth is, I'd love for it to be a real date. But that's just not in the cards for me. My brother is my top priority with the studio coming a distant, but necessary, second. And I pass out most nights as soon as I put Tommy to bed. That just screams you should be dating a professional football player, doesn't it? I drop my head in my hands, as shame washes over me for the pity party I'm throwing myself.

Fuck today.

Time to get over it.

I plaster a smile on my face and make my way out to the front of the studio to greet the parents. Once I'm seated behind the front desk, I chitchat with most of the moms and dads as they take the coats off their little ones and kiss their cheeks. Some talk longer than others. Some write checks for their monthly bill. Others want to talk about their little ones and how much they enjoy class. Most move through quickly.

Hart & Soul has two dance studios, one smaller and one bigger. I have a room in front of the bigger studio we call the fishbowl. It has glass walls so parents can watch without interrupting class. The desk I'm currently sitting at is in front of that room, so most are just passing through.

Noah Monroe is the exception to this rule. He was a few years ahead of me when we were in school, but I didn't know him as a kid because I moved to New York to attend a ballet school before high school. He's classically handsome, and he knows it. His daughter is a beautiful little blondie with big blue eyes that looks just like her daddy and not at all like her former prom queen momma. Apparently, Noah and his high school sweetheart dated throughout college and got married right after graduation. They had Olivia a few months later and got divorced a year after that. He likes to talk to me during the lesson instead of watching his daughter.

Noah walks over to me, carrying two cups of coffee and hands me my favorite pumpkin spice. I can't help it, I'm a basic bitch when it comes to my coffee. I love all things pumpkin spice this time of year. Thanking him, I take a sip and smile as the sweet, tasty goodness hits my tongue. Noah lets his eyes roam over me, and I quirk an eyebrow at him. He's made no attempt to hide that he'd like to take me out on a date. And I've let him know more than once that I don't have time for any complications in my life.

Tommy and the studio are it.

"Noah, you're an angel sent from God above. I spent my afternoon up to my eyeballs in taxes and desperately needed this."

He smiles at me, and I swear, the panties melt right off

girls three states away because that smile is so damn potent. "I'm happy to give you anything you desperately need, Annabelle. All you have to do is say the word." Noah winks like the cocky SOB he is.

I shake my head from side to side and roll my eyes for good measure. "Yes. You've mentioned that before. I appreciate the offer and will definitely let you know if I get desperate enough."

"When, Annabelle. You make sure to let me know *when*, not if." He looks over his coffee cup and cocks his brow.

The bell above the door jingles again, only this time when I look up, Tommy's walking in, and he's not alone. Nattie's boyfriend, Brady, is on one side of him, and Declan Sinclair is on his other.

What the hell is Declan doing in my studio?

Tommy is talking Declan's ear off, and Dec is giving him his full attention. Hopefully, my little brother isn't telling him how to improve his game this week. Although it wouldn't be the first time. Tommy is a walking, talking encyclopedia of football facts and stats, not to mention a little sponge. If it gets said in front of the kid, it's getting repeated.

Coach Sinclair learned that the hard way.

If Declan feels the stares of every man and woman currently in the fishbowl, he isn't letting it interrupt his conversation with my brother.

The parents start to whisper. I'm sure some know who he is, while others just know that the most beautiful man they've ever seen has just walked into the studio.

Thick chocolate-brown hair that's a little too long frames Declan's strong, scruff-covered jaw, and eyes so blue they're almost navy are currently looking at Tommy. He always appears to be super serious, but if I've learned anything from Brady Ryan in the time I've known him, it's that being the starting quarterback for a football team means you walk around with added pressures on your shoulders.

Something I can commiserate with.

Noah looks from me to them and then moves closer to my desk. I'm not sure if he thinks he's being protective or staking his claim. Neither works for me.

I stand up and ruffle Tommy's hair. "Hey, munchkin. How was your Minecraft club? Did you have fun?"

He shrugs me off, drops his book bag to the floor, and plops down in my chair before announcing, "I'm hungry."

Brady and Declan laugh.

This is my life.

I'm always ready for his appetite, and my Mary Poppins bag is stocked. "I'll grab your snack from my office and be back out in a minute, okay?"

Tommy already has his folder out of his book bag and is spreading his homework worksheets out on my desk with Brady moving behind him. He typically stops by on the nights Nattie is teaching and helps Tommy with his homework. It's like his very own Big Brother program.

A sexy throat clears behind me. "Annabelle." I turn back to Declan. "Can we talk?"

Noah moves slightly, and I glance between the two men. "Declan, this is Noah. His daughter is in the class your sister is teaching right now."

Declan shakes Noah's hand and focuses those indigo eyes back on me. "You want to follow me back to my office?" Dec nods and moves next to me. I turn back and wave to Noah. "See you next week." Then I lead Declan down the hall and into my office, closing the door behind me.

My office isn't huge, but I never considered it small before I had this six-foot-six, massive man taking up all the space and oxygen inside it. I can't help the laugh that bubbles up my throat. "I think you just sent the moms out there into heat, Dec."

"What?" He looks utterly confused and so fucking sexy in dark blue jeans and a white long-sleeved Henley tee that's hugging his muscles just enough to make a good girl think dirty thoughts.

I swear one of his biceps is bigger than my thigh. Who knew big, bulky athletes would be my weakness after being attracted to lean dancers my whole life? Thinking about what those massive hands would feel like on my body has me making a mental note to stop and get more batteries tonight.

I really should invest in a rechargeable vibrator . . . or maybe two.

"Nothing. Forget it. You wanted to talk?" I sit down, grab a water bottle and a juice box out of my bag and offer him both. Declan takes the water with a laugh. Then I'm treated to watching the column of his throat work while he drinks.

It's been far too long since I've had an orgasm I didn't give myself if I'm reacting this way to a man drinking water.

Sure, he's a sexy man, but he's just a man.

"Yeah. I wanted to thank you for agreeing to go with me this weekend. Did you get the email I forwarded you earlier?"

I nod. "Yup."

He puts the bottle of water down on my desk and walks around to where I'm sitting. Bracing himself on the edge of the desk, he leans in facing me. So much for getting some space. "Did Nattie agree to watch Tommy for you?"

"Yes." My voice comes out annoyingly breathy. "She wants him to sleep over at their house. I'm not sure though. Tommy hasn't spent a night away from me since . . . Well . . . since I moved home. It makes me a little nervous."

He thinks about that for a moment. "Well, you could always ask Nattie to watch him at your house."

I'm not sure who's going to have a harder time being apart that night, me or Tommy. "I know, but I don't want to deny him something he might enjoy. I'm just . . . Well, I guess I'm just freaking out a little bit. Parenting sucks. It's just so easy to second-guess yourself."

"Jesus, Belle, I'm sorry. I didn't mean to put you in an uncomfortable position."

Dear God, the positions I would like this man to put me in. "No, you didn't. If I don't force the two of us to try new things, Tommy and I would just live in our routine forever. He might really enjoy himself. And if he doesn't, just be warned that we might need to make a hasty exit."

"Like I told you earlier, that's fine with me. Having you there might be the only thing that makes the night bearable." His leg brushes against my tights, sending an electric current crackling through my skin.

I should move my leg away. But I just don't want to. "Okay, you just redeemed yourself for saying I was one step above an escort." I begrudgingly adjust myself so our bodies are no longer touching, no longer able to handle the way every single nerve feels like a live wire.

Why is this particular man so damn potent?

I absolutely hate the way I react to Declan. It's been like this since the very first time I watched him walk into his father's backyard last summer.

If I wanted a relationship, he'd be at the top of the list. Hell, he'd be the entire list. But what am I supposed to take time away from in order to date? The studio that's barely keeping its head above water? My brother, who needs me to be a mother and a father? And what if we try it and it goes bad? Do I risk losing the only friends we have because they're his family?

But what if...

What if he's worth it?

Today, of all days, I'm reminded of how short life is.

How good the reward can be if you take the risk.

I'm just not sure Declan Sinclair is a risk I can afford to take.

5

DECLAN

Annabelle graces me with one of those smiles that has a dimple popping deep in both of her cheeks before she tries to push my leg away from her on a laugh. It's cute she thinks she can move me. This woman might possibly weigh a hundred and twenty pounds soaking wet. Thinking about Annabelle soaking wet has me sucking in my breath while trying to keep my face neutral as I imagine her in front of me...

In the shower.

On her knees.

I stand up and shove my hands in my pockets so she doesn't notice the way my cock is now straining painfully against the zipper of my jeans. "I promise you, Belle, I don't think you're one step above a call girl." Reaching down, I tuck a lock of her warm caramel-brown hair behind her ear and whisper, "You're at least two or three steps above that."

I laugh and allow her to think she's successfully pushed me away this time.

"Get the hell out of here, Sinclair, before I change my

mind and find you an escort service for this weekend." There go those damn dimples again.

I don't know why I do what I do next.

I don't know what made me think it was a good move.

I lean down to say goodbye, to kiss her cheek. But Annabelle stands at the same time as I lean in, and my lips graze hers before she jumps back like she's just been electrocuted. Those long lashes of hers flutter before she starts laughing.

Hysterically.

I don't know whether to be pissed that she thinks this is funny or grateful that she's not pissed. Instinct has me raising both hands in an *I surrender* motion as I back up.

Her fingers quickly touch her lips before she smiles, laughs, and then points toward the door. "Out. Now, Sinclair. Before I make sure it's an ugly escort."

I salute her as I back out through the door, trying to hold my smile back. "See ya Saturday, Belle."

Walking back out through the studio, I stop at the desk to say goodbye to Tommy and Brady. Tommy has his headphones on while he works on a worksheet while Brady leans against the wall behind him. Reaching out, I grip his shoulder. "Hey, man. I'm outta here. I've got tape to watch tonight."

The noise level around me explodes as a room full of tiny girls dressed in pink run excitedly into the waiting room, looking for their parents. I glance back over to Brady and know, based on the expression on his face, that my sister must have walked through the door.

I didn't love finding out that my sister was involved with such a high-profile quarterback, but I was wrong to prejudge the guy. He may be the starting quarterback for

Kroydon University, but he's not the same guy I was during my freshman year at Notre Dame.

I had it thrown at me from more girls and guys than I could count the minute I set foot on campus.

I tried to do the serious girlfriend thing that year, but it blew up in my face. Leighton was the first and only girl I dated seriously in college. I liked her, but I wasn't in love with her. She professed her love for me a few weeks after we started dating. I like to think I tried, but I was an immature college freshman with the world at my feet and the weight of it on my shoulders. I didn't like having a nagging girlfriend distracting me from football. I wasn't ready to try to balance football with anything else.

I could have handled it better.

At least I learned from my mistakes.

I no longer expect Brady Ryan to make those same mistakes I did. After getting to know him this summer, I realized he's head over heels in love with my sister. As long as he keeps her happy, I guess he'll get to live another day.

After a few minutes, Nattie comes dancing over to us.

She's literally dancing instead of walking.

She's always been a little extra.

"Dec! I didn't know you were stopping by today." She leans in and hugs my waist. Cooper and I got all the height in the Sinclair family. Poor Nat is only five-foot-two. She used to think she'd be tall like our supermodel mother. Instead, she stopped growing in the eighth grade.

"Hey, kid. If you'd bother to check your messages once in a while, you'd know I was stopping by. I texted earlier." No way she didn't see it. My sister is attached to her phone.

Annabelle walks down the hall, moving next to Tommy. "Oh, she checks her messages even when she isn't supposed to have her phone on her." Belle raises her brow. "Isn't that right, Nattie?"

Nat looks from Belle to me and then decides it's time to get the hell out of the firing zone. She leans up on her toes and plants a kiss on my cheek. "Good talk. See ya soon." She grabs Brady's hand then pulls him behind her down the hall.

Laughter echoes behind the two of them.

Noah, that guy from earlier, walks over, holding the hand of a tiny blonde ballerina. He looks from me to Belle then back to me again. Guess I'm supposed to take the hint. I tap the desk, grabbing Tommy's attention. "See ya, Tommy."

This kid smiles, looking off to the side, then yells, "Bye, Dec," about ten decibels above typical levels. Having never taken his headphones off, he has no idea just how loud he is.

I smile one more time at Belle. "See ya Saturday, Belle." Yup. Just like I thought, douchey dude doesn't look happy.

Oh fucking well.

Sucks to be him.

I've been thinking about this woman for months. I might not be thrilled with what brought this date about, but it's a date I've wanted since I moved to this town. And this guy isn't gonna get his chance if I have anything to say about it.

~

I'm halfway home when my cell phone rings. There's no Bluetooth in my truck, and I like it that way. One of the first things I did when I moved to town was buy my baby. It's a metallic blue and white 1968 Ford Bronco. She's been restored to mint condition, and I fucking love it. She's my baby. So instead of having Bluetooth installed, my phone sits in its holder, and I hit the speaker button.

I'm greeted by the voice of my agent, Hunter. He and I played ball for Notre Dame my freshman year. Hunt was a senior who was getting ready for law school. He was a cool guy who knew exactly what he wanted—to be a sports agent. By the time I was getting ready for the draft, Hunter was knocking on my door with one of the partners of the firm he was interning with. I agreed to sign with them if Hunt was my guy. I trust him, and that's not something that comes easily for me.

"Jesus Christ, Dec. Are you seriously not gonna get Bluetooth in that ancient fucking truck? The connection sounds like shit before you even speak."

"Don't talk about my baby like that, asshole. What's up?" I turn into the parking garage of my condo, pulling into my spot.

"Okay. Straight to it. I like it. Did you find a date for Saturday? If not, I got a few contacts set up for some Instagram influencers. Shouldn't be too hard to get one lined up. We're gonna need an NDA signed, though, so we've got to get the jump on it now."

"I'm good, man." I see no point in letting him go on. "I'm not a complete idiot. I can get my own date."

Hunter hesitates. "Okay, I can have the NDA couriered over tomorrow..."

"No need. She's a good friend of the family. I'm not having her sign an NDA."

Hunt's quick to say, "I don't know if that's a good idea."

"Seriously, it's fine. If I have to go to this dog and pony show, Annabelle is the only date I want. No NDA." I pop my earbuds in and hop out of the truck.

I hear a deep sigh from Hunt's end of the line. "Alright. Did you look at the sponsor information I had sent over? Nike's not going to wait forever, Dec." I hear paper shuffling. "Neither is Tag Heuer. Seriously, Dec, this is how you pad your retirement fund. I need answers."

"Yeah, man. I hear you. Listen, I'm about to walk into the elevator. I'll call you tomorrow."

"Do not hang up on me, Declan. I'll be in the city tomorrow, and we're meeting in the afternoon. Four o'clock. Don't forget."

"Yeah, yeah. I hear ya." I walk into my silent condo, kick my shoes off by the front door, and head to the kitchen to throw one of my premade meals into the microwave. I stayed with my dad for a few weeks after moving to Philadelphia last summer. After four years of basically being on my own, I needed my own space. It only took a week for my realtor to find me a fully furnished condo in Center City Philly with a view of the riverfront and security. I'm renting for now. I'm a little hesitant to buy. I need to see how this season goes first.

I drop my keys and wallet on my kitchen counter and make my way to my bedroom to get changed into sweats before I eat and look through the folder sitting on my table. I know these companies want answers. I just don't know if the money is worth the privacy I'll have to give up.

I've always held my privacy close. I've seen what the media can do to a person's life. Perception means more than truth.

Everybody wants me to start to put myself out there, and all I want to do is play football.

～

Group Chat:

Sabrina: What time are we meeting at your house tonight, Belles?
Nattie: Want me to bring pizza?
Chloe: Meat lovers, please.
Nattie: I heard you're starting to like sausage more. Huh, Chloe?
Chloe: Shut the fuck up, Nat!
Sabrina: Plain cheese for me.
Annabelle: You know I'm capable of dressing myself, right???
Nattie: You need to look HAWT.
Sabrina: Please don't spell it like that. Just . . . no.
Chloe: Bahahaha
Annabelle: Fine. Tommy needs a plain cheese pizza and a side of cheese fries.
Nattie: And . . .
Annabelle: And be here at 6pm.
Nattie: There. Now was that so painful?
Annabelle: I'm gonna show you painful later, Natalie!
Nattie: You know you love me.
Annabelle: You're lucky I love you!
Annabelle: XOXO See you soon.

6

ANNABELLE

Thursday afternoons are the closest thing I get to "me time" all week. The studio closes at noon, and I don't have to pick Tommy up from school until three. That's three whole hours to myself. Granted, I usually spend them grocery shopping and cleaning up around the house. Still, I didn't realize how much I enjoyed having a few minutes to myself until they started to come fewer and further between.

The girls are coming over tonight to help me pick out a dress for Sabrina's dad's fundraiser this weekend, and I may never admit it to them, but I'm excited about it. It's been a while since we've had a girl's night and even longer since I've put on one of the many pretty dresses hanging in my closet. When I was dancing in New York, I needed to get dressed up for formal functions on a regular basis. It comes with being a ballerina. The company needed to frequently show us off. But it's been two years since I've slipped into something dressier than skinny jeans and a sweater.

Most days, it's more like yoga pants and a band tee. If I'm home, it's long socks, short shorts, and a soft tank or tee.

Nobody's ever accused me of being the most stylish person they knew.

The sun is still sitting high in a pretty blue sky dotted with wispy white clouds when I lock the studio up and take a step toward my car. The cool autumn breeze is whipping through the small parking lot that sits behind Hart & Soul, bringing the heavenly smell of coffee and sugary sweet goodness with it. A bakery moved into the old deli that used to be two buildings down from the studio last week. I've been meaning to stop in and welcome them to town, and that heavenly smell is telling me now is the perfect time to do it. Hoisting my Mary Poppins bag higher up on my shoulder, I cut through the alley between our buildings and walk around to the front. Pretty pink and minty green awnings have been added above the window and door and cover the front of the shop. A giant pink cupcake and the words "Sweet Temptations" curved underneath it in the same minty green decorate most of the large window.

The chimes jingle above the door as I step into an explosion of mouthwatering smells. I glance quickly around the small shop. The walls are pale mint green with pink accents. A few small tables with mismatched chairs and a few comfy-looking couches are scattered throughout. The smell of freshly brewed coffee drags my attention to the glass cases with their counters full of gorgeously decorated cupcakes. Behind those cases, I spy the coffee machines which have my stomach growling in anticipation and are surrounded by beautiful glass canisters full of an assortment of coffee beans, but I don't see any employees.

I find a small bell to ring next to the register on the counter and tap it once. Yeah, that would be dangerous if Tommy were with me. He'd have a field day tapping that thing. Note to self—don't let Tommy have a bell.

"I'll be right there," a voice yells from behind swinging double doors that only cover half of the opening leading back to the kitchen.

"No rush." I continue perusing the cupcakes, trying to pick out a few to bring home with me. There are a few basic flavors, vanilla bean, carrot cake, and death by chocolate. Some unique flavors line the other shelves, like maple cinnamon bacon, peanut butter cup and apple pie. A loud crash from the back startles me.

"Son of a . . ." A girl resembling a real-life version of Snow White comes through the door covered in white powder. I'm guessing it's flour. She rubs her hands on her apron, pushes her shoulders back, and pastes the fakest smile I've ever seen on her face. "Hi. Welcome to Sweet Temptations. What can I help you with today?" She blows her black bangs out of her eyes, and flour puffs out around her.

I can't help but giggle. The look she gives me in return isn't nearly as funny. I reach my hand out over the counter toward her. "Hi, I'm Annabelle. I own the dance studio at the corner. I meant to stop by sooner, but I'm usually rushing or late for everything." My hand is left hanging in the air while Snow White eyes it like it's a snake ready to attack.

Finally, her eyes move to my face. "You sure you want to shake?" She holds her flour-covered hands up in front of herself and smiles. This time it doesn't look quite as forced.

"Trust me, my hands get messier than that all the time." I push my hand closer to her.

"Nice to meet you, Annabelle, I'm Amelia." She wipes her hand on her minty green apron again, attempting to get them clean, then shakes mine. "So, what brings you in today?"

"Honestly?" I point over her shoulder to her coffee machines. "That did. I want the biggest cup of whatever you have brewing back there. If heaven has a smell, I hope it's that." Then I glance back down to the cases. "And a dozen cupcakes. I'll take whatever variety you feel like throwing in there as long as one of them is that vanilla bean with vanilla icing, please. My brother is a plain kinda kid. He'd never want to try any of these fancy flavors."

"He doesn't know what he's missing. They're all original recipes." Amelia gets to work making my coffee, then glances over her shoulder. "So, Annabelle... How long have you owned the dance studio?"

"About two years now." Oh, jackpot! As I check out the goodies Amelia has lining the top of the counters, I find boxes of chocolate-covered pretzels. My favorite. Yup. Need these too. "I haven't seen you around before. Are you from Kroydon Hills?"

My coffee is handed to me before Amelia grabs a pink bakery box and starts to pick out cupcakes as she answers, "No, I'm new to town. I wanted to get out of the city, so when I started looking for a place to open the shop, I started with the smaller towns around Philly. This place was the right price, and the apartment above it made it perfect. Who knew living in the 'burbs could be so expensive?" She picks up a final exquisite-looking little cupcake.

"Oh! What flavor is that?" I ask, already knowing this shop is going to be dangerous for my waistline.

Closing the door to the bakery case, Amelia walks over to the register. "That was a S'mores cupcake. Triple chocolate fudge cake, sitting on a baked, graham cracker crust, with a whipped, toasted meringue icing, and topped off with a square of Hershey's chocolate and a square of a honey graham cracker." She rings me up and hands me a pink bag with her Sweet Temptations logo stamped on the front. "Thanks for stopping in, Annabelle. Maybe I'll see you again."

"You'll definitely be seeing me again. Welcome to the neighborhood, Amelia."

~

I'm folding the final towel from my laundry basket when the doorbell rings later that night. Tommy jumps up off the couch and runs to the door. "Thomas David Hart, do not open that door!" I walk over and grab his hand to stop him from reaching for the handle. Then I tilt my head to catch his eyes. "What do we do before we open the door?"

Tommy looks down at his feet, his deep voice grumbling, "We look through the window and ask who it is?"

"Right. You never just open the door, bud. It's not safe." I shift the curtain to the side so he can see the girls standing on the front step.

"Who is it?" Tommy yells. We've been trying to work on volume control, but it's not clicking yet.

"It's Nattie, Chloe, and Brina, Tommy boy. Can we come in?" Nattie makes sure she speaks clearly and loud enough for him to hear.

Tommy looks to me for permission, then opens the door and accepts the hugs these incredible women force on him. He's come a long way over the last year. Still preferring high fives to hugs, he allows the women in this room the privilege of hugging him, and my beautiful friends absolutely consider it a privilege. Once he's stood still longer than he can usually manage, he runs off into the family room and plops back down on the sofa, un-pauses the TV and smiles happily as *Jumanji: Welcome to the Jungle* continues to play.

The girls and I make our way into the kitchen to lay out the pizzas and fries.

Tommy must smell it because in the next second, he's standing next to me with a paper plate in hand. "Can I have a picnic, Belles?"

"Sure, bud. Just make sure you lay the blanket out on the rug first, please." Tommy isn't allowed to eat on the furniture in the family room, so we've taken to throwing his giant *Toy Story* blanket down on the floor and having what he calls picnics when we want to eat in there.

It works for us.

The girls and I grab our pizzas and move to the kitchen table. On the outside, these women couldn't look more like polar opposites. Chloe's hair is purple this week. Her Doc Martens make her tiny feet look huge, boyfriend jeans hide her curves, and a gray t-shirt that says "Shh, No One Cares," in light pink script, is two sizes too big. She's Brady's little sister and a year younger than Sabrina and Nattie, making her the only one of us still in high school. Chloe and Sabrina have been best friends since they were little, and they both got close to Nat after she moved to town last year.

Sabrina is dressed in dark-wash skinny jeans, and a pretty red cashmere sweater with black-and-white polka dot ballet flats. Her dark brown hair is tied up in a bouncy ponytail with a red ribbon tied in a bow around it. Brina is the super-serious one of our little group. She's a beautiful old soul.

Nattie reminds me the most of me. She's got her black yoga pants on with an oversized, comfy Kroydon Kings hoodie hanging down to her knees. Tall Ugg boots that lace up the back make her tiny legs look even tinier, and her wild blonde locks are hanging down past her shoulders.

These ladies are my tribe. It took me a while to accept that. I was used to doing things on my own and really struggled with letting them in. But they pushed and shoved until I opened my doors, and I couldn't be more grateful.

"Okay, ladies. What's going on in your worlds?" I ask as I grab our drinks.

Chloe licks the grease from her finger before answering, "My mother is still being all Stepford Wife. She's all over me all the time. I can't take much more of it. Brady has no idea how lucky he is that he moved out when he did."

"Suck it up, buttercup. You've got the rest of the school year to deal with it." I pass her a bottle of water. "I know you don't want to hear it but enjoy the next few months and let her take care of you. Adulting sucks. Don't rush it."

The face Chloe gives me reminds me of something I'd see one of my baby ballerinas doing. It's scrunched up, pissed off, and has her tongue sticking out. "Belles, we've gotta get you laid. You need to loosen up."

"I'll cheers to that!" Nattie raises her bottle of water like it's a shot glass, and she and Chloe tap bottles before turning to me. "So, what are you thinking about wearing this weekend?"

"I don't know. I have a few options to choose from." I bite my bottom lip, trying to hide my excitement about getting to dress up.

Nattie's face lights up. "It gonna be like dressing up a life-sized Barbie!"

Maybe I spoke too soon.

After dinner, we all head to my bedroom and get to work. Chloe is lying on my white wrought iron bed. Nat's sitting at my vanity, and Sabrina's zipping me up. The first dress they insisted I try on is a bright red, high necked, satin sheath dress. It always made me think of Meghan Markle's second wedding dress, and I loved it as soon as I saw it in the window at Bergdorf's a few years ago. I'm not feeling it right now though.

Sabrina ties the ribbon at the back of my neck and looks at me in the mirror in my en suite bathroom. "Well . . . It's beautiful, Belles, but I don't think it's the right dress for this weekend."

I meet her eyes through the reflection. "I think you're right."

We're cut off by Nattie banging on the door. "Hello? We want to see it too, ladies!" A distinct clapping sound is added for dramatic effect. "Chop, chop! We don't have all night."

Brina and I shake our heads as I lean down to slip on the heels that go with this gown. Swinging the door open dramatically, I walk into my room like I'm walking a catwalk in Milan. I stop at the far corner and strike a pose before turning and facing the girls, who are cheering me on. "You guys are crazy." Laughing like this always feels damn good though.

Thank God for good friends.

"Damn, girl! That dress is smokin! I'd do you." Leave it to Chloe to make me blush.

Nattie motions for me to spin again. "Yeah, if I swung that way, I'd give your old ass a try."

"Natalie! I'm not old, thank you very much. And," I spin around so I can see my ass in the mirror, "I have a great ass." I might have tiny little boobs, but they make me appreciate my booty even more.

The laughter from the peanut gallery stops when Sabrina walks out of my closet holding a gown I never got the chance to wear, bringing a tear to my eye as I sink down onto my bed. The girls quickly surround me.

Nat sits down and grabs my hand. "Hey, hey. What's going on?"

"Wow." I wipe the tears from my face. "Sorry. I wasn't expecting to have that reaction. Woo." I wave my hands in front of my face, trying to cool myself down. Lifting my head, I look at Brina and that beautiful dress. "I was supposed to wear that gown to the after-party for the opening night of *Giselle*." My voice trembles. "It would have been the night after my parents died. A flurry of memories assaults my mind. I spent so many months preparing for an opening night I never got to experience. Years of training to dance a principal role.

So many early mornings and late nights spent perfecting every move.

Pushing through the pain from hours spent dancing on a miniscule box of satin and canvas.

Trying to be perfect.

To fly.

Learning to fly took my childhood and accomplishing my dreams took my parents. They would have never been in that car that night if they hadn't been on their way to the airport.

I've tried to let that go, to move on. Maybe this is another step in the process.

"It was two years ago this week," I tell them.

Sabrina turns to put it back in the closet, but I stop her. "No. Don't. I think I want to try it on." Maybe this can be another step in moving on.

"You don't have to, Belles. You have a ton of other dresses in there. My mother would love your closet." Sabrina eyes me warily.

Nattie squeezes my hand, giving me the strength to do this. "Nope. I'm not sure, but let's give it a try."

"It really is a pretty dress, Belles." Nattie stands up, taking the gorgeous gown from Sabrina and hanging it on the bathroom door.

Chloe walks into my closet. "I'll bet you have a killer pair of shoes in here too." She looks back at us. "Brina, help me find some shoes."

Nattie is sitting on my counter when I walk into the bathroom. Turning my back to her, she unties the bow at the back of my neck, and I slip out of my dress.

Once I have the new gown on, Nat zips the small zipper up, her breath catching in her throat. I turn my head and see unshed tears glistening in her sky-blue eyes. "Annabelle, this dress is perfection. You would have made such a beautiful Giselle."

Smiling a sad smile, I turn and grasp her shoulders. "Chase your dreams, Nattie. Chase every single one of them because you never know when they're going to change."

When I walk back out into my bedroom, I'm met by Chloe whistling, "Damn, bitch."

"Seriously, Belles, you look fierce." Sabrina holds up a shoebox and purse. "These were together. They looked like they matched the dress."

I slip the shoes on, then turn to look at myself in the white wrought iron cheval mirror in the corner of my room. The gown is a gorgeous champagne color with a high square neckline and skinny beaded straps. It's entirely backless and fits tightly, then it flares into a trumpet skirt with just the hint of a train. It matches my skin perfectly, giving a sexy illusion to it.

"Annabelle, you give a whole new meaning to business up front and party in the back. I'd definitely do you now."

Chloe's smiling and not paying any attention to Sabrina as she knocks her off the bed.

"I think you found the dress, Belles." Sabrina glares at Chloe, who's gotten up and is now trying to wrestle Brina to the floor.

Nattie walks up behind me and gently pulls my hair up, tucking it into a bun. Her voice drops low. "Flawless, Belles."

The tears are right there, but I force them down. With trembling lips, I smile. "Thanks, Nattie."

Her fingers find mine, and she squeezes my hand again.

I think it's time to make some new memories.

7

DECLAN

By eleven-thirty Saturday morning, the special teams and the offense and defense walkthroughs have wrapped up, and we're free to leave the practice facility. I'm shoving my phone in my pocket when my center, Jasper, walks around the corner.

This guy makes me feel small, and at six-foot-six, two hundred and forty pounds, very few people make me feel that way. Jasper sits down on the bench in front of me, drops his bag on the floor, and runs his hands through his damp blonde hair. "So, the game's not 'til eight tomorrow night. What are you doing with your Saturday, Dec?"

"I've got to go to a fundraiser tonight. The Kings bought a table and told me to be there." I've gotten less bitter about it as the week rolled to an end. I've decided to look at this as the kick in the ass I needed to finally make a move on Annabelle. We've seen each other a handful of times since I've moved to Philly, and every single time there's been a magnetic energy attracting me to her. But we're always surrounded by my family and their friends, not to mention

Tommy. There's never been a time that seemed like the right time to talk to her.

My family loves her. Nattie even said she was like a sister.

The feelings I have for Annabelle are far from sisterly.

I needed to make sure I had my job under control, that I wasn't going to let my new team down before I could focus on anything besides football.

My gut's telling me she's worth it, splitting that focus. And it's never steered me wrong before.

I just wish it didn't have to be in the public eye.

I'd rather order takeout and stay in than parade us in front of a line of reporters.

Fucking reporters. "I had a meeting with Scarlet Kingston. It's time to start getting my image out there."

"Oh, yeah? Well, you have fun with that. Sounds like the seventh circle of Hell to me, but to each his own. Everyone wants a piece of the quarterback. They leave us linemen alone, man."

Shutting my locker, I shoulder my bag. "Yeah, we'll see." I'm trying to be optimistic here.

The locker across from us slams shut, and Dean Watkins turns around. "Dude, if you don't want the press, I'll take it."

"You may need to get to play more than a quarter of a game for the press to be interested, Watkins." Jasper blows Dean off.

Watkins and I were both drafted last spring. But where I was brought on board specifically to be the starting quarterback, Dean was picked up at the end of the draft as a backup for the team's starting tight end, Curt Kenny. Curt and I have a shit relationship. My junior year, I let the Heisman bullshit all get to me and it exploded one night at a bar. It shouldn't have been that big of a deal. It was a fucking shoving match.

Fists were never even thrown, but that's not how it got reported. One day, I was a shoo-in for the Heisman, and the next fucking day, I was a hotheaded athlete with no control.

Curt was a senior. He was predicted to go in the second or third round of the draft the following spring but was labeled a troublemaker after the incident. He didn't go until late in the sixth round, potentially costing him millions.

As luck would have it, we're back to playing on the same team. We coexist. We're professionals. But we fucking hate each other.

Jasper and I manage to walk out of the building before anyone else can stop us. "You at least got a hot date for this thing tonight, Dec?"

I don't answer but can't hide my grin.

"Ooh-hoo! Who's the lucky lady, and does she have a friend?" I side-eye him as we make it to the parking lot that has already started to clear out.

"She's a family friend, and most of her friends are too young for you or they're related to me, so that's a no." This fucker's smile grows bigger. "Just no."

Jasper veers off toward his car. "Well, don't stay out too late. I don't wanna hear you bitchin about being tired out there in the huddle tomorrow."

"Fuck off, man." I smile, shoot my middle finger over my shoulder, and get in my Bronco.

~

A few hours later, I've showered, shaved, and I'm dressed in my custom tux. The guy at the shop I talked to earlier in the week was nice enough until I mentioned that Scarlet Kingston had sent me. Then, he looked like he was going to shit himself. After that, everything was "yes, sir," "right away, sir," "anything you need, sir." She strikes me as the type to get off on making men scared of her.

Not gonna lie. It worked.

When my phone pings with a text telling me the driver I hired is here, I check myself one more time and then shoot off a text to Annabelle.

Declan: Hey, Belle. Leaving now. Should be at your house in twenty mins.
Annabelle: K. I'll be the one with a dress on.
Declan: Oh good. I was worried I wouldn't be able to find you.

Fuck.

Was that seriously the best I could come up with?

Smooth, Dec. Real smooth.

Annabelle Hart turns me into a tongue-tied teenager.

Hell, my little brother could come up with a smoother line.

Getting into the back of the limo my father's fiancée, Katherine, insisted I use for the night, I'm trying to remember the last time I had to work to get a woman's attention. When she didn't just throw herself at me because of who I am. It's pretty fucked up when I can't think of a single time. I haven't spent any time with anyone worth the effort in as long as I can remember.

Before long, we're pulling up to a two-story white center hall colonial house. It looks homey and is as opposite to the McMansions my mother insisted on living in as it possibly can be.

When the driver starts to get out, I stop him. "Thanks, man. I've got it from here."

He nods and closes his door as I walk along the brick path to the fire-engine-red door of Annabelle's home. I don't see a doorbell, but there's a brass knocker below the curtain-covered window on the top half of the door. I tap it a few times and wait.

"Coming, coming, coming." I hear the muffled words before the door is flung open, and the goddess in front of me takes my breath away. "Hey, Declan. Come in. I just need to find my purse." She spins away from me on the hunt, and I'm left standing there staring after her. Her dress is on, but she's got a silky white robe on over it.

I'll never understand why women do that.

Once I get it together and force one foot in front of the other, I pull the door shut behind me and walk through her foyer into the family room. She has built-in bookcases full of pictures of Tommy and her, and some people who I'm assuming are her parents. The older woman in these pictures looks like she could be Belle's older sister. Tall and thin with light brown hair and warm brown eyes. Her father appears a few years older with sandy-blonde hair and Belle and Tommy's emerald-green eyes. They looked happy, and my heart sinks at the realization that they're gone. I know her parents are dead and that she's taking care of Tommy, but seeing these family photos makes that hit home harder.

Annabelle Hart is a package deal. Dating her . . . getting serious with her—because, let's face it, she's not the kind of girl who accepts casual—means being in Tommy's life too.

The question is am I ready for that?

I don't get a chance to analyze that thought before Belle comes back down the stairs, robe off, and glittery purse in hand. She's stunning in a sparkly dress the same color as her golden skin. Her long caramel locks are parted down the middle and hanging in loose waves down her back. When she gets to the bottom of the stairs, she does a little twirl, so I can see all the angles, and holy hell, there's no back at all. The champagne-colored dress dips down to just above her tight little ass, showing off two perfect dimples that I want to drop down to my knees and worship.

"It's not nice to make a girl fish for a compliment, Declan." She runs her fingers gently through her hair and looks into my eyes.

I think my heart may have just skipped a damn beat.

"Sorry." I stare at her at a complete loss for words. "Sorry, Belle. It's just ... You just ..."

She turns to walk away, not letting me finish my thought. "Do I need a coat?"

"Annabelle, stop. Please." She listens but doesn't turn to look at me. In two steps, I'm standing behind her, trying to resist spinning her to look at me. "Jesus, I'm screwing this up. Annabelle, you're breathtaking. I've never seen a more beautiful woman in my life."

I see a tremor travel down her spine before she steps forward and looks at me over her shoulder. "Thanks," she whispers quietly before she's reaching for a long coat out of her hall closet. "We should get going. Nattie just texted that Tommy's happy and watching *Jurassic World*, but I don't know how long that's going to last." She grabs keys off a hook by the door and stares at me.

I walk over, taking her coat from her and drape it over her back. "Your chariot awaits."

Seriously, I used to be smooth. What the fuck happened to me?

8
ANNABELLE

As I slide onto the cool leather seat of the ridiculously big white stretch limo Declan rented for the evening, I'm suddenly very aware of the fact that this dress dips so low in the back there was absolutely no way I could wear even the tiniest thong under it. I'm also aware that feeling the heat rolling off Declan Sinclair while he stood behind me and told me that I was the sexiest woman he'd ever seen has me drenched.

For Declan Sinclair!

Holy shit, I'm so screwed.

This is Natalie's brother. Of course, I think he's sex on a stick because, well, who doesn't? Seriously, he brings tall, dark, and handsome to a whole new level. He's a nice guy because he's a Sinclair, and while Nattie's mom seems like a whack-a-doo, the rest of them are salt of the earth, amazing people. He's so sweet to my brother. He probably even helps little old ladies cross the damn street too.

I didn't need to know that feeling his breath on my bare skin was going to wake up something that's been lying dormant for two damn years.

Need.

Yearning.

Desire.

Dec slides in next to me, has a quick conversation with the driver, then leans back and smiles.

Damn. That smile...

"Do you want a glass of champagne? I think there's a stocked bar back here somewhere." He pushes a button, and a cabinet opens. There's a bottle of champagne already chilling in an ice bucket next to a few cans of soda, bottled water, and a few bottles of top-shelf liquor all above a tiny refrigerator stocked with bottles of beer. "Ladies choice."

"Sure. Why not? I'll take a glass of champagne." I quickly check my phone to make sure there are no missed calls or texts from Nattie. I guess that means Tommy's okay so far.

I offer up a silent prayer. *Please let him be okay tonight.*

Declan pops the cork on the champagne and angles the bubbles spilling out of it away from us before handing me a crystal flute. He raises his glass, holding it there until I do the same. "A toast."

I angle myself to face him. "What are we toasting?"

"To you."

"Declan..." I drag out his name.

Damn him. Those full lips tip up on one side, giving me the sexiest smile. I swear I want to straddle his lap right here, right now.

"To you, Annabelle Hart. Thank you for saving me from what would have been an excruciating night without you." He touches his flute to mine, takes a small sip, and then holds it down at his side.

I nod toward the flute. "Not into champagne?"

"I don't drink during the season." There's no hesitation in his voice.

"Mind if I ask why?"

"I keep to a pretty strict diet. I want to keep my body as healthy as possible so I can play the game as long as I want to. That means staying in peak condition. Part of that is what I put into my body." His eyes linger on mine. "You were a professional dancer. I'd imagine you couldn't eat whatever you wanted or do whatever you wanted without it effecting your performance."

I sip my champagne and enjoy the sweet bubbles as they tickle my throat. "True. But that was a long time ago."

"It's still the same thing. When your career is based on your physical ability, you have to take care of yourself. Now, I'm not saying everyone agrees with me. Half the guys on the team eat shit and booze it up all season, but they'll be the guys who have careers that span the average length for the league."

I have to ask. "How long does the average player get to play?"

"Three years." Declan leans forward and places his champagne flute in a cup holder before facing me fully. "They train all their lives and only get three years."

I tilt my head and study this man who is a contradiction in confidence and self-consciousness. Cockiness and modesty. "And how long do you want to play, Dec?"

"Twenty years."

The limo jerks, causing me to brace myself by grabbing the seat. At least I try to grab the seat but instead, end up grabbing Dec's thigh. Jesus, it doesn't budge. The seat would have been softer. And that thought has my mind going to a completely different part of his anatomy I'd love to grab, that I'm pretty sure would feel like steel wrapped in velvet. I guess my vibrator is going to get a workout tonight. My face flames as the temperature in the limo rises. I slide my hand to the space next to him, whispering, "Sorry."

We hear the driver's voice through a speaker, "Sorry about that, Mr. Sinclair. We hit a pothole. We'll be pulling up to the Union League in just a moment. Please leave anything you'd like in the vehicle. I'll be the only one with access until you're ready to leave."

Slipping my coat off my shoulders, I lay it on the bench seat across from the bar area and place my clutch in my lap.

As the limo starts to slow, Dec turns to me. The confidence he had moments ago has faded, leaving discomfort in its place. "Is my tie straight?"

I reach up to fix his black bowtie. My hands grazing his chiseled jaw. "Have I told you how incredibly handsome you look tonight, Mr. Sinclair?" A beautifully cut suit on a beautifully built man is my personal kryptonite.

His hand grips my wrist gently before he turns his head and places a kiss on my open palm.

I swear to God, my heart skips a beat. Indigo blue eyes lock on mine and refuse to release me. "You call my dad 'Mr. Sinclair,' Belle." Ohmygosh . . . That deep voice. It's dropped lower. Sexier. "When you're with me, I want to be the only Sinclair you're thinking about."

Oh. My. God.

The door opens, causing Declan to pull away briefly. He flashes me a quick megawatt smile. "Showtime, Belles." Dec steps out, stands to his full height, then turns, offering me his hand.

He's a perfect gentlemen, but I'm beginning to think there's another side to Declan that I wouldn't mind getting to know better.

Lordy. I'm giving myself whiplash with my warring

emotions.

I slip my hand in his and clutch my purse to my chest, so no one gets a peep show as I get out of the limo. I learned that move years ago. If you ever need etiquette lessons, just watch British royalty. They know all the tricks.

I'm momentarily blinded by the flashing lights once I'm out and standing next to Declan. A few reporters stand off to the side of the golden ropes lining either side of the black carpet running from the drop-off spot to the beautifully curved staircase that leads up to the gorgeous brick building where the fundraiser is being held.

Declan moves his hand to the small of my back as we start to walk the carpet, and dear God, the heat emanating from his big hand feels divine against my sensitive skin.

This part is a piece of cake for me. I'm a trained ballerina. Walking an event carpet is nothing new. Maybe not something I've done recently, but my muscle memory kicks in. My job tonight is to smile and follow Dec's lead. The problem is that he hasn't stopped to answer any of the questions being thrown his way. I'm fairly sure he's supposed to be working this a little.

I try to whisper out of the corner of my mouth so I don't draw too much attention. "Dec, you need to answer a question or two. This is all PR."

His eyes meet mine. They're hard to read, but he stops. I decide to help out a little and take a step closer to one of the reporters on our right. Declan follows.

The reporter's eyes light up like the Fourth-of-July fireworks they set off over the Delaware River each year. "Declan Sinclair. Great to see you here tonight. Are you a fan of Senator Cabot's? Who's this beautiful lady with you? Should you really be here tonight when we're playing Dallas tomorrow? Are you ready for the game? Are we gonna win?"

"Slow down, man. Take a breath." Okay, not bad. He's trying. "It's great to be here tonight to support Senator Cabot and the Kings. Max Kingston himself invited me, so I'm fairly certain I'm safe for the night. And yes, we're ready for Dallas. It should be a good game." Declan laughs, but I can tell it's forced.

A mic is shoved in my face, causing me to take a step back and Declan to slide his hand to my hip to steady me. "Declan, who's your date? Is this your girlfriend? Is it serious? How long have you been together?"

I feel Declan's hand squeeze ever so gently, before answering. "This is Annabelle Hart. She's an extremely good friend."

More flashes go off. Someone else yells over, "Is she your girlfriend, Declan?"

His calloused palm slowly slides back to the small of my back before he offers them a smile. It's real this time and reminds me of his sister's. Mischievous. Beautiful. "Have a nice night, folks." Dec leads us to the end of the carpet and then, takes my hand in his and guides us up the stairs.

With one hand in his and the other holding the small train of my dress, we ascend the beautiful historic winding staircase. "Declan," I say admonishingly. "They're going to think we're together." Damn. Maybe I should have looked this place up before I decided to wear four-inch heels to walk up a million stairs.

"Let them think whatever they want, Annabelle." When we get to the top step, he lifts the hand he's been holding to his lips and presses a kiss to my knuckles.

Flashes go off in the distance, and my heart skips another beat.

Damn, Declan Sinclair isn't what I was expecting.

9

DECLAN

As Annabelle and I enter the ornate ballroom, I spot Murphy and Sabrina standing off to the side, next to one of the white linen-covered tables. A waiter dressed in a black tux with tails and white gloves is about to hand Murphy a glass of champagne. I might hate the press, but I've been schooled in it enough over the years to know they're everywhere. And a high-profile, underage college football player cannot be photographed drinking champagne at a political fundraiser. Pressing my hand against the small of Annabelle's back, I ignore the zing of anticipation that shoots up my arm and guide her quickly to my soon-to-be stepbrother.

Our parents got engaged two months ago, surprising us all.

Once we're next to the waiter, I lift both crystal glasses off his tray. "These two aren't twenty-one. You might want to get them some soda." The poor guy glances uncomfortably between Murphy and me before walking away.

As I hand a flute to Annabelle, I hear Murphy whisper, "dick," to which I answer back with "asshole." In our world, these are terms of endearment. Placing my glass down on the high-top table, I look over at the asshole in question. "Don't let anyone catch you grabbing a drink, Murph. You're not twenty-one. You can't be photographed like that."

"I'm not that stupid, Dec." Murphy smiles like the goofball he likes the world to assume he is, but I'm pretty sure he's smarter than that. At least, I hope so. He laces his fingers with Sabrina's, then turns to Annabelle, exaggeratedly looking her over. "Damn, Belle. You look smokin.'"

Belle twirls in a small circle and curtsies. "Why, thank you, Mr. Murphy." She winks at him. "Looking mighty fine yourself."

As the waiter comes back with what I'm assuming are two sodas, I take one from his tray and hand it to Sabrina. "You look very nice tonight, Sabrina." And she does look pretty in an emerald-green ball gown with her dark hair in curls piled on top of her head. Motioning to Murph, I add, "Much too nice to be here with this oaf."

She blushes. "Thanks, Declan. It's nice of you to come." Sabrina's definitely the quiet one of that group. I guess opposites really do attract because quiet is not a word anyone would ever use to describe Murphy.

A guy walks over, underdressed in a mismatched sports coat and dress slacks and smelling like whiskey. "Sabrina. How are you, kid?" He grabs her hand and kisses it. I watch with amusement when Murphy steps forward like he's going to throw down with this guy who looks older than our parents. Jesus, keeping an eye on him is harder than making sure Cooper didn't get in to trouble when we were younger.

The drunk guy walks away a few minutes later with Murphy glaring daggers at him as he leaves. "Who was that?"

Sabrina spins, laughing. "Aiden Murphy. You are not seriously jealous of Pat Donovan, are you? He's a harmless ward leader from South Philly. Nice guy, but he's got to be forty years old, and he's only being sweet because of my dad."

"Aww, Murphy. Are you jealous? Who knew you could be so cute?" Annabelle is facing Murphy and giving me an unobstructed view of the creamy, soft skin of her bare back. The tiny straps look like they could snap with a flick of my fingers, and I have to fight the urge to find out.

"I am not cute, Belles." Murph puffs up his chest, making the rest of us laugh. "I'm manly."

"Never good when you have to announce to anyone that you're manly, Murphy." Dad slaps a hand down on Murphy's shoulder and squeezes. Katherine, Dad's fiancée and Murph's mom, joins us, as well. She's a pretty, older woman in her early forties with auburn hair the color of Murphy's, wearing a red strapless dress. She seems to make the old man happy, and that's all that matters to me.

"Be nice, Joe," Katherine scolds my dad. She turns to Murph. "You are so very manly, sweetie." She leans in and kisses his cheek, then she reaches over and hugs me.

"You might want to lick your thumb to get the lipstick off his cheek now, Katherine." I try to rub his cheek, but he shoves me away.

"You all suck," Murph announces, sulking.

Dad clears his throat and then smiles sweetly at the girls. "Sabrina, Annabelle, you both look lovely tonight. Is Nattie watching Tommy for you, Annabelle?"

Belle steps into my side giving me an excuse to rest my hand on the soft skin of her back again. "Yes. He's supposed to be spending the night there tonight. He and Brady concocted the idea. I'm expecting to get a call when he refuses to go to sleep. He's never slept anywhere else before."

Katherine smiles warmly at Belle. "Annabelle, if you ever need a break, I'd be happy to have Tommy spend time with me. I've really enjoyed getting to know him, and I think he may have a bit of a crush on my daughter, Carys."

"Thanks so much, Katherine. I appreciate it. I don't really have much time for a break." Belle laughs self-deprecatingly and glances quickly at me. "Wow, when I say that out loud, I realize how sad it sounds." As her green eyes glitter in the low light of the ballroom, I can't help but wonder if she'd be willing to make time for me.

"Nonsense. You have to take some time for yourself. Carys and I are moving in with Joe next week. Tommy already knows that house well. I'm sure we could make sure he was comfy and happy, and you could get a little alone time." Katherine is pushing for her to take her up on the offer, but from what I know of Belle, she's not good at accepting help.

Sabrina's father joins our growing corner of the ballroom. A conversation takes place that I'm not paying attention to. Instead, I'm studying my gorgeous date. There's absolutely no way I'm letting this night be a one and done. I'm Declan fucking Sinclair. I've never not accomplished something I've set my mind to, and I've waited long enough to make this move.

With a lowered voice, I lean into Belle, brushing her long hair over her shoulder. "You ready to find our table?"

She hesitates momentarily, her eyes searching my face before tipping her head back and smiling. She links her arm through mine. "Lead the way."

I guess she found what she was looking for.

We say our goodbyes and locate our table as Scarlet

Kingston approaches. She's in a sleek black gown with a slit up the leg that would make any man look twice. Her dark hair is pulled back off her face, and there's a calculating glint in her pale blue eyes. "Declan Sinclair. You clean up nice." She leans over and kisses my cheek, then offers her hand to Belle. "And you must be 'Family Friend, No NDA.'"

Annabelle takes her hand, smiling. "Can't say I've been called that before. Annabelle Hart. Pleased to meet you . . ." She lets her voice hang until Scarlet offers her name.

Scarlet turns to me. "I like her." Then she faces Belle. "Scarlet Kingston. Nice to meet you, Annabelle. How do you know Philly's favorite quarterback?"

Watching these women talk is like watching a tennis match. No one wants to give up a point. It's one part awkward and one part sexy.

Belle's laughter is light. "I think part of the reason I'm here tonight is because we're still working on him becoming Philly's favorite quarterback." She lifts one brow, and Scarlet smiles—point one for Belle. "I'm a friend of the family. Declan's sister works at my dance studio."

"A dancer?" I can see the wheels turning in Scarlet's mind. I'm not sure what she's thinking, but she seems to be plotting.

"Scarlet," I say warningly.

Never taking her eyes off Belle, she answers, "Calm down, Declan. I'm just trying to get to know your date."

"Scarlet," Becket Kingston cuts his sister off as he joins the conversation. "Behave, Scar. You're not on the clock tonight."

She pierces him with an icy stare, then runs her hands over his lapels. "I'm behaving, Becks. I'm just trying to get to know Declan's date better. Jesus. You guys act like I was going to cross-examine her or something. I'll leave the lawyering to you, brother dear. I'm better at PR anyway." She glances back at Belle briefly before settling her eyes on me. "I can sell the hell out of the ballerina and the baller."

"I never mentioned that I was a ballerina." All eyes turn toward Belle and the cold tone in her voice. She sounds . . . annoyed? Maybe pissed. Definitely not happy.

"Oh, Declan. I like her." Scarlet looks between the two of us appraisingly. "She has a brain, a business, and the cameras love her. She'll work."

Belle clears her throat and crosses her arms protectively. "Excuse me, I'm standing right here. Care to fill me in here?"

"I have no idea what she's plotting over there," I say with honesty, then place my hand on her hip and squeeze.

Becket tracks the move with his eyes before turning to his sister. "Come on, Scarlet. Take the night off." He pulls out a seat at the large round table and waits for her to sit down.

Instead of sitting, Scarlet tips her glass to Annabelle. "I apologize for running your background, but the organization has invested quite a bit in Declan. This is our first real step in creating his image. I had to make sure that whoever he was bringing tonight would fit in with that image. And you, Ms. Hart, are perfect. Hometown girl and former professional ballerina who gave up her career to take care of her autistic brother when her parents died tragically. The press is going to eat you up."

I hear the gasp from Annabelle as I cut in sharply. "Scarlet . . ." The word comes out angrier than it probably should, considering she is part-owner of my team.

Belle's small hand comes to rest on my chest. She smiles sweetly at me then morphs into a pissed-off momma bear before my eyes. "Miss Kingston, I'm here for my friend, and I'm happy to help in whatever way I can. So long as that doesn't involve my brother. Not only is he more than his diagnosis, but he's been through enough and doesn't need to be brought into the spotlight for anyone. If you can respect that, we can be friends. If not, I'm sure that my background report showed that my father was a state trooper, and my mother was a partner in a law firm. I don't scare easily, and I allow myself and my family to be manipulated even less easily. I'd also be happy to have one of my friends help me explain just how you can go fuck yourself if need be." She sips the remainder of her champagne before placing it on a tray of a waiter passing by and grabbing two new ones.

Annabelle offers one to Scarlet. She accepts it, turning to me. "Oh, Declan, I really like her." Then she clinks glasses with Annabelle. "You've just won my respect, Ms. Hart. That's not something I give out freely."

Belle's beautiful smile returns. "You haven't earned mine yet, Miss. Kingston. You've got a long way to go."

Jesus, I take a deep breath and murmur to Becks, "Your sister is scary."

"She's a raging bitch most of the time, but she's loyal to a fault, and she's damn good at her job." He slaps a hand on my back then reaches out to Annabelle. "Becket Kingston, nice to meet you, Ms. Hart."

"Nice to meet you, Becket. Please call me Annabelle."

An hour later, dinner has been served and the senator has given his speech when the band begins to play. Out of the corner of my eye, I see a photographer coming toward us. A few have been inside the event tonight, and they've ignored me for the most part. This one looks like he's got his lasers locked and I'm his target. Pushing my chair back, I stand and offer Belle my hand. "May I have this dance?"

"I thought you'd never ask." She excuses herself from

the conversation she was having with my father and Katherine and allows me to escort her to the dance floor. The woman singing has a breathy voice and is doing a haunting version of "Iris" by the Goo Goo Dolls.

Wrapping one arm around her waist and grasping her other hand to my chest, I lean my head down to her ear whispering, "Think you can make me look good out here? I'm a lousy dancer."

Belle laughs at me but does as I ask. Her arm rests on my shoulder, and her body rests flush against mine. She's leading without it showing, and I'm happy to let her take control.

I wonder how much control she'd want in other areas.

The beat is slow and sultry. This woman fits perfectly in my arms. Her head rests under my chin, and the scent of lavender and vanilla is invading my senses. My hand spans the entire width of her delicate back as my fingers dance along the tiny strap.

"I'm sorry for what Scarlet did, Belle." She pulls her head back to look up at me. "I know you don't know me that well yet, but I'd never let anyone use Tommy or you for their own agenda. I hate the fucking media and would never let either of you get hurt because of me."

The hand wrapped around my shoulder travels into the hair at the nape of my neck. "I appreciate that, Declan. I know you'd never let anyone hurt Tommy, and that means the world to me. He's a special kid, and before I met your sister, I was all he had. Now, he has all of you too. He's a lucky kid to have been taken in by the Sinclairs. Nattie gave us a second chance at a family." She takes a shaky breath and dips her head so she's shielded by her hair. "We're both lucky."

Letting go of the hand on my chest, I tuck her hair

behind her ear then cradle her head in my hand. "I've seen three-hundred-pound defensive linemen cower in front of Scarlet Kingston. Is it okay to admit watching you cut her off at the knees was fucking hot as hell?" The twin dimples in her cheeks pop deeply as her beautiful smile stretches across her face. My voice drops one step above a whisper, "You're incredible, Annabelle Hart."

The hand on my chest grabs the front of my shirt and our bodies erase the small space that was left. "Declan." Her voice comes out soft before she drops her head to my chest and whispers, "everyone's watching us."

I make a split-second decision. "Want to get out of here?"

Belle doesn't answer. Her fingers continue to play with my hair, while her body stays pressed against mine. Shit, maybe I read the situation wrong.

"Annabelle?" My voice comes out questioning.

"I don't want to break the spell, Declan." She lifts her eyes to mine. "I'm scared if we walk off this dance floor, the spell will be broken. Right now, I'm your date. I'm having fun. A lot of fun. Right now, I'm anticipating all the ways you could make my body sing. And I'm scared the minute we walk off this dance floor, the bubble we're magically in will burst and I'll realize this isn't my reality." She swallows before adding, "And I want this to be my reality tonight. One night, Dec. That's all I can give you."

My thumb skims her cheek before I lean in and brush my lips over hers. Once. Twice. When I go in for the third time, she pushes me back and my hope comes crashing down.

"Declan." Her voice is breathy. Needy. "Let's go somewhere that cameras can't follow."

Cradling her face in my hands, I realize I'd completely forgotten about the cameras. "My place is closer."

She nuzzles her cheek against my hand. "Just let me run to the ladies' room."

We walk off the dance floor together, Annabelle heading to the ladies' room and me to the table. I tell my dad we're leaving and turn to catch Murphy as he heads out of the ballroom. He moves the way Annabelle just left, so I follow. When I enter the hall, I see a smaller room set up with a fire roaring and a group of men smoking cigars. What I didn't expect to see was Sabrina's mom ripping into Murphy. I can just barely make out her voice from where I'm standing.

"Her father will sit in the White House one day, and Sabrina will be right there by his side. Who knows how far she will be able to go when it's her turn? What I do know is that you will only drag her down." Damn. The look on Murphy's face as Mrs. Cabot lays into him makes me want to rip her to shreds.

Shit.

Instead, I look around until I find Sabrina near the door of the ballroom. Moving quickly and quietly, I grab her attention. "Sabrina, I need you to come with me."

Her doe eyes look confused. "What's going on, Declan?"

"I'm not sure. But I think Murphy might need your help." I lead her into the smoking lounge just in time for us to hear Mrs. Cabot threaten Murphy.

"No, you are not going to be given the chance to destroy my daughter's life the way he destroyed your mother's." Her mother's words echo like a slap throughout the room.

Sabrina cuts her off. "Mother!"

I wait a few moments to make sure the situation is handled before I leave the room. Shooting off a text to Murphy, I ask him to let me know that everything's okay and try to find Annabelle. She's not near the ladies' room. Walking through the ballroom, I find our table empty and scan the room. Annabelle's on the dance floor with Becket. There's plenty of space between them, and she isn't smiling at him like she's been smiling at me, but something primal in me still wants to rip his heart out. I don't like his hands on her.

As I get to the dance floor to interrupt, my cell phone rings, alerting me to a text.

Murphy: Dec, can you grab Sabrina's purse off the table we were sitting at? It's silver and sparkly. She says Belles will know which one it is.
Declan: Sure. Where are we bringing it?
Murphy: We're in the attached hotel. Room 104.
Declan: Okay. Be there in 5.

As I shove my phone back in my pocket, I see Annabelle and Becket crossing the room to me. "Hey, Dec. Is everything okay?" She reaches out and runs her hand down my arm before grabbing my forearm. "I couldn't find you."

I glance over to Becket and then back to Belle. "Hey, Becks, we've gotta get out of here. I'll catch up with you next week, okay?"

Becks nods his head to me and smiles at Belle. "Ms. Hart, it was a pleasure to meet you. Dec, I'll see you later."

Linking my finger with hers, I pull Belles behind me, moving us toward Sabrina and Murphy's table. "There was a bit of an issue with Sabrina's mom and Murphy. I'm sorry you couldn't find me, but I was trying to help avoid a scene."

Annabelle gasps, "Oh, no! What happened?"

"Do you know which purse is Sabrina's? Murph said it's silver and sparkly."

Her eyes scan the table before she picks up a tiny bag. "Got it. Now spill, Sinclair. What happened?"

I guide us out of the ballroom and down the long hallway. "I'm not sure exactly what caused it or what was said before I got there, but Murphy was getting attacked by Sabrina's mom. I grabbed Sabrina. I can't imagine that Murphy was going to speak up for himself to his girlfriend's mother. Not here. Once Sabrina was there, she didn't care who could hear her or what they thought. She tore her mother to pieces. I left the room. I felt like it needed to be a private moment and they didn't need an audience."

"Holy Hell. I wasn't even in the ladies' room for five minutes. How did I miss all that?"

When we knock on their door, Annabelle steps in front of me, tension radiating off her in waves. Murphy cracks the door open, and she holds the purse out of his reach. "How's our girl, Murph?"

He steps outside, keeping his hand on the door so it doesn't shut completely behind him. "It's been a fucked-up night, Belles. I'm sure Brina will fill you in tomorrow, but for now, I need to get back in there." He leans in and kisses Belle's cheek, then puts his hand out for the purse. "Thanks for bringing this up here."

"Let me know if you need anything, Murph." I clap his shoulder.

"Thanks, man. I will." He steps back into the room, and the door shuts behind him.

Belle and I step back and momentarily stand in silence.

"Well, damn." I run my fingers through my hair. Probably should have gotten a cut before tonight. "This wasn't how I was expecting the night to end."

Annabelle places her small hand in mine. "Who says it has to end now?"

10

ANNABELLE

I'm nowhere near ready for this night to end.

Declan's hands move to my face as I'm backed into the wall of the hallway outside Murphy and Sabrina's hotel room. His lips crash down on mine, fanning the flames he's been stoking all night. Every synapse I have starts firing at once. They're all screaming, "*Get this man into a room and get naked right this second.*" His lips are firm as he kisses me. But when his tongue invades my mouth and I feel my toes lifting off the floor, I push him back slightly, thanking God I still have a little mental strength left and that it didn't abandon me in the same way my breath did.

"Dec," I pant, "we need to get out of here." Suddenly not sure if I'm trying to push him away or pull him closer, I refuse to let go of the hold I have on his tux jacket.

He drops his head to mine and takes a deep breath. "Jesus. I'm sorry. You're right." He kisses my forehead so sweetly, I want to melt. "I texted the driver before we left the ballroom and asked him to pull the car around."

My fingers travel to his strong palm, and I try to pull him away, but it's no use. Declan is twice my size and one gigantic muscle. He doesn't budge unless he wants to. And that thought, right there, has me wishing, yet again, that I'd found panties to wear tonight.

"Declan . . ." Here goes nothing. "If you don't get me out of here soon, I'm going to get myself off in this hallway, and I really, really don't want to do that. So, please . . . Move."

He brushes his lips over mine one more time before he pulls his head back. "We better get moving then because the only one getting you off tonight is me, Annabelle. When we're done, you're going to feel me between your thighs for days." He squeezes my hand, then straightens his jacket before we hurry to the elevator.

We wait for the elevator doors to open for what feels like an eternity but is actually only seconds. Declan guides me inside in front of him. Once the doors slide closed, he inspects the elevator walls then hits the emergency stop button before spinning on me. "Let's see how fast I can do this."

"What?" My question is muffled by Declan as he picks me up, pressing my bare back against the cool wall of the elevator.

My dress is too tight for me to wrap my legs around his waist, but that doesn't stop him.

He pushes it up to my waist. "No panties tonight, Belle?" Dec comments with absolutely no surprise in his voice as he drops to his knees and licks my pussy with his flattened tongue before he bites. That's it. That's all it takes for the world to stand still and go eerily quiet, with only the sound of my ragged breathing echoing within the elevator as everything else simply ceases to exist.

As I begin to come down from that beautiful high, a noise begins to seep into my head. "Declan." I pull at his hair, but he doesn't stop. "Declan, stop. There's an alarm going off."

Standing to his full height, he wipes his mouth with the back of his hand before leaning in to kiss me deeply. Tasting myself on his lips, I wish I could drop to my knees right here and return the favor. Declan hits the same emergency button, and the elevator jolts as it resumes its descent.

Those strong hands run over my hair and pull just the slightest bit. The sting at my scalp mixes with the euphoria still coursing through me. "You taste better than I ever dreamed you could, Annabelle."

Oh, wow.

The doors slide open. Luckily for us, no one is standing on the other side and waiting to get on. I'm guided out of the elevator and through a side door leading to the parking lot behind the building. "How did you know this was here?" This isn't the way we came in.

Dec's lips tip up on one side. "I can't give you all my secrets." The driver is waiting for us, leaning against the door that he hurriedly opens once he sees us approach. Before Declan steps aside, he asks, "Can you take us back to my place?" He's addressing the driver, but his eyes haven't left mine, waiting for consent.

I don't know if it's my smile or the red creeping up my face, but he must get the consent he's looking for. As I slide into the limo, I hear Declan quietly tell the driver not to open the privacy window, and my soaking wet core weeps with anticipation.

If I'm going to allow myself this one night to have fun . . .

To escape reality . . .

I'm going to enjoy every single second of it.

Moments later, Declan joins me in the back seat. This time, I'm not caught entirely off guard. I shimmy my dress up to my waist and straddle his lap. My hands dig into his hair as I lick Declan's lips. His mouth opens, and our tongues dance in exploration. His hands grip my hips bruisingly over my dress, the bite of his fingers making me feel more alive than I have in years.

"Belle." My name comes out on a sexy, desperate groan. "I don't have a condom. I mean, I have a box at my condo, but I don't have one on me now."

Our mouths are a breath apart—neither of us wanting to move. "Declan, I have an IUD, and I'm clean." My cheeks flame as I add, "I haven't had sex in over two years, which you probably figured out when I orgasmed from one touch."

The straps of my dress are slipped off my shoulders as the hot suction of Dec's lips on my breasts brings me right back to the edge of the world before his low voice breaks the silence. "I don't think that's why you came so hard or that you're soaking my pants right now. I think it's because it's us, Annabelle. I've wanted you since the first minute I saw you in my father's back yard." The feel of his rough, calloused fingers against the soft skin of my breasts is the perfect mix of pleasure and pain. "I'm clean, Belle. I get tested religiously for the team. But are you sure? We can wait until we get to my place."

Reaching down, I unzip Declan's pants, and he shoves them and his boxer briefs down just enough. His hands go back to my hips as I begin to sink down on the thickest cock I've ever felt.

Velvety smooth steel. Just like I thought.

His ocean blue eyes hold mine captive. "Oh, Dec." It's been so long, it stings as my body stretches to accommodate his size. "Oh. My. God."

We both moan as he fills me completely. There are no

words to describe how good, how right, this feels. His mouth finds my neck, and his hands go back to my chest.

"Annabelle, baby, you've got to move." His thumb rolls my nipple, pulling a tight string straight down to my core.

"I don't know if I can," I gasp, panting.

Declan's warm hands slip under my dress and move to grip my hips, branding my skin. Jesus, I don't know how I ever thought a dancer's manicured hands felt good on my body now that I know what Declan's hands feel like.

He starts to lift his hips and fuck me, controlling me as if I weigh nothing.

My nails dig into his shoulders, my head thrown back, my body vibrating. "Declan . . . You feel . . . Oh God, Dec."

He licks up my throat, moving his lips to mine and swallowing my moan.

"Belles, you feel so hot. So tight. So fucking good." Each thought is punctuated with another thrust.

Dec's arms wrap tightly around me until I'm forced to wrap mine around his shoulders. There's no space between us as I finally start to rock my hips in time with his. "Don't stop." Holy shit, I can't complete a thought. I claw at his back, glad he has his jacket on so I'm not scarring him but nevertheless annoyed at the barrier between my hands and his skin.

"Fuck, Belle. I need you to get there. I need to feel you come on my cock the way you came on my tongue, baby."

He fists my hair and pulls me down as he surges up, hitting a spot deep inside. My body convulses around him as my eyes water from the power of my orgasm. "Declan," I gasp. But he swallows it as he pushes up once more, and I'm overwhelmed by the incredible sensation of Declan Sinclair losing control.

I have no idea how many hours have gone by while I lay with my head on Declan's gorgeous, gloriously muscled, naked chest. I should be sound asleep. I lost track of how many times this man has made me come sometime after the fifth or sixth time. There was once in the elevator, once in the limo. Once against the door of his condo. Once bent over the table. Hmm . . . I think it was actually twice bent over the dining room table. Definitely twice in the shower.

His fingers play with my hair. "Belle. What are you thinking about so hard?"

Leaning one elbow against his chest, I rest my head on my hand so I have a better view of his perfectly chiseled face. "Hmm?" Yeah, that's about as articulate as I can be right now.

"I said your name twice before you finally heard me. If you can think that hard right now, I must have done something wrong." He sits up, taking me with him. Strong hands lift me so I'm straddling him, much like I did earlier in the limo. "Annabelle, is something wrong?"

Holy hell, it's hard to think when I'm straddling a naked Declan Sinclair. His body is a work of art. Strong and defined. His movements hold purpose. He doesn't falter.

My hands trace the planes of his chest. "No, Dec. I just don't want this night to end."

The ends of my hair are curled around his fingers as he tugs. He seems to like doing that, and I've got to say, I don't mind it either. My hair has been pulled, caressed, and wrapped around his fist. Each one a bigger turn-on than the last.

"Belle, just because we have to get out of bed soon

doesn't mean this has to end. I know my schedule sucks, but I want to see you again. I want to see where this goes."

Shit. "Declan . . ." I drag out his name.

He must know he's not going to like what I'm about to say because I'm flipped onto my back before I can even finish the thought that was trickling in.

His strength is gentle.

It's contained.

I'm not thrown around like a rag doll. I'm moved with a reverence that makes tonight so much more than I was expecting.

My knees bend, and my toes point as they wrap around his lean hips.

With one hand, my wrists are grabbed and held above my head while his other hand goes to my throat. There's no real pressure being used, just control, and fuck, it's so hot.

Silence surrounds us, locking us in our own world.

There are no hurried sounds of skin on skin. No moans. Just whispered words.

Declan sinks slowly into me. So slowly, it's nearly excruciating.

He kisses me so tenderly I want to cry because I know this is all we can ever have.

"Jesus, Belle. You can't tell me you don't feel this. You were made to be mine."

"Oh, God," I cry out as he hits the spot I didn't believe existed before tonight. "Harder, Dec. I need it harder."

"No." He lets go of my wrists and wraps himself around me.

"Please, Dec," I beg, needing this to be less intimate.

Declan refuses to give in to my frantic plea. Taking his time. Worshiping me.

He snaps his hips, and oh dear God. His hand tightens on my throat. "Your pussy is fucking perfect."

And then he's kissing me as I'm clamping down on him. Again.

His orgasm chases me over the edge without his lips leaving my mouth.

Dec is taking so much more than I'm willing to give.

I was ready to give him tonight. To give him my body.

Giving him my heart is not an option.

11

DECLAN

Christ, the woman lying in my arms is fucking perfect. Her body was made to fit mine. I don't think I'll ever get enough. I wrap my arms around her, tucking her into my chest. Nothing has ever felt so natural. Not even football, and I took my first steps with a ball in my hands.

Annabelle's long legs tangle with mine as she draws lazy circles on my chest.

There's something about waking up with her here. In my home. In my bed. It's comfortable and exciting. It's fucking insane how much I still want her, as if we hadn't spent the entire night exploring all the ways to make each other scream before morning came and threatened to break the spell.

Lifting her chin, I ask, "Tell me you feel it, this crazy connection we've got? I felt it in June and every single time I've seen you since. I've never felt this before."

My words hang in the air unanswered, causing the post-sex euphoria I felt moments ago to crash and burn.

Annabelle sits up, holding the soft black sheet in front of her. "Declan . . ." she trails off, her eyes scanning the room, the ceiling, the bed. Looking anywhere but at me.

I mirror her, sitting up and leaning against the oversized black leather headboard. "Annabelle, please look at me."

Slowly, she lifts her glistening emerald eyes to mine. What the fuck? Is she crying? "Annabelle?" I reach for her, but she pulls away.

"No, Dec. If you touch me, I'm going to fall right back into your arms, and I can't do that. I need to get through this." She spins the gold infinity band she wears on her middle finger before wiping away her tears and pushing her hair out of her face. "I feel the electricity. Of course, I feel it too. But that's all it can be, Dec. You're a great guy, and you deserve so much more than the baggage I bring to the table."

I interrupt her, "You've got to know that I don't think of Tommy as baggage."

Bright green eyes flame in front of me. "I was not calling my brother baggage." For a moment, I think she's about to go to war, but she deflates before my eyes. "My whole life is baggage, Declan. I survive day-to-day. Most days, I thank God I kept it together long enough to get to the next day. I've got the studio, and I've got Tommy. And I've got a whole heap of guilt and regret. I am the oldest twenty-three-year-old you'll ever meet. I could keep a psychologist in business for years, talking through my issues, Dec. You deserve someone who can be all-in, and that's not me."

"Annabelle." I reach for her again, but she stands, wrapping herself in the sheet.

"No, Dec." She tightens the sheet around her chest. "You're Philly's newest football god. You're the real King of

Kroydon Hills. You could have any girl you wanted. You deserve someone who can help you bear the weight of that crown. Someone who can make you a priority. Someone who's not scared every day of losing another person she loves." A tear falls down her cheek. "And that's not me. This was so much fun, but that's all it can be. I don't have room in my life for a relationship, and that's not going to change."

"But Belle." My voice softens as I see more tears well in her eyes. "I'm not a god, I'm a man. I may not be the smartest man you've ever met, but I know enough to know that a connection like ours doesn't happen all the time. Don't you want to see where this can go?"

"I can't, Dec. I just can't right now," her voice cracks. "I'm sorry." She turns and starts looking for her dress just as I hear a phone ringing in the other room. "Shit. That's my cell." She begins frantically searching through our discarded clothes lying on the dark hardwood floor. "Where the hell did I leave my purse?"

"I think it's near the front door," I tell her as I jump out of bed.

Belle runs out of the room, so I pull on a pair of boxers and follow her down the hall.

By the time I get to the living room, she's sitting on the couch, wearing my sheet like a strapless toga and wrapped in the soft gray throw blanket that sits on the back of a chair. The sun is beginning to trickle in through the curtains, reminding me that it's later than I thought.

The phone is at her ear, but her eyes swing to me as a gasp escapes her lips, "Oh my God, Natalie. What happened?"

Coming to a stop in front of her, I watch the color drain from her face.

"Are Nattie and Tommy okay?" I ask, sitting down next to her. My heart hammers in my chest as I wait for her answer.

She nods and continues listening to whatever my sister is telling her. "Okay. I'll be there as soon as I can. Give me a few minutes." She's listening to Nattie as her eyes dart nervously around the room. "Right. Be there soon." Once the call ends, the first tear falls right before she climbs into my lap and wraps her arms around me.

"Jesus, Belle. What happened? Is everyone okay?" I start to cycle through all the people we care about who could be hurt right now.

Sniffling, she says, "Our friends are okay, but their friends aren't."

I haven't slept enough to decipher this. "What are you trying to tell me?" I ask as I cradle her face.

"One of the guys from the Kroydon University team and his fiancée were in a car accident this morning. She's dead, and he's in surgery. They don't know if he's going to make it."

"Nattie, Tommy, and the guys are fine though, right? My sister and your brother are fine?" I wipe her tears away with my thumbs, and she nods again.

"They're fine. Thank God, they're okay. It just hits a little too close to home. I remember getting that call. I remember Tommy waking up in the hospital and having to tell my scared little brother that our parents were gone." She takes a shaky breath. "It makes my heart hurt thinking about it. Plus, Nat and the guys are really upset. She said I should probably come get Tommy. He's okay. Well actually, he's totally oblivious right now. Obliviousness is his superpower." She buries her face in my neck and lets me hold her while she pulls herself together—the discussion from a few minutes before seemingly forgotten.

I stand, scooping her into my arms and walk back into my bedroom, placing her on my bed. Then, I go into my closet to grab a hoodie and sweats. "Sorry, I don't really have anything that's gonna fit you."

"Oh, crap. I hadn't thought about that. Do you mind dropping me off at your sister's place?" She stands and pulls the sweats up and then rolls them over so many times she'd look ridiculous if it weren't for how big the hoodie is once she puts that on. "Oh my God, these are huge."

"Sorry. At least the hoodie is too big to notice you have an extra roll around your hips." As soon as the words leave my mouth, I hear my mistake. If I hadn't realized it yet, the pissed-off glare I'm getting would definitely clue me in.

"Dec, you might not want to tell the woman you just spent the night fucking that she has a roll around her hips." She turns, storming into my master bath, looking like the cutest thing I've ever seen.

I holler through the door, "There's a box of toothbrushes under the sink."

A minute later, the door flies open, and the gorgeous mess in front of me is still glaring. Her head is cocked to the side, her soft brown hair falling around her shoulders and toothpaste frothing from her lips. "Are these for all your overnight guests, Dec? I didn't realize you were so full-service." Her feisty attitude makes me want to strip her right back out of those clothes.

Oh, fuck no. I take the toothbrush out of her hand and throw her over my shoulder in a fireman's hold, then slap her ass, no doubt leaving a nice red handprint on her creamy skin under those ridiculously oversized sweats.

"Declan!" she manages to yell before laughter overtakes her, and she pinches my ass. "Put me down."

I deposit her on the bathroom counter, next to the sink,

and watch her squirm to relieve the pressure from sitting on her stinging cheek. She spits her toothpaste out, then bends her head to rinse her mouth with water. "You shit. I got toothpaste on your rug when you picked me up."

I shrug. "The cleaning lady will get it." I step between her legs and rest my hands on either side of her thighs. "Listen to me, Annabelle Hart. Last night was incredible. You may not want more..."

Belle tries to cut me off, but it's my turn to glare, only mine has been perfected against three-hundred-pound linemen. "I'll give you a little space, but I'm not giving up on this thing until we get a chance to see what's there." I grab the box of unused toothbrushes and hold them in front of her face. "I have extra toothbrushes because I bought them in bulk when I moved. There were ten in a pack, and I've only used two since I came to Philly. You're the first woman to walk into my home who isn't related to me or about to be related to me." I crowd her space so she has to tilt her head back to look at me. "I don't do this. Ever. You're the first woman I've slept with in nearly a year."

Annabelle looks at me through her long black lashes, then mumbles, "Sorry." Her hands let go of the marble countertop she's been gripping, and flat palms splay against my chest. "I still can't give you what you want, Dec. But I know you're a good guy." She looks like she wants to say more but doesn't.

Stepping back, I hold her gaze a little longer before accepting that I lost this battle. "I'm gonna go throw some clothes on so we can get to Nattie's. We can grab Tommy, then I'll drop the two of you off. I've got to catch a few hours of sleep before I'm due at the stadium this afternoon for tonight's game."

Always Earned, Never Given

I turn to walk away as I hear "I'm sorry," whispered in the air.

She's crazy if she thinks I'm giving up this easily.

Anything worth being given has to be earned.

And I'm gonna earn Annabelle's heart.

12

ANNABELLE

Declan and I are quiet on the drive over to Nattie's house. She shares it with her boyfriend, Brady, and their two roommates, her soon-to-be stepbrother, Murphy, and Sebastian Beneventi. I can't even process what just happened this morning between Declan and me, let alone figure out how the hell to explain to everyone there why I'm wearing his clothes. Nattie is like a dog with a bone. Once she catches even a whiff of something happening between her brother and me, she's not gonna let go.

Let go. That's comical. I'm so good at letting go, I could be Elsa.

Let go of any feelings I may have briefly allowed myself to catch last night.

Let go of the fact that Declan managed to make me feel more in one night than I've felt in years. More like myself. More like I was actually living in my own skin. More alive.

I can tell myself, *"Oh well, Belle. Better let go of that too."*

I can remind myself to keep that boxed up for later when I'm alone and can handle thinking about it. Break it down, compartmentalize, and pack it away to the far recesses of my mind to only be thought of again years from now.

Lock it away and throw away the damn key. That's my best course of action. That's what I'm good at.

Because Declan Sinclair is dangerous.

No one realizes I'm hanging on by only a thread. They don't know that some days I fall into bed so grateful to have made it through the day at all. That control and sheer willpower are the only things getting me through. How much control would I have to give up to allow someone like Declan into my life? Someone forced to live his life in the public eye. I've been there and done that when I lived in New York. It was hard enough then, without the metric ton of baggage I've now got weighing me down added to the fucked-up equation.

The second Dec pulls to a stop in front of Nattie's brick house near Kroydon University, I throw open the door of the Bronco and am halfway out by the time he turns the ignition off. I catch him out of the corner of my eye and see he's getting out too.

Oh, no. No. No. No.

"Uh, Declan," my voice comes out a little too loudly. "You don't need to walk me to the door. I'm good. I appreciate the lift." And all the orgasms. And a whole lot more, if I'm being brutally honest, which I'm not.

This gorgeous god of a man ignores me, slams the door of the Bronco, and walks around to my side. "I'm not just leaving you here, Belle. Let's go see how everyone's doing. I want to check on my sister, then we can grab Tommy, and I'll take you guys home." He places his hand at the small of my back and guides me to the door.

Damn him.

That crazy zap of electricity courses between us even through my bulky clothes.

Declan's knuckles barely graze the door before it swings open and Nattie throws her arms around her brother's neck. I take my chance to sneak by her and take in the surroundings. Tommy is happily sitting on the couch . . . petting a dog.

When did they get a dog?

Looking around, I don't see Brady, Murphy, or Sebastian anywhere. I stand behind the couch and lean down, kissing my brother on the top of his head. "Hey, munchkin. I missed you."

Emerald-green eyes that mirror mine look up at me briefly. He brings his finger to his lips. "Shh, Belles. Me and Rocky are watching *Jurassic World*."

Wouldn't want to interrupt a movie this kid's seen a million times already. Guess he didn't miss me. Maybe overnights could be a thing? "Oh, you and Rocky?" I put my hand in front of the chubby little brown and white bulldog's nose so it can smell me. "Who does Rocky belong to?" I'm at this house at least once a week, and this cutie is a new addition.

Tommy shrugs his shoulders and turns back to the movie, effectively dismissing me.

Rocky looks from me to Tommy and plops her head back down on his lap.

Guess I see where I rank.

I follow the scent of coffee into the kitchen and blessedly see a full pot, freshly brewed. Come to Momma. On the ride over, I started coming down from the adrenaline rush I ran on all last night and well into this morning. I don't think we slept more than an hour, maybe two. My head is throbbing, and my eyes are dry and tired. My first order of business is getting a big cup of coffee. Then, I should be able to function enough to figure out what's next.

Moments later, Declan enters the kitchen alone, and I see Murphy heading up the stairs.

Nattie steps into the kitchen, and I watch Declan hand her a cup of coffee. She shakes her head no and leans against his shoulder.

Wow.

This girl never turns down coffee.

She wraps her arms around his waist before asking, "Don't you have to get to the stadium?"

He rubs her back. "Game's not 'til eight tonight." He's talking to her, but his eyes are locked on mine. I shouldn't love the way he does that. "I've got time. I let Dad know what's going on. I'm good for now."

"I'm glad you're here, Declan." She pulls back and looks at her brother adoringly.

"Me too, kid. Me too."

My attention is taken away from the gorgeous man in front of me by Sabrina when she sits down next to me. I'm glad to see she seems okay after whatever hell her mother put her through last night. My relief disappears when she snatches my coffee away. I reach for it, but she takes a quick sip. "Hey! Give that back. My head is killing me in a way only caffeine can fix."

She moves it further out of my reach. "I'll give it back when you tell me what Declan is doing here."

Damn it. Of course, Sabrina's going to pick up on it right away. She's too smart for her own good. Or well, at least for *my* own good right now.

She takes a second to look me over head to toe, then squeaks, "You're wearing his clothes. You slept with him!"

I grab her hand and drag her off the stool and into the

dining room. "Could you please keep it down? I don't think Nat has caught on to that yet, and I'd like to keep it that way if I can."

"Oh, come on, Belles. You're wearing his clothes. I've never seen you in men's sweatpants before, and I'm fairly sure you didn't play football for Notre Dame." The shock from seconds ago morphs into excitement, followed by confusion. "Seriously, where are your shoes?"

"Yeah well, I didn't exactly pack a bag for last night." I start pacing around the dining room, trying to calm my nerves. It's not working. "He was supposed to drop me off after the fundraiser. But then, one thing led to another, and we ended up going back to his place instead. Even then, I thought he'd be dropping me off at my own house this morning. I thought I'd have time to change before I came to get Tommy. I figured I'd just wear my dress from last night home. It was supposed to be a classy walk of shame, okay?" My voice is getting louder with each word.

Sabrina smiles a very self-satisfied smile. "So, you giving up those batteries?"

"No. It was a onetime only thing. A mistake that will not be repeated. What sucks is it was a really good mistake. Like, fucking amazingly good. Seriously—I'm going to have to buy a new vibrator and back-up batteries, I've never come so hard in my life—good." Leaning against the wall, I thunk my head as reality sets in, and I groan, "Declan Sinclair ruined me. Fuck me."

"Nope." Sabrina raises her hands up in front of herself. "Not fucking you. Sounds like Declan's already been there and done that, and I'm not into sloppy seconds." She flicks her hair over her shoulder dramatically and smiles proudly at her comeback.

"What the hell, Brina?" My chest shakes with quiet

laughter. "Just do me a favor, and don't mention this to Nattie. I'd like to pretend it never happened." For my own sanity as well as my patience with Little Sinclair.

We hear Rocky howl, and I spin around. "Oh shit, Tommy." We rush into the family room to find Tommy still happily sitting on the couch, but Rocky's now scratching to be let outside with Nattie trying unsuccessfully to attach the leash.

I stop next to her just as Murphy, Bash, and Brady walk down the stairs and head toward the kitchen. Nat grabs my hand and squeezes before she crosses the room to stand with Brady.

Tommy doesn't need to be here to listen to this, so I attach the leash to Rocky's collar and call out to Tommy, "Come on, bud. Let's take Rocky for a walk. Grab your coat."

~

When we finally drag Tommy away from Rocky and get him into Declan's beloved Bronco, exhaustion is weighing me down. My emotions are all over the place, and I would love nothing more than to allow myself to fall into Declan Sinclair's arms and let him tell me that we've got this right before we slept away the rest of the day. I don't remember what it's like to have someone tell me everything will be okay. My dad used to be so good at that. It didn't matter what time of day I called, he'd drop everything to talk to me and tell me we've got this.

I miss those comforting words.

I realize I've been staring out the window, lost in my thoughts, when I feel Dec's hand on my knee. "Belle . . . Is it okay with you?"

Son of a bitch. I guess I checked out. "Sure. It's okay." I have no idea what I'm agreeing to.

"Sounds good. I'll bring the pizza, kiddo. You pick the movie." Declan is smiling at my brother through the rearview mirror.

I turn my head and catch a beautiful smile spread across Tommy's face. "Plain pizza, please." He asks so nicely I kinda want to do a happy dance. Yeah, I definitely need to get some sleep.

"Plain pizza. Gotcha." Then he quickly glances my way. "Any special request for you, Belle?" God, his face is so perfect. I see his supermodel mother in his features when I look closely, but for the most part, he's all chiseled sexy man. Coach and his ex-wife made a trio of beautiful children.

I spin the ring on my finger, the smooth gold band reminding me to slow down. It's a habit I picked up years ago when I had to learn to think before I speak. "And when exactly are we doing this pizza and movie night?" I raise my brows in question but can't be annoyed when Tommy is happily bouncing in his seat in the back.

Declan grins back into the rearview mirror before answering, "Friday night." He pulls into my driveway and turns to face me. "It's a date."

"It's a date, Belles. It's a date," Tommy happily sings as he unbuckles and grabs his Rex and the dinosaur book-bag he took with him last night before he runs to the front door.

Declan's voice drops low, "You heard the man, Belles. It's a date."

If I had panties on, they'd be damp from his voice alone.

How does he do that?

Reaching down, I grab the canvas grocery bag filled with my dress, purse, and shoes. So much for a classy walk of shame. Then I turn in my seat and stare into those blue eyes that remind me of the color of the ocean after sunset. Eyes I could so easily get lost in. "That sounds like a perfect date for you and my favorite guy. Let me know what time you're coming, and I'll make sure I'm scarce," I say, giggling.

Declan glances at Tommy, who's standing outside our front door. He reaches one hand under my hair and cups the back of my head. "We'll see about that, Belles."

I rest my face briefly against his arm and then turn back to open the door. "I had an amazing night, Declan. Thank you for giving me back a piece of myself for a few hours."

God, how I wish it could be for more.

13

ANNABELLE

*A*fter spending the rest of Sunday afternoon overanalyzing every moment of the last twenty-four hours and fighting with Tommy over whether he should be allowed to stay up for the eight o'clock Kings game, I'm running on far too little sleep to wage a war, so we compromised. I allowed Tommy to stay up until half-time.

Of course, this resulted in a full-blown meltdown when I did put him to bed.

I should know better. In all reality, I do know better.

His routine is crucial to both of us. It's the only thing that keeps us functioning. He usually does pretty well with small tweaks, especially for things he wants. But he did not want to miss the rest of the game, and the result was me spending the next hour trying to calm him and get him to relax for bed. By the time he finally falls asleep and I drop back down on the couch, the game is ending, and Declan is running off the field, having just won thirty-six to seven.

Go, Kings!

He has his helmet in his hand, and his sweaty dark hair

is plastered to his gorgeous face. I guess that smile can make me melt even through a TV screen.

At least, I melt until a microphone is shoved in front of him and his mask slips in place. The perky sideline reporter asks a few questions about the game, but then she asks about me.

"So, Declan, does the beautiful ballerina who was on your arm last night have anything to do with the beast we saw on the field tonight? Is she in the stands cheering you on?" the reporter asks cheerfully.

I really don't want to be annoyed that she's touching his arm while asking him this or that her cleavage is a little too shoved in his face for my tastes, but I can't help myself. Dammit. I try to shove that down. Jealousy has no business in a friendship, and that's all Declan and I can ever be.

Friends.

I wonder if friends with benefits is still a thing.

~

Monday morning rolls around way too fast. Sleep deprivation is a real thing, and I'm seriously feeling the effects of having barely slept two nights in a row. Yup, two nights. Saturday night, because I was in Declan's bed, and Sunday night because I couldn't stop thinking about how I spent Saturday night. More specifically, what I was doing Saturday night. I don't want it to be a mistake. It was a onetime thing. It was amazing. But now, it's going to be a distraction—a massive reminder of what I don't have room for in my life.

Tommy was grouchy and harder than usual to get moving this morning, which already had me in a mood before my phone rings as I'm pulling into the parking lot behind the studio. A glance at the screen shows me it's Nattie. I hit the car's Bluetooth and brace myself for hurricane Nattie. "Hey, Nat. I was going to call you later today. Listen, I can take over your class tonight if you need to be with Brady. How are the guys doing?"

"Hey, Belles," she singsongs my name in typical Nattie fashion. "Brady hasn't woken up yet. When Brina and I came downstairs today, we found an empty bottle of Jack, three empty shot glasses, and a sticky table. I'm thinking the guys tried to drink away their pain, and they're apparently missing class this morning. I'll let you know later how they're doing. I should be okay to teach class tonight, but thanks for the offer."

There's an uncomfortable silence lingering in the air. "What's on your mind, Nat? You're never quiet."

"So . . ." she drags the word out dramatically. "How was it?"

"How was what?" Son of a bitch. I spoke to Sabrina earlier this morning, and she promised she wouldn't mention anything about Declan and me to Nat.

I can feel her eye roll through the phone. "Don't play dumb with me, Annabelle Hart. I'm the blonde in this friendship, and I play that part better than you. First, the whole freaking world saw the pictures of you and my brother from the fundraiser. He was kissing your hand at the top of the staircase, and you two looked like you were going to light the city on fire. I mean, seriously, it was the most romantic picture I've ever seen. Then you show up at my house yesterday, with Declan in tow. Not to mention, you were in his clothes. And why the fuck weren't you wearing shoes?"

"Jesus, Natalie. Take a damn breath."

"Stop stalling, Belles. Was it good? Are you guys official?

Does this make me Tommy's aunt? I would rock being the favorite auntie," she exclaims, excitement lacing each word.

"Nattie," I cut her off before she has the chance to continue down the crazy-train tracks. "It was a onetime thing. It was a great night. We had a fun time. We're friends, and we're going to stay friends." The words taste like lies, but I refuse to focus on that. "Besides, you're basically Tommy's aunt already. He adores you and doesn't need me dating a member of your family to change that."

"What the hell, Belles? Is my brother not good enough for you?" Natalie Sinclair can talk a girl in circles.

"Nat, listen to me. I'm only going to say this one time. Your brother's a great guy, and I'm sure he'll find his perfect soul mate when the time comes, but that's not me. I don't have the mental capacity for anything more than a friendship right now. Can we please move on to a different subject?"

She huffs out an annoyed breath. "Fine. But this conversation is not over, Belles."

The call ends, and I'm left staring at the building in front of me.

What the hell just happened?

I grab my Mary Poppins bag off the front seat and decide to make a detour into Sweet Temptations for a cup of coffee . . . and maybe a donut or two.

When the bell over the door announces my entrance, I hear a voice from the back call out, "I'll be with you in just a sec."

It may smell even better in here today than it did on Friday. Amelia pushes through the swinging doors from the back, carrying a tray of muffins. "You are going to be so bad for my waistline," I laugh. The muffins look like they're ready for a photoshoot. Decadent and picture-perfect. The scent of vanilla and cinnamon swirls through the air, and I'm pretty sure I want to move my dance studio inside this building.

Amelia laughs at me. Her jet-black hair is pulled up high in a ponytail with a red bandana holding it out of her face. Another flour-covered apron is covering her today, revealing only her frayed jeans and red Converse tennis shoes. I like this girl's style. She fills the empty spot in the display case with her muffins and then turns to me. "So, what'll it be?"

I point to the coffee pot. "I'll take the biggest cup you offer of that." Then, I study the muffins. "And can I have one of the coffee cake muffins, please? I can already tell it's going to be a long day."

Amelia turns her back to me while she makes my coffee. "Sure. So, did those pics I saw of you last night during the Kings game make your day longer?" She turns to hand me the coffee, but I'm staring at her, dumbfounded.

"I'm sorry, what? What pictures?" Then, I remember Nattie mentioned a picture too. Fuck. Fuck. Fuckity-Fuck.

"Oh, come on. If you're dating the quarterback, do you actually expect me to believe you didn't watch the game? Oh wait, were you there? At the game? I guess you wouldn't have seen the halftime show then."

Amelia stares at me, waiting for me to answer, but it takes me a minute to catch up. "No, I wasn't at the game. I was home, and I watched it with my little brother, but we missed the half-time show and most of the second half. I missed the pictures," I groan.

Placing my muffin in a bag, Amelia rings me up. "Well, it was a good picture. You guys might as well have lit my television on fire, you looked so hot. I didn't realize you ran in those kinds of circles."

My head whips toward her. "Oh, no. I don't. I mean, I

guess I do. I'm friends of the family. Declan and I aren't dating." How many times am I going to have to say this today?

"Does he know that? Because if a man looked at me that way, I'd climb him like a tree."

Everyone's got a damn opinion today. "Yeah. That's the popular opinion. Thanks for my breakfast. I'll catch up with you later this week."

I push through the front door and head down to my studio.

Great.

Another reason to relive Saturday night.

~

My toddler tap class has just ended, giving me a two-hour break before the next group of tiny dancers make their way through my doors. Please, God, let me have replenished the Tylenol I keep in my bag. My head is throbbing. Two days of very little sleep do not agree with spending an hour listening to ten little girls try to make as much noise as possible with their black patent-leather tap shoes.

I think my head may actually explode today.

After grabbing a bottle of water, I sit at my desk, pop two pills, move the overdue bills aside and pull up the Internet. I've been debating with myself all morning about whether to search for those photos Nattie and Amelia mentioned. I might as well have had an angel on one shoulder and a devil on the other. Or in ballet speak, a white swan and a black swan.

My little white swan is perfectly put together. Her tutu is starched and pristine. Her bun is tight, not a hair out of place. She's warning me, "*Protect your heart. You don't need to see those pictures. You know what happened, and you know it needed to be a one-time thing.*"

My black swan, who is equally as beautiful, but is the dark to her light, laughs at her, "*Girl, you know you need to see those pictures. Let's get another glimpse of that panty-melting man. While we're at it, maybe we go for round . . . what round is it now? Oh, who cares. When the sex is that good there can never be too many rounds!*"

Stupid swans.

It only takes one search to drown in images of us from Saturday night. The first ones to appear are when we walked the red carpet, and they're stunning. We look perfect together. Declan really is magnificent in that tux. I scroll through a few before I get to the one at the top of the curved staircase. The one I knew in my heart would be a perfect shot when he did it. Declan holds my hand to his lips while he drops a kiss on it. The beautiful old brick building is the perfect backdrop with the glittering lights of the city surrounding us.

Good grief, I'm swooning just from looking at it. My fingers hover over my mouse, as I internally debate whether I want to save it as my screensaver before forcing myself to hold strong and keep scrolling.

A bit further down are images of us dancing, and we don't look like friends in these images either. We look intimate. I flush, remembering what happened after these pictures were taken.

I don't know how long I've been sitting in a daze in my chair when my phone buzzes.

Declan: Hey, Belles. I'm not sure if you caught the post-

game press conference last night. I'm sorry they asked about you.
Annabelle: Hi, Dec! I missed that. I had some stuff going on and didn't catch most of the second half of the game. Congrats on the win though.
Declan: We still good for pizza and a movie Friday night?
Annabelle: We are. Tommy talked about it all night last night. He's ready.
Declan: Oh, yeah? And what about you, Belles?
Annabelle: See you Friday, Dec.

My white swan perks up. "*He's so dreamy, and he's not going to make this easy. Maybe we should give him a chance.*"

My black swan smacks her down. "*The only thing that man needs a chance to do is give you more orgasms.*"

I drop my head down onto my desk, close my eyes and remind myself I don't have room in my life for a relationship.

No matter how dreamy Declan Sinclair is.

Why does everything always have to be so damn hard?

14

DECLAN

When my dad summoned me to his house on Tuesday, he failed to mention there would be a giant moving van in the driveway. I shouldn't be surprised. Katherine mentioned that she and Carys were moving in this week, but I hadn't realized it was today. I make my way around a few boxes and into the kitchen to find Dad and Katherine kissing. Her arms are around his neck, and his hands are on her ass.

While this might skeeve Murphy out because it's his mom, I'm forced to resist high fiving my dad. I don't remember my mom and dad ever being overly affectionate with each other when they were married. So seeing my dad like this is strange, but I'm glad for him.

I clear my throat and fold my arms over my chest.

When they pull apart, my father glares at me, but Katherine, ever the hostess, turns around with a rosy tint to her cheeks. "Declan, we didn't know you were coming over today."

"Sorry, Katherine. Dad asked me to stop by." I glance

around the kitchen and down the hall to see more movers coming in through the front door. "This is me, stopping by."

Dad grumbles, "I asked you to stop by this morning, Dec." He raises his wrist and glances at his watch. "Morning," he emphasizes, "not afternoon."

"It's eleven fifty, Dad. Technically, it's still morning, and it's Tuesday. You're making a habit of consuming my day off." I watch Katherine move to the stove and turn on a tea kettle.

"Does anyone want some tea?" She still looks nervous, like I almost caught them the way Murphy did a few months ago when he walked in on them having sex in Katherine's kitchen.

Not a day any of us are likely to ever forget. Dad proposed a few hours later.

My father smiles at his fiancée. "No, thank you, sweetheart. Declan and I will be in my office if you need anything."

"Thanks anyway, Katherine. I'm glad you're moving in. Someone needs to keep the old man in line now that we're all out of the house." I hear her snickering behind me as I make my way down the hall and into my father's office.

Dad has lived in this house for almost two years, and this office still has boxes scattered throughout the room. The built-in shelves lining the wall behind his desk are covered with pictures of Cooper, Natalie, and me through the years. Christmas mornings, graduations, ballet recitals, and more football games than I remember line these shelves. A framed jersey we gave him when he retired from playing pro ball leans against a wall. Other than that, the office is a mess. Papers litter his big desk. There's a jacket flung over a chair, and a football that looks to be a hundred years old is sitting against one of the big windows. "You think you're ever going to unpack this room, old man?"

He sits down and laughs at me. "I'm barely twenty years older than you, and let me tell you, those twenty flew by in the blink of an eye. Be careful because someone's going to be calling you 'old man' before you know it."

"Yeah, yeah." I move the jacket off the chair and sit down across from him. "So, what's up? I'm assuming it's not as serious as last week since we're not meeting in your office at the stadium. What's going on?"

Dad studies me for a minute before casually leaning back in his high-backed leather chair. "Care to tell me what's going on with you and Annabelle?"

Well, I sure as hell didn't see that coming. "I'm sorry, what?"

"Don't play coy with me, son. I saw the way you looked at her last weekend. I watched the two of you together. We all saw you on the dance floor, and then you both were together at your sister's house the next morning." He doesn't continue. Just waits for me to respond.

"Uh-huh," I breathe out an annoyed breath. "I brought Annabelle as my date." I lean forward and rest my elbows on his desk. "A date you forced me to bring, by the way. So, I really don't know where you're going with this?"

Dad sits up, mirroring my position. "Don't get defensive, Declan. I'm talking to you as your father, not your coach. I love Annabelle and Tommy. This is me giving you a friendly reminder that dating Annabelle Hart isn't like dating anyone you've ever been with before."

"Yeah, Dad. I know." The hostility in my voice is loud and clear, so I force myself to back off.

"Do you though? She's basically part of our family. If things go bad, you'll still have to see her at family functions because I won't take our family away from the two of them. They've lost too much already."

Nervous energy has me standing from the chair. "I'm aware, Dad. She and I have already discussed this. She's got it in her head that her life is too much for me and that she has too much baggage."

"And what did you say?" Dad walks around the desk and leans against it, next to me.

I glance at him. When I was young, my dad seemed like the biggest guy in any room. He exuded strength and power. He was either playing football or coaching it. Everyone always stopped and listened when Joe Sinclair spoke, and I've never been any different. I've idolized my father my entire life, and the answer to this question matters to him.

I think back to Sunday morning and the feel of Belle in my arms. "I told her that Tommy wasn't baggage and that I wasn't going anywhere. She thinks she blew me off, but Tommy and I have a date to watch a movie and eat pizza Friday night. She might not be ready to let me all the way in yet, but those walls are getting knocked down, one way or another."

Dad's eyes are calculating. "Are you using Tommy to get close to Annabelle, son?"

"Wow, Dad. Guess I know what you really think of me. No. Tommy invited me over, and I told him I'd bring pizza. He's a cool little kid. And if I'm going to be in Annabelle's life, then I'm going to be in Tommy's life. He and I need to get to know each other better."

Dad nods in approval. "Good answer, Dec. I just wanted to make sure you know what you're getting into. Annabelle and Tommy are a package deal. I've watched that girl struggle for the last year. She doesn't like to ask for help. She also isn't impressed by you at all . . . And that's a good thing,

Dec." He slaps his arm around my shoulder. "When you decide to get into a serious relationship, it needs to be with someone who doesn't care about your fame or the money. Those things come and go. It needs to be with someone who'll fight for you—Declan the man, not Declan the quarterback. Annabelle could care less about all the extras, and money and fame don't impress her at all. But I've watched the two of you circle each other for a few months now." He taps his fingers against his desk. "And I'm telling you, that girl is worth the fight."

"Thanks, Dad. I appreciate your advice." I wasn't expecting it today, but I appreciate it more than he knows. Any doubts I had about trying to get Belle out of her comfort zone were just erased.

"Good. Now, what're you going to do about it?" he laughs, his eyes twinkling with the same mischief Nattie's eyes get when she's up to something.

Thoughts of Saturday night play out in my mind like an old home movie. "I think I'm going to stop by the dance studio."

~

When I pull my Bronco over to park in front of Annabelle's studio, I take a minute to study the building. The old, whitewashed brick building has arching white windows covering the front of the studio. They must be one-way windows because I can't see inside, and I only see "Hart & Soul Academy of Dance" scrolled across the glass in rose gold. Little girls bundled up in coats and hats are exiting the front door with their parents, chatting excitedly. The door swings open a little wider, and I spot Belle standing there, wearing a pair of tiny navy blue shorts, white leg warmers, and a white fuzzy sweater. She's there one second and gone the next as the rest of the girls filter out.

I texted my partner in crime, Nattie, a little while ago to see if Belle has any free time today. According to Nat, she's free for the next hour and a half. I wait for what feels like forever until the last little girl clears the door before walking up to the front of the building to find Belle has flipped the sign to "Closed." I give the door a push, and it opens easily. Stepping in, I flick the lock behind me.

She's not at the front desk.

Christ, anyone could walk in, and she wouldn't know.

"Never Enough" from *The Greatest Showman* is playing through the speakers. Nattie used to listen to this song on repeat back in the day. I walk further into the studio, past the front desk, but don't find her until I get to the dance room. It's off to the right. It's the room with all the windows, and I was right. You can see out, but anyone outside can't see in. There's also a big window between the waiting area where I'm standing and the dance room, so I can see her perfectly. She's breathtaking. I've never seen anyone or anything in my life as beautiful as Annabelle Hart dancing.

This isn't ballet. My sister grew up dancing ballet. I know what it looks like. This is different. This is grittier. She's gotten rid of her sweater, leaving her in those short shorts and a sports bra. She's dancing barefoot. Her caramel-colored hair is down and whipping around her as she effortlessly flies through the air.

I'm not sure when I stepped through the door into the room where she's dancing, but I catch myself standing there in amazement. As the last few beats of the song play out and she brings her foot down to stop spinning, I let go of the breath I hadn't realized I was holding.

Annabelle lifts her head in shock when she hears the noise in the otherwise now silent room.

"Declan?" Her voice is raspy and strained. God, she sounds sexy. "What the hell are you doing here?"

Well, that's not exactly the welcome I was hoping for.

15

ANNABELLE

"Jesus, Dec. You scared the hell out of me." My hands fly to my chest, trying to calm the wild beating of my heart. I move to the sound system and power it down, then spin on my not-so-little intruder. "Mind telling me how exactly you got in here?"

Declan stiffens before my eyes. He looks good. Really good. Worn jeans and a navy blue peacoat over a gray thermal shirt. He's got a Notre Dame ball cap on, covering his dark brown locks I had so much fun holding on to Saturday night.

Shit. How am I supposed to handle him in my space when I'm trying so desperately to push him out of my head?

"I came in the front door. It was unlocked." He holds up a brown paper bag. "I was at my Dad's and thought I'd see if you needed lunch. I grabbed us sandwiches from the place on the corner."

He brought me lunch? I have to stop myself from crying. Over. Lunch.

What the hell?

I can't remember how long it's been since anyone has brought me a meal that wasn't pizza for a girl's night.

Declan mistakes my silence for annoyance and drops his hand and the bag down by his jeans-clad thigh. "Sorry, Belle." He sounds cold. Distant. "I just wanted to do something nice for you. You know, since you helped me out last weekend."

I reach for him but come up short when he steps back at the same time. "I shouldn't have presumed."

Dammit. "Declan . . ." I step forward, a pleading tone in my voice. I want to beg him to stay. Instead, I opt for, "Want to eat in my office?" I check the front door to make sure it's locked and then walk down the hallway to my office before pushing him down on the gray sofa and grabbing us each a bottle of water from my bag.

"I wasn't trying to intrude, Annabelle. Friends need lunch." The hard edge to his voice tells me I'm screwing this up, but he tries to hide it behind a crooked smile.

I hand him a bottle of water and sit on the arm of the couch. "Three years ago . . ." I whisper softly.

Declan has no idea what I'm trying to tell him. I honestly have no idea why I'm even trying to tell him this, but I want him to know. Declan leans back against the couch and gives me his full attention.

He's good at that.

Making you feel like you're the only thing that matters.

"Three years ago, I danced the Sugar Plum Fairy in *The Nutcracker*. I couldn't come home for Christmas because we had a show the day before and the day after. I came home the first week in January for five days. It was the last time someone brought me lunch." I catch myself nervously playing with the bottle in my hand and force myself to stop and meet Declan's eyes. "I'm not used to this, Dec. I take care of Tommy, and I run this studio . . ." I don't even know what I'm trying to tell him.

"Annabelle." Declan pulls on my calf until I scooch down next to him on the couch. "I'm trying to respect your wishes here. You want to be friends, and that's what I'm trying to give you." There's sincerity in his voice, but it's the twinkle in his eyes that's telling me that's not all he wants. "Make no mistake, Belles, I want more. But if being friends is all you can do right now, then friends works for me. In case you haven't noticed, I don't have a ton of them in this city either."

Feeling a weight lift from my shoulders, I relax into the couch. "So, what did you bring for lunch?"

~

The next night, I'm soaking in a bubble bath with a glass of wine, my kindle synched to my favorite sexy book series, and a candle burning when my phone pings, alerting me to a text. I've only just gotten Tommy to bed and slipped into the warm water, so I ignore the first ping. My eyes close, and I rest my head back, enjoying the momentary peace and quiet before two more pings interrupt my silence.

It's got to be the girls. They're the only ones who ever text me. Grumbling, I grab my phone.

This better be important.

When I look down at my phone and see that there's a name assigned to the text chain, I chuckle, knowing it's definitely not the girls.

This has to be Coach's doing.

Sinclair/Murphy Family Group Text:

Coach Sinclair: Sorry for the group text. This seemed like the best way to get this information out. We got a letter from Cooper today. It appears he'll be home a week before Christmas until January second. Katie and I would like to get married on New Year's Eve at a private estate north of the city. We want to start off the new year as a family. We've reserved every room they offer for the weekend.

Declan: Did you really name the text chain, Dad?

Nattie: Aww, Dad! That's perfect!

Coach Sinclair: You and Brady will have two rooms.

Nattie: What?

Declan: Don't waste your money, Dad.

Coach Sinclair: I'm ignoring everything you say, Dec.

Declan: I feel the love, Dad.

Katherine: Aiden, feel free to invite Sabrina. The girls can room together.

Annabelle: I don't think I'm supposed to be on this text chain, but congrats!!

Coach Sinclair: I added you to this, Annabelle. You and Tommy are family, and we'd really like it if you'd both be there.

Annabelle: I . . . I don't know what to say.

Nattie: Say you'll come, Belles. It'll be fun, and you already closed the studio for that week.

Annabelle: We would love to. Thank you so much! Tommy will be so excited.

Katherine: Annabelle, we'd really like Tommy to be the ring bearer if he'd want to.

Annabelle: He would love that. (BTW I'm not crying right now. That's someone else)

Mom: Aiden, please tell Sebastian we'd like him to come as well.

Carys: Can I bring a friend?

Katherine: We can discuss that later.
Carys: How's that fair?
Murphy: Sucks to be the youngest, Care Bear
Nattie: I love you, Daddy!
Coach Sinclair: I love you too, honey. Now go tell your boyfriend he's bunking with Murphy!

Wiping the very real tears from my face, I force myself to pull it together and smile at the thought of celebrating Coach and Katherine's wedding with all our friends. Then I start to think about how Tommy will handle a night like that. My spiraling thoughts are interrupted by another ping on my phone. My smile comes back in full force when I see that this time it really is the girls.

Group Text:

Nattie: Hey, Hey, Ladies. My dad just announced the wedding date, and it's New Year's Eve.
Chloe: Woo-hoo! Big Daddy Sinclair's really putting a ring on it!
Nattie: Zip it, Chloe. Kathrine's had a ring on it for months now.
Chloe: Maybe he's putting a ring somewhere else. I hear older guys are all about the Prince Alberts.
Nattie: Oh, gross!
Sabrina: Yay! That's great, Nat.
Nattie: Oh, Annabelle?
Annabelle: I knew this was coming ... What, Nattie?
Nattie: Should we expect you and Declan to sneak away for some secret nookie?
Chloe: WTF! When did Belles and Dec have secret nookie? Why didn't anyone tell me?

Sabrina: If everyone knew, it wouldn't be a secret.
Nattie: It was last Saturday!
Annabelle: IT WAS ONE TIME!!!
Nattie: We'll see about that.

My black swan is back on my shoulder doing a little bootie shakin' dance and telling me, *"You could work on the secret part of secret nookie tomorrow night. Hell, just work on the nookie part. Figure out the rest after a few orgasms."*

My white swan flicks her off, pirouettes, then tells me, *"Forget secret nookie. Stay strong. That man may be perfection wrapped in Greek god tissue paper, but he is more than you can handle right now. Stay focused. No distractions."*

Okay. I think I'm losing my mind.

Before giving any of this nonsense more thought, I sink under the water and try to drown both of them.

∼

Friday morning, I step into Sweet Temptations for what's become my new morning routine. Coffee, sweets, and a quick chat with Amelia if she isn't too crowded. I typically catch her after she's done with the morning rush and starting to restock for the day. However, when I walk in, a tall brunette is there, looking at the cupcakes in the cases while Amelia makes her a cappuccino. Her shiny hair is hanging loose down her back, and a beige raincoat is tied around her waist. She's wearing pretty patent leather black pumps that give her a few extra inches, making her about my height.

Both of them look up when the bells chime over the front door. "Hey, Annabelle. I'll be with you in just a minute," Amelia throws over her shoulder as she finishes

Always Earned, Never Given

up. Today's bandana is hot pink and holding her black curls out of her face. And her ever-present flour-covered minty green apron covers her clothes.

"No rush. My first class isn't for another hour or so." I peruse the muffins and feel eyes watching me. When I look over, it's to catch the brunette looking at me curiously. Years of being on stage and in the public eye have me plastering a smile on my face. "Good morning," I say as I hoist my bag up higher on my shoulder.

She looks at me for a long moment before smiling a little too big and offering me her hand. "I'm sorry. You look so familiar." She drags the words out as if she's trying to place me.

"Well, you're looking at a local. I've lived here on and off my whole life. Maybe we've crossed paths." I shake her hand. "Annabelle Hart. Nice to meet you."

"Leah," she offers. "Nice to meet you, Annabelle Hart." She holds my hand for a second too long before dropping it. "Hart. Like the dance studio on the corner? Hart & Soul?"

"Yup. That's me. Are you looking for classes? We have a class for every age and skill level."

Amelia hands Leah her cappuccino then looks at me. "The usual, Belle?"

I feel the blush climb up my cheeks. I guess I really have made this part of my new morning routine if the owner knows my usual. "Yes, please."

Amelia rings up Leah, who turns to me before leaving. "You know, I was thinking about taking some kind of class at the gym, but if you offer adult dance classes, maybe I'll take you up on that."

I reach into my bag, pull out a business card, and offer it to Leah. "We'd love to have you. Check out my website when you get a chance. All the classes are listed there with the times and the number of the studio. Feel free to give me a call with any questions."

She flips my card over in her fingers. "I'll make sure to do that. Thanks."

Amelia and I both watch her leave before Amelia whistles. "I've got a pretty good whacko radar, and that girl seemed off."

I turn back to look out the window, but Leah's already gone. "She seemed okay to me."

"Maybe . . ." She hands me my cup of coffee then leans in with her elbows on the counter. "So, tonight's the night, right?"

"Oh, please stop. He's coming over to watch a movie with my brother. Nothing else." At least, this is what I keep telling myself.

Maybe if I say it enough, I'll believe it.

Amelia nods her head slowly. "Sure. Keep telling yourself that." She grabs the rag hanging off the back of her apron and starts wiping down the counter. "We'll see what tune you're singing Monday morning."

"Yeah, yeah. I hear ya." I start to cross to the door before turning back to Amelia. "You sure you don't want to come with Tommy and me to the Kroydon University football game tomorrow? My friends are all going. You're more than welcome to join us if you don't mind listening to my friends ogle their hot boyfriends the whole time."

Her laughter echoes throughout the empty bakery. "As much fun as that sounds, I'll pass this time. I can't close the shop early tomorrow."

I nod and open the door, just before hearing, "But maybe next time?" asked softly. I don't think Amelia is comfortable with having friends. I get it. I don't know her story yet, but there's unquestionably a story under the surface.

"Definitely next time." I wave and head over to my studio, hoping that spending my day teaching will help me forget I'm supposed to spend a few hours tonight acting unaffected by Declan Sinclair.

16

DECLAN

When my center, Jasper, and I sit down to eat lunch in the cafeteria Friday afternoon, it's already been a shit day. We're both quiet while we inhale our perfectly prepared, perfectly tasteless chicken, brown rice, and broccoli without speaking. We fly out tomorrow morning for our game Sunday against our division rivals in Dallas. It's going to be a tough game, and the staff has hammered that home all morning. I'm about to stand up when Jasper chokes on his water before hissing. "Ice Queen at two o'clock."

I stare at him for a beat, having no fucking clue what he's talking about before I hear the staccato clicking of stilettos against the linoleum floor. Glancing over my shoulder, I see Scarlet Kingston heading our way. She looks entirely out of place in her sleek black pantsuit with blood-red heels. Her hair is pulled back off her face, and her glasses are perched on her nose.

She and I met on Monday to discuss the fundraiser's press coverage and what to expect this week. Then she wanted to plan out the rest of the season, but I was saved by the bell. Coach needed me, and I've never been so happy to be summoned by my dad. Is it possible to have PTSD around one person?

Scarlet stops next to the table and examines it like a bug on her perfectly polished fingernails before she glances at Jasper and waits impatiently for him to excuse himself.

Jasper makes it a habit to avoid the press and Scarlet as much as possible. He happily stands, nods at her, and then turns to me with a stupid grin on his face. "Catch you on the other side, Dec." He might as well have said, *"Better you than me,"* before he escaped.

Scarlet leans against the table and crosses her stilettoed feet at her ankles and her arms over her chest. "Declan, I've spoken with your agent and sent him a list of interviews I'd like you to do." She appears to be waiting for a response but continues with a huff when I don't give her one. "Last weekend was a nice start to changing the narrative, but we need more. The organization needs you to pick at least one of the reporters from the list to sit down with and do an in-depth piece. Hunter has all the information. I need an answer by Monday morning." She unclasps her arms and moves her hands to her hips, irritated by my lack of response. "Declan . . . Are you hearing me? Did you get hit on the head earlier?"

When I've finally had enough of this conversation, I stand and hold my ground, which is not an easy thing to do with Scarlet. "I'll talk to Hunter after practice. Anything else?"

I know I shouldn't be this short with an owner of the team, but I'm a football player, not a damn trained monkey.

"No. But I need to know Monday. If I don't hear from you or Hunter, I'll pick the interview myself."

I nod and turn to leave when I hear her call, "And pick

your damn sponsorship deals, Declan." The click-clack of her heels goes out the same way they came in, and I cringe.

I fucking hate the press.

~

I can't help the smile stretches across my face later that day when my phone rings with a text from my brother.

Coop: Hey man. I got my phone and computer back – so I can finally text and email again.
Declan: Hey there, little brother. Still loving the Navy?
Coop: Yeah, man. Looking forward to the next step of training.
Declan: Did you see Dad set a date?
Coop: Yup. I'll be there. Think one of the guys is coming home with me too.
Declan: You finally coming out?
Coop: STFU.
Declan: Nothing wrong with liking guys, bro.
Coop: Nope, nothing wrong with it, except I'm more of a pussy man.
Coop: Speaking of – Did I hear you hooked up with Belles?
Declan: What the hell is wrong with you?
Declan: Jesus Christ, I'm gonna kill Nattie.
Coop: Might want to kill Murphy while you're at it.
Declan: Fuck me.
Coop: Is it serious?
Declan: It's Annabelle.
Coop: Exactly. It's Annabelle and Tommy. Don't fuck this up, man. She's perfect. If I weren't going to be away for the next 8 years, I would've gone for it.

Declan: Yeah, that's not fucking happening. Keep dreaming.
Coop: Fuck off, asshole. I'll see you next month.
Declan: Stay safe, Coop.

Coop's out of his damn mind if he thinks I'd ever let him have a shot with Annabelle. There's only one Sinclair for her, and that's me, even if she doesn't know it yet.

~

When Belle answers her door that night, she's wearing a pair of black leggings and an old worn Bon Jovi concert tee hanging off one bare shoulder. Fuzzy cream socks are on her feet, and her caramel-colored hair hangs down her back. I stand outside the open door, momentarily stuck in place while I drink her in. It may have only been a few days since I've seen her, but that was a few too many.

I itch to touch the bare skin peeking out at her shoulder. Lick it. Suck it. Bite it . . . I'm torn from my quickly turning X-rated thoughts by her voice. "Hey, Dec. Want me to take that?"

Oh, shit. Yeah. The pizza. "No, I'm good. Just point me in a direction."

Belle leads me into the kitchen, giving me the perfect view of her delicious ass as we go. I place the pizza box and bag of cheese fries on the counter. When I look around, I realize the house is quiet. "Hey, where's my date for the night? I don't hear Tommy."

Her smile ignites something in me, and I shove my hands in my pockets to stop from reaching out to touch her. I'm determined to show her I can be her friend, and showing her my hard dick might not really help my cause here.

"He's in his room playing on his iPad. Probably has his headphones on." Annabelle hops up onto the counter next to me, putting her at the perfect height. "I swear he blocks out the world when he has those things on."

Damn, what I wouldn't give to move between her legs and kiss her right now. I settle for leaning against the counter next to her.

"So . . ." she sighs. "You ready for the game this weekend? When do you guys fly out?" I guess we're gonna talk shop.

"Yeah. It should be a tough game. Dallas is good this year. We fly out late tomorrow morning."

She kicks me softly. "How about you give me the uncanned response? I'm not a reporter, Dec."

I blow out a deep breath. "Well, let's see. Scarlet Kingston is working with my agent to pick what interviews I have to do. 'Have to do,' being the operative phrase. I have no choice in the matter. I talked to Hunter, my agent, earlier today, and I lost the battle on sponsorship deals."

"Oh, no. Your sponsors dropped you?" She grabs my arm.

I place my hand on hers. "Nope. They've been trying to get me to sign for three months, and I wasn't ready to sign. My hand's being forced now," I groan.

"Declan, listen to yourself. You sound like a little boy having a fit because he's not getting his own way. Man up."

I turn so I'm looking into her pissed-off eyes. "The hell, Annabelle?"

"Listen to me. I've been there. It's not the same as football, but I've had to deal with the media circus when I danced in New York. It's all part of the game, Dec. I get it.

You hate this part. But you need to own it and control it yourself. Stop giving power to Scarlet Kingston. Her priority is the team. Take control and make yourself your own damn priority."

Belle jumps down off the counter when we hear the heavy thumping of feet running down the stairs, followed by Tommy's voice. "Belles, Belles, Belles, is Dec here? Is the pizza here? Is the movie ready?"

By the time he makes it to us in the kitchen, I think I've gotten over the wake-up call I've been handed and manage to focus on Tommy. This kid's energy runs at a crazy high level.

He skids to a halt when he sees me, zips his lips, and looks over at Belle before grabbing paper plates out of the pantry and dropping them down next to the pizza box and white paper bag. He picks at the masking tape holding the bag closed. "Are there cheese fries in there?" he asks Belle, who shrugs before running her hand through Tommy's hair.

"I'm not sure." The patience in her voice was certainly not there a minute ago. Jesus. I'm jealous of a kid. "How about you ask Declan?"

I know they're always working on eye contact, so I try to catch his eyes as he asks, "Are there fries in there, Declan?" His focus darts over my shoulder as quickly as it came.

"Yeah, bud. They're in the bag. Cheese on the side, just like you like it."

Tommy grabs napkins and puts them next to the plates before he gets three bottles of water. Definitely a routine he's done before.

Once Annabelle gets his pizza and fries on his plate, he turns, asking, "Can we have a picnic with the movie now, Belles?"

"Slow down, little man. Tell me again what we're watching tonight?" I ask, trying to get him to talk to me.

He huffs out a little sigh, and the attitude plastered on his face is 100 percent all Anabelle. Impatience is radiating from his body. "We're watching *Jurassic World*. Not to be confused with *Jurassic Park*. This one's better 'cause it has an Indominous rex." He spins on his heel and marches into the family room.

I watch, taken by his methodical movements. He places his plate and water on the coffee table while he lays out a blanket on the floor, plops down, and turns to grab his food and drink from the table. "Hurry up, guys."

Belle hands me a plate and a bottle of water. "You don't want to keep your date waiting, Dec. Patience is not a virtue Tommy has."

I reach over and tuck a lock of her soft hair behind her ear and then lean in and whisper, "If I remember correctly, patience isn't a virtue either Hart sibling possesses." I watch her green eyes dilate and try to hold back a smile.

She reminded me all week that this date is for Tommy and me. It's her way of telling me I'm supposed to stay on my side of the fifty-yard line. She doesn't realize all the best games are won in inches, not yards, and I'm gonna earn this win inch by inch.

17
DECLAN

Saturday night, I end the call with Hunter and feel surprisingly good about the conversation we just had. Annabelle was right. I needed to take control of the PR situation and own it. I've never let anything own me before, but that was exactly what I was doing with Scarlet and the media. On the plane to Dallas, I looked over the folders Hunter had been shoving down my throat for weeks. I picked two of the five sponsorship deals that were on the table and told Hunter precisely what I was willing and not willing to do promotionally for both companies. If they want me bad enough, they'll agree to my terms. I also picked two of the interviews Scarlet had on the list and told him to get a list of questions ahead of time.

It's time for me to control the damn narrative.

I climb into bed in my hotel room at nine o'clock and grab my phone.

Declan: I took your advice today.

I see the little dots stop and start a few times before Annabelle's response comes through.

Annabelle: What advice?
Declan: To take control of the PR situation. It was good advice. Thanks for the push.

Again with those damn dots before her response pops up and my phone rings.

Annabelle: Glad I could be helpful.

I'm surprised when a picture of her appears on my screen. She's FaceTiming me. "Hey, friend." Holy shit! Annabelle's soaking in a tub, surrounded by candles. Her damp hair is thrown on top of her head, and her cheeks are flushed a deep red.

"Shit, Dec." She looks totally shocked to see me. "I didn't mean to hit the FaceTime button." I watch her angle the phone so I can only see her face. Damn. If she could just angle it a little lower.

"You sure about that, Belles?" I groan and adjust my dick.

"Declan..."

"Friends don't FaceTime each other naked, Belles. You're looking kinda warm there. You feeling okay?" I love torturing this woman. It's so much fun.

She blows her hair out of her face, and the angle of the phone slips slightly. "I didn't mean to!"

"Okay. I believe you." This little tease licks her lips, and images flash through my mind of what she can do with that damn tongue. My voice drops low, demanding, "So, what are you doing in that tub, Annabelle?"

She sighs a soft sigh. "I was trying to relax before you texted." Her voice is as soft as her sigh and so fucking sexy.

"Were you touching yourself, Annabelle?" The twin patches of red on her cheeks is all the answer I need. I push harder. "Were you thinking about last weekend, Belle? I've lost count of how many times I've gotten myself off this week, thinking about your pretty pussy." I grip my cock and squeeze.

Her rapid breathing increases.

"Tell me, Belle. Tell me what you were thinking about."

Belle bites down on her lower lip, and another sigh carries through the phone. "Declan . . ." she groans in a mix between a beg and a denial.

"Tell me, Belle." The words are being ripped from me. I'm trying to keep it together, but God, I want this woman.

"I had to order a new vibrator this week. I haven't been able to get myself off since our night together." Her voice is pleading. "I've tried so hard. But my body is a bitch, and nothing is working."

"Remember what it felt like when I ate your pussy, Belle? Remember how hard you came that first time? Remember how you tried to push me away after your first orgasm in my apartment, but I just kept licking your clit until you came again?" There's no way she can't tell I'm jerking my cock now. Just picturing her from last week gets me off these days.

"Keep going," she pleads.

"Remember what it felt like when you sank down on my dick in the limo? Your tight fucking heat was the hottest thing I've ever felt, Belle. Or fuck, when we finally made it to the bed, when I had you under me?"

"Yes," she keens. "I'll never forget what it felt like," she says, her voice trembling. Our heavy breathing blends together.

"You ready to come for me, baby? I wish I were there to make you come with my mouth. My hands. My cock." Her head lolls back against the tub, and her eyes close as she moans, and I come long and hard.

When she opens her eyes, I'm expecting to see her blissed-out, but instead, she looks worried. "What the fuck? Dec, I'll call you back. The Kroydon Hills Police Department is calling me."

I'm not sure whether she hears me order her to call me back as she ends the call.

What the hell does the police department want?

I jump out of bed and look for my pants like I'm not half a country away with no way to help her. What the fuck do the police want at . . . I check my phone. If it's nine o'clock here, it's ten back home. Why the fuck are the police calling her at ten o'clock at night?

After a few minutes of pacing around the hotel room, which feels more like an hour, the phone rings again. Belle looks scared this time. She's thrown a pale pink robe on and is throwing decidedly upset vibes my way. "Sorry about that. The alarm was going off at the studio, and the alarm company couldn't reach me. Apparently, they had the wrong number on file."

"Was there a break-in?"

She shakes her head. "The cops are there now. They said the doors are locked. They wanted to know if I wanted to come down and meet them there or if I just wanted to call the alarm company."

"Do not go there alone, Annabelle."

Belle's eyes flash with fury. "I'll do whatever I want,

Declan Sinclair. I knew how to take care of myself by the time I was a teenager. I don't need you telling me what I should or shouldn't do." It looks like she sits down as she blows out a breath and her big eyes glass over.

"I'm sorry. I just wish I were there to go with you. Can you please call one of the guys? You'll need someone to stay with Tommy anyway."

I've already come to realize that Annabelle has a tell. When she lifts her eyebrows, she's basically calling me a dumbass. "I'm not going tonight. Tommy's asleep, and the guys played a hard game today. I'm not asking any of them to come over here. I already called the alarm company and asked them to turn it off. They said it looks like it was a tripped wire or something. None of the doors were opened, and none of the motion sensors were set off."

"Okay, good. I still think you should ask one of the guys to go with you tomorrow to check it out. Please. Just to be safe," I all but beg her. "I fucking hate that I'm halfway across the country right now."

"I'm a big girl, Declan. I don't need one of the guys to go with me. It's all good. I swear. I'm not going anywhere tonight." She smiles, and both dimples pop deep in her cheeks.

"Please just be safe, okay?"

"I will. You just worry about winning the game. Tommy is even more excited to watch now that his best friend is the quarterback," she laughs, and the vice around my heart starts to loosen.

"Will do, Belles. Will you text me tomorrow? Just to let me know everything's okay." I hate how badly I need her to agree to this.

Her smile disappears before she purses her lips and

nods. "Sure, Dec. Now get some rest. You've got a game to win tomorrow."

Her bravado falters slightly when she quietly adds, "Sweet dreams, Dec," right before ending the call.

I needed that. To hear her calm and okay. But I'm gonna make sure she stays that way. I open the running group text message that I've got with my brother and the guys.

Group Text:

Declan: Hey, guys. Annabelle just got a call from the cops about the alarm going off at the studio. She doesn't need to rush over tonight, but they want her to check everything out. Can one of you go with her tomorrow after she drops Tommy off with Nattie?
Bash: I can go check it out tonight.
Brady: I'm up for either.
Murphy: Me too.
Declan: Thanks, guys. She said not to worry about it tonight. She just wants to pop in tomorrow before the game.
Cooper: And how do you know she got a call from the cops, Dec? You're in a different state.
Declan: We were on the phone when the call came through.
Cooper: Doing what?
Declan: Talking, asshat!
Murphy: Wasted opportunity, man. Phone sex is the bomb.
Brady: Wonder if that's what your Mom's doing with Coach right now, Murph?
Cooper: Make sure my sister's safe before you kill him, asshole.
Bash: Ignore the fuckers. I'm gonna ask my brother, Sammy, to have someone check out the studio tonight. And I'll go

with Belle tomorrow, man. Go to bed and win the damn game.
Declan: Thanks, guys.

Why can I breathe easier knowing she'll be safe tomorrow but still feel irrational rage at the idea of it being with Bash instead of me?

18

ANNABELLE

"Thanks for coming with me. I'm sorry Declan made you feel like you had to," I tell Bash as I hop out of his oversized Hummer, heading for the backdoor of the studio.

"Gotta tell you, Belles, I'm glad Declan texted last night. A lot of bad shit goes down in this city. Whether you hear about it or not, it's there. You've got to be safe, and as your friend, I don't want you checking this shit out alone. If you were my girl, I'd have done exactly what Declan did." Bash drops that bomb then hangs back, looking around the parking lot while I'm unlocking the back door and disarming the alarm.

I'm not Declan's girl.

Even thinking that sounds whiney.

"It's all clear outside." He walks in behind me and continues down the hall when I make a left into my office.

"Nothing looks out of place in here," I yell down the hall. "I don't keep any cash here. I can't imagine what someone would want from the studio." I leave my office and pull the door closed behind me. By the time I meet Bash by the front desk, he's checked the locker room and both studios.

"Yeah, it all looks good up here too. Must have been a tripped wire." He checks something on his phone, then smiles. "Let's get out of here. The game's gonna start soon, and I think your man needs to hear that everything's okay before he goes on that field."

I whip my head around, hand on hip. "I don't have a man, thank you very much, Sebastian."

Bash fails to hide his laughter. "Yeah, Belles. Whatever you gotta tell yourself."

"Fuck off, Bash." I flick his ear.

He grabs the keys out of my hand and holds them above my head. Sebastian Beneventi is six-foot-seven. If he doesn't want you reaching something, you're not getting it. "Call Declan. Put him out of his misery, please. I want the Kings to win today." His eyes dare me to fight him before he adds, "I'll be waiting in the Hummer." He heads back the way we came, leaving me alone in the lobby.

I grab the phone out of my pocket and huff out an annoyed breath. I'm not used to high-handed guys. I grew up around dancers. I was friends with dancers and dated dancers. I don't think any of the guys I dated could be referred to as an alpha male. If anything, I think I may have been more alpha than them. It always seemed hot when I read about the elusive alpha male in my romance books. The guy who took what he wanted, protected how he wanted, and claimed a girl for the whole world to see.

In real life, these guys are a giant pain in my ass.

I dial Declan's number and wait to hear his voicemail. I'm completely shocked when he answers, "Are you okay?" The worry in his voice hurts my heart to hear.

Maybe they're not *quite* a giant pain in my ass.

It's really noisy wherever he is. I'm guessing it's the locker room.

"I'm fine. Sebastian came with me after I left Tommy with Nattie at the house. Everything looks good at the studio. Must have been some kind of error."

"God, it's so good to hear your voice, Belle."

This man... "I'm fine, Declan. You didn't need to bother the guys. Now hang up the phone and win the game." I hear the noise from his end of the call get quieter.

"Can I call you later, Belle?" It's twenty-five minutes before kick-off, and he's worried about me.

"What am I going to do with you, Declan Sinclair?"

"We can talk about it later, Belles. I gotta go." He ends the call, and I feel a tiny piece of my wall start to crumble.

～

Tuesday morning, I pop into Sweet Temptations and am greeted by my new favorite scent of coffee and chocolate. And oh boy, does it smell fan-freaking-tastic!

"Amelia," I call out.

"I'll be out in a minute, Belle," she yells through the doors. This seems to be how our daily chats start each day. I hear a giggle coming from the corner of the room and turn to see the girl from last week sitting on the funky brown suede chair in the corner of the shop, sipping something that has steam coming off it and a chocolate muffin sitting in front of her.

Damn. I wonder if that's what smells so good?

Standing, Leah leaves her things at the table and crosses the room to me. "I've been here for a while, and she only just slowed down a few minutes ago. You just missed the crowd."

I drop my bag next to the register and lean against the counter. "Good grief, it's already been an insane morning. It's a full moon tonight. I guess the crazies are coming out early."

"Yeah, must be." She looks as pretty and put together today as she did last week. Knee-high heeled boots and skinny jeans show under a cute leather bomber jacket. The girl's got great taste. "I was hoping to see you today. I wanted to know if I could sign up for your Friday morning adult beginner's class."

"Sure. I'm heading over to the studio once I get my caffeine fix. Why don't you follow me over and we can get you registered? I just have a few releases I need you to sign."

Amelia pops out of the swinging doors. "Okay, Annabelle, let me guess. Large pumpkin spice?"

"You know me so well already," I laugh and pick up my bag. "Can you throw a muffin in there too, please?"

She turns around to make my coffee. "I sure can. Did Tommy get to give the doggy cookies to his new buddy this weekend?" Amelia's face lights up. My brother sure can win over the pretty girls.

"He did, and Rocky loved them. We saw them Saturday before the Kroydon Crusaders game. You've really got to come with us next time. It's a lot of fun." We stopped in to get the cookies for Rocky on our way to Nattie's before the game Saturday. Tommy hasn't stopped talking about the pudgy bulldog for a week.

"Oh, yeah. What about the Kings? Are you going to be watching that man of yours in person anytime soon?" I swear to God everyone has turned into Natalie this week.

"He's not my man," I mumble. "But I think we might be going to the game next weekend. I'll let you know if we get tickets."

Amelia's entire face lights up. "Yes! I love football. The food, the lights, the hot players in tight pants."

When I look at her in shock, she laughs and holds up her hands. "No worries. I know not to look at the quarterback. But does he have any friends? You may be in denial, but I'd be happy to climb a few trees." Amelia winks at me, hands me my coffee and muffin, and then rings me up.

Leah, who I forgot was still in the room, clears her throat and then laughs. "Wow. You're dating the Kings' quarterback? The one from Notre Dame?" she asks.

"Jesus. You girls are way bigger football fans than me. I don't think I'd have a clue where Declan went if it weren't for his family," I tell them both and then look at Leah. "We're really just good friends, but everyone keeps getting that mixed up."

"Sure you are, Belle. Maybe if you tell yourself that enough you might actually start to believe it. Was he, or was he not at your house Friday night?" Amelia crosses her arms over her chest and waits for an answer.

"Oh, wow. He was at your house?" Leah asks, more to herself than to me. "The Kings' quarterback?"

I glance between her and Amelia. I'm not sure who I'm more annoyed with. Amelia for being a little right or me for having to admit that to myself. "Whatever. Thanks for the sustenance. I'll catch up with you tomorrow, Amelia." Turning around, I ask Leah, "Are you ready to head to the studio, or do you want to drop by later?"

She smiles an overly excited smile, leaving me to wonder how much coffee she's already consumed. "Lead the way."

19

DECLAN

Wednesday night, I decided to swing by Hart & Soul after a meeting with Scarlet and Hunter. We hammered out the final details of both interviews I agreed to. Hunter gave Scarlet all the information on my endorsements and thinks I might finally be on Ms. Kingston's good side. According to her, this will be as good for the organization as it will be for me.

I wanted to ask if we were talking about sex because she was talking about it like we were about to fuck, but I managed to keep my inner sixteen-year-old quiet and sat back, counting down the minutes until I could get the hell out of there.

When I got into the Bronco, my phone was already ringing with a call from Hunter, who had joined the meeting via Skype. When I finally swipe to answer, the asshole is laughing. "Jesus, Declan. Could you have possibly looked less interested in there? We just signed two deals that are going to make your children's children rich, and you looked like you couldn't get the hell out of there fast enough, man."

"Just make sure we get the questions for both interviews ahead of time and tell me where I need to be and when." I end the call as I pull in front of the studio and get out of the Bronco. I haven't talked to Belle since Sunday morning. I did speak to Nattie earlier today, and she was more than happy to help me with a little recon on Belle's schedule. She should be here tonight for another hour or so.

The lobby is full of parents putting coats on excited tiny ballerinas, but my attention is immediately drawn to the front desk when I hear my name exclaimed above all the noise. Tommy is sitting in the chair with Brady next to him. He's bouncing in his seat when he turns to Brady and tells him, "My best friend, Declan, is here."

"Tommy boy, I thought I was your best friend." Brady feigns hurt.

Tommy's head bobs up and down in agreement. "I have lots of best friends and one girlfriend."

Brady and I exchange shocked looks before I lean on the desk. "So tell me, who's this girlfriend? Does your sister know?"

Tommy goes back to playing on his iPad. "Well, it used to be Nattie. Then it was Carys. But now, it's Amelia." Those Hart dimples pop in his cheeks. "Amelia makes the best cupcakes." He never looks up at either of us, which is a good thing because both Brady and I are trying hard not to laugh.

"Yeah, kid. It's important to like your girl's cupcakes." Brady's grin grows as he says that before he steps behind Tommy so I can't hit him.

Instead, I glare. "No talking about my sister's cupcakes in front of me. I like to think she doesn't have cupcakes. Got it, Ryan?"

"Uh-oh, you just got last-named by Declan. What'd you do, Brady?" Nattie wraps an arm around my waist then stretches to kiss my cheek. "Hey, Dec. Brady and I are grabbing pizza after this. Wanna come?"

"Thanks for the invite, kid. I've got to get home. Long day." Annabelle comes out of her office, followed by the douchey dad from last week, and my urge to grab her is strong. Kinda proud of myself for not just throwing her over my shoulder and taking her right back into the office for a few minutes of alone time.

"Declan, are you coming over to our house again this Friday? Can we do pizza and a movie again? Please?" Tommy asks excitedly, quickly glancing up as he bounces in his seat.

I could kiss this kid for his perfect timing. Douchey Dad just heard that, and it looks like he sucked a lemon.

Good. Asshole.

Annabelle moves in next to Tommy and runs her fingers through his hair. "Tommy, Declan may be busy Friday."

"Nope. My Friday is completely open for you, little man."

Tommy's hand shoots up in the air for a high-five, and Annabelle sucks in a quick breath.

I high-five his chubby hand, and she looks shocked.

I try to get her to look at me, but she smiles and shakes her head as if to clear her thoughts. When she turns to Douchey Dad and thanks him for his help, his smile is arrogant in return. "Anything for you, Annabelle." He looks down at his little girl and squeezes her hand. "Alright, Livvie. Say goodbye."

The little girl smiles. "See you next week, Miss Annabelle. Bye, Miss Natalie."

Nattie fakes a shiver once they're out the door. "I don't know how such a sweet little girl can have such a slimy dad."

"He's not slimy, Nat," Belle admonishes.

"Whatever. He gives me the creeps." Moving around the desk, Nat kisses the top of Tommy's head. "Give me a minute to get my stuff together, QB, and I'll be ready to go home." She practically skips down the hall to Belle's office and shuts the door behind her.

Annabelle finally looks at me. "Hey, Dec. What's up?"

Brady clears his throat. "I'm gonna go see if Nattie needs help." Then he follows my sister down the hall.

"Smooth, Ryan. Real smooth," I chuckle. "Don't eat any cupcakes in Belle's office."

"What the fu— fish sticks are you talking about?" Belle asks.

"Fish sticks?" I ask, confused.

She shakes her head and nods towards Tommy. "Oh . . . Fish sticks. Gotcha." I hadn't thought about the fact that she needs to watch what she says in front of her brother and all her baby ballerinas. I guess that has to get sticky when he's around the guys. I cannot imagine any of the guys being good at watching what they say. I'm sure they try, but still . . .

"Remind me to tell you about the cupcakes later." I move next to her and push her hair away from her face, shocked when she only tilts her head up to look at me but doesn't back away. I lower my voice, "I was worried about you this weekend."

She glances quickly at Tommy. "We're fine, Dec. I told you that Saturday night and Sunday morning."

"You okay with me coming over again Friday night?" I twirl her soft hair absently around my finger, and she nods her head.

"Yes," she whispers. "Will you let me make dinner this time? You didn't touch the pizza last week."

"Yeah, pizza's not really on my approved food list during the season. How about you pick a place and I'll order take out? Just make sure to pick a place Tommy likes. Better yet, just text me what I should order." I move my hand under her hair and start to rub her neck.

Belle hums and tilts her head. "Sounds good." Her hand grips my wrist before she adds, "Thank you."

I lean down and kiss her forehead. "See ya Friday, Annabelle." I gently rap my knuckles on the desk in front of Tommy to get his attention. When he looks up, I add, "Friday night, little man. Pick out a good movie, okay?"

"*Jurassic World!*" he announces . . . loudly with an infectious smile plastered on his face.

Annabelle laughs, and I know I just earned an inch.

～

We actually sat down to dinner at the dining room table Friday night since Tommy picked spaghetti and meatballs from his favorite Italian place for take-out. Not exactly a picnic kinda meal. This meant the movie started later than last week, and by the time his favorite raptor, Blue, is saving the day at the end of the movie, little man is starting to fall asleep on the blanket he's wrapped up in on the floor.

This kid cracks me up. He knows exactly how many millions of years ago each species of dinosaur lived, whether they were from the Jurassic or Crustaceous period, and what their real names are. Apparently, a brontosaurus was also thought to be an apatosaurus at some point, but those scientists were wrong. This week, Tommy told me all about wanting to be a paleontologist when he grows up so he can make sure no dinosaur is forgotten. I think I might have fallen in love a little bit right then.

When the credits roll and Tommy doesn't move, Belle,

who's been sitting next to me and painting her nails, whispers, "I think he's asleep."

"Want me to carry him upstairs?" I offer.

She shakes her head no. "He needs to go to the bathroom before he goes to bed. Let me just get him moving, then I'll be back down."

Once the two of them are upstairs, I move into the kitchen and clean up what little mess we left earlier before slipping my feet back in my boots. Tonight was a good night. I wasn't sure how Belle would act around me after our FaceTiming session last weekend. But she wasn't awkward, and I think I'm starting to gain a little ground. I'm still in the friend zone, but I'd say I'm getting closer to crossing the fifty-yard line.

When she finds me lacing my boots up, she looks a little disappointed.

"You heading home already?" She moves further into the kitchen and leans against the counter.

I lean against the edge of the kitchen table across from her. "Yeah. We've got a walk-through tomorrow. Gotta get some sleep tonight." I take a chance and reach out, grabbing her hand and pulling her between my legs. "Are you and Tommy coming to the game Sunday? I know Dad said his box isn't even close to being full this week."

Belle's palms rest on my chest, not pushing me away. "Well, I can't exactly tell your biggest fan that we're going to miss it, now, can I?"

I move my hands to her hips, a current of electricity drawing me to her. "Nope. That little man can get whatever he wants, and he knows it." I'd give him the world if I could. I'd give them both everything if she'd let me.

Annabelle tips her head up and flutters her long black

lashes. "What are we doing, Declan? I don't think I'm ready for this yet."

My heart soars and sinks at the same time. I can handle her not being ready for this because my girl put "yet" on the end of that sentence. I hold her face in my hands and kiss the top of her head. "We're becoming really good friends, Belle, so that when you're ready for more, we've already built the foundation we need."

With strength I didn't know I possessed, I stand to my full height, force myself to drop my hands, and pull my keys out of my pocket. "Will you guys stick around Sunday after the game? Maybe I could take Tommy on a tour of the locker room."

She nods gently.

"Night, Belles."

"Sweet dreams, Dec."

20

ANNABELLE

The next two weeks fly by much the same as the last two did. Tommy and I have one routine between home, school, and the studio. Nattie and I have another routine at the studio. She keeps bugging me to add another teacher because we're turning students away since we're stretched so thin. But it's just not something I can afford yet, not that I tell her that.

Even Declan and I have settled into a little bit of a routine. He drops by on Tuesday afternoons with lunch, and we do dinner and a movie with Tommy on Friday nights. I think he's trying to prove to me that I have room in my life for more. For him. But I'm not sure I'm ready to take the chance yet. Although I do find myself looking forward to those precious few hours we get to spend together.

We've both been good about keeping things where I'm comfortable. Dec does a good job of not pushing, but I don't know how long he's going to be willing to settle for sitting next to me on a couch or watching me work on the studio's books while he eats lunch.

Today, however, I'm trying out a new routine. One of the

universities in the city has a school of autism studies. Tommy already takes social skills classes there weekly, and this week, we've added Saturday sports and skills camp. They offer all-day sessions, which is perfect for a Saturday. This means he doesn't have to come to the studio with me, and maybe he'll enjoy himself and get to learn a new sport. He's going to spend his morning there while I teach three classes at Hart & Soul.

The sky is the color of an angry bruise this morning. It's not really dark blue, more like deep purple with hints of blacks and darker blues, warning us the heavens are going to open up and soak the world at any minute. I took a chance last night and told the girls I'd meet them this morning for coffee at Amelia's shop. I have one hour before I have to be in the studio and jumped at the chance for a little girl time. I'm just hoping that I don't get a call that Tommy needs me to pick him up.

Chloe and I are the first to arrive at the shop. We're sitting at a table in the back corner, waiting for Nattie and Sabrina when Amelia finally gets a lull in customers and decides to sit with us for a minute. She looks Chloe over, assessing. "So . . ." She drags the word out. "You're not the peppy dance teacher who brings Tommy in, and I've seen the senator's daughter on the news, that must make you Chloe."

Chloe cracks up, "Um, yeah. Definitely not the peppy dance teacher because she's banging my brother. So, ick. And the senator's daughter has a name. It's Sabrina. If you're trying to get a feel for Belle's friends, I'm the youngest and loudest of the bunch. Don't be judgy, and it'll be nice to meet you, Amelia." Chloe offers her hand, and Amelia shakes it and smiles at me.

"Damn, Belle, you have a crazy crew, don't you?" she asks

as a buzzer goes off in the kitchen, causing her to disappear behind the swinging doors.

Chloe relaxes back in her crushed-velvet burgundy wingback chair. I love the funky furniture Amelia has in the shop. It's got a very Central Perk vibe.

"Well, that's Amelia. I think she likes to act tough on the outside, but she's really a softy deep down," I tell Chloe.

"I'm not soft," is hollered from the kitchen, before Amelia adds, "and I've got great hearing and even better acoustics. Might want to keep that in mind, Belle." Then she cackles.

Swear to God, she cackles like a witch.

Chloe leans back and sips her hot chocolate. "I think I'm gonna like her."

When the front door opens, the howling wind bounces off the walls of the shop as Sabrina and Nattie hurry in and shake the rain off their coats. They both drop down onto the couch opposite Chloe and me. Nattie helps herself to my coffee before I smack her hand. "Give it back, brat."

"You love me, and you know it." She sticks her tongue out at me. "I need more caffeine. I never sleep when Brady's traveling for a game." She takes another big sip, then stands and pulls Sabrina up. "Come on. Let's go order so we can gossip before Belles has to go."

A few minutes later, we're all munching on sweets and sipping liquid gold when Chloe breaks the calm. "Sooooo . . ." Her eyes zero in on Sabrina. "Brina. All good now with your parents and Murphy? Has Mommy Dearest sucked it up yet and apologized?"

Sabrina's parents had an issue with her dating Murphy that led to a huge family fight. They seemed to have straightened it out but were recently all in a room together for the first time since it happened.

"Yeah, she's good now." Brina thinks about it for a minute. "Well, as good as she's going to be. You know my family. Dad was just reelected, and he's already strategizing his next move. Murphy and I have both been given parts to play."

Brina turns to me. "How about you, Belles? What's going on with you and Declan?"

"Yeah, Belles." Nattie wastes no time jumping on this bandwagon. "What's going on with you and my brother?"

Of course, this is when Amelia comes out of the kitchen, wiping her hands on her apron. Today, it's chocolate-brown with a minty-green cupcake on the front. Guess she felt like switching it up. "Why yes, Annabelle. I haven't been able to get an answer to that question yet either."

My head snaps to Amelia. "Hey! You're supposed to be on my side. You don't even know these little traitors." I glare at my three laughing friends.

She points at each girl. "Chloe, Sabrina, and peppy dance teacher."

"Hey," Nattie pouts. "I've introduced myself to you before."

"I know. You strike me as the eternally happy cheerleader type. And, since I'm not, I may enjoy giving you a hard time about it." She shrugs her shoulders and cocks her head to the side. "Sorry, not sorry?" It sounds like a question but it's not.

"Okay." Nat nods. "That's fair. I can deal with that." Then the blonde brat turns back to me. "Come on, Belles. What's up with you and my brother?"

I put my cup down on the table and my hands in my lap in an attempt to not strangle Nattie. "I know it's not the answer you all want, but we're just very good friends. I'm telling you guys, I have enough on my plate. I don't think I can handle much more than that."

"Oh, I'm sure there's a whole lot of Declan to handle too." Chloe taps her hot chocolate against Brina's cup as if to say *"Cheers,"* and I choke on my coffee.

Amelia shakes her head and huffs. "Maybe you guys can talk some sense into her. I'm telling you, Belle, you need to make time." She heads back into the kitchen.

"Damn, she's blunt. I like her," Nattie laughs, before taking a sip of coffee, then adding "and she's basically my new crack dealer with this coffee. It's so good."

"Good. I like her too. I convinced her to come with us to the game tomorrow." I pick at my muffin and check the time on my cell. "Ugh, guys. I've got to get moving."

There are a few groans, but we agree to meet at the stadium tomorrow, and I leave them in the dry bakery while I dart through the rain down to the studio.

I step into the studio, turning on the lights and the sound system as I make my way to my office in the back. I drop my Mary Poppins bag on the couch and sit down at my desk to check my voice mails when I notice the drawer isn't closed all the way. It sounds silly in my head, but I'm a little obsessive about keeping my desk organized. I can only control so many things in my life, and my office space is one of those things. I never leave it messy. I never leave a drawer open or a paper out.

I glance around the room, and everything else looks fine. Maybe I was in such a rush to get home last night I didn't notice that I'd left it open.

My black swan is back, telling me, *"Of course, you were in a rush. The GOAT was coming over last night for another orgasm-less non-date. Maybe if you'd let him test out how limber you are, you'd be able to concentrate better."*

My white swan tour jetes over and kicks her counterpart right off my shoulder. *"Ignore her. You don't need a man to help you concentrate. He already knows exactly how limber you are. And he can't be the GOAT after half of one season. Let's see if the cutie-patootie can win the game tomorrow. Maybe he can be a baby goat after that. Or one of those fainting goats. Those little guys are adorable."*

The chimes over the front door ring, pulling me from my spiraling thoughts.

Okay, bring on the day!

~

Fuck this day!

Four hours later, I'm done.

The kids have been awful. The parents have all had issues today. I had to talk to one parent who was three months behind on tuition, and she managed to tell me off. I thought that was the icing on this shit-tastic day until I locked the studio up in the pouring rain and saw I have a flat tire. And not a little flat. More like sitting on the rim and totally flat.

I officially give up. I'm supposed to pick Tommy up in thirty minutes. It's going to take me twenty minutes to get from here to there, and I didn't renew my roadside service a few months ago because I didn't want to spend the extra money. So basically, I'm screwed.

I jump into my car to get out of the rain and dial Nattie. She picks up on the second ring. "Hey, Belles. What's up?"

"Nattie, I've got a flat at the studio, and I'm supposed to be picking Tommy up. Is there any way you can pick him up for me? I'm so sorry to ask." I lean my head against the steering wheel and close my eyes.

"Annabelle, stop. It's not a big deal. I can be there in twenty minutes. Do I go to the same place we picked him up from last time?" I hear the rustle of the couch as she gets up.

"Yes. I'm so sorry, Nat. Thank you so much."

"No problem. I'll call you once I have him. How about I bring him back to my house? Just text me when you've got the car straightened out, okay? We're ordering pizza for dinner since the guys won't be home. I've got you covered."

"Thanks, Nat. I'll let the school know that you're allowed to pick him up." I lift my head and watch fat raindrops hitting the windshield.

"K. Talk soon," she ends the call.

After I've called the school to make sure they add Nattie's name to the sheet I filled out a few months ago, giving her permission to pick him up, I sit in my car, stumped as to my next move.

Damn it.

I'm far from a damsel in distress, but I have no clue how to change a tire. I spent my teens in New York City. Learning how to change a tire was not at the top of the how-to list when I didn't even have a car in the city. I didn't need one. I look up the number for the roadside assistance company and give them a call to see if I can renew my subscription or just get a new one.

No problem, they say.

Easy peasy, they say.

Credit card given and renewal complete, they finally look to see who they can send my way. That's when they inform me that it's a two- to four-hour window before someone can change my tire.

Son of a bitch.

Annabelle: Thanks for getting Tommy, Nat. Roadside

assistance is going to be a few hours. Can you drop Tommy off here? I don't want you to have to babysit all afternoon.
Nattie: Nope. I've got him. We picked up pizza and are going to watch Brady's football game on TV. He's good. I'll bring him to your house when the game's over. No worries.
Annabelle: I don't know what I did to deserve you. But I'm super grateful for you, Nat.
Nattie: Remember you said that, Belles. TTL.

Thunder crashes above me as lightning pierces the dark sky. I'm already upset and on edge when a knock against my window rips a terrified scream from my throat.

"Jesus Christ, Declan." I pocket my keys and swing the door open. Then I grab his hand and pull him behind me under the awning above the building's back door. "What are you doing here?"

Dressed in a navy blue Notre Dame football hoodie with his hat pulled low, he exudes comfort and confidence. He looks good. Damn good.

"Nattie called. She thought you may need help changing a tire." He pulls me into him, wrapping those massive arms around me and giving me the comfort I'm desperate for.

"Dec, it's pouring. You don't need to change my tire. I called roadside assistance." I lean my head against his chest and soak in his warmth. He smells clean and masculine and all Declan.

"Not a big deal, Belle. It'll take me five minutes." He pulls back and kisses my head, then puts his hand out. "Keys."

I drop the keys in his hand, then watch the first-round draft pick for the Philadelphia Kings change my tire in the rain. This man who could buy my car a million times over dropped whatever he was doing to make sure I was okay. He didn't flash his money or fame to get someone else to help. He's doing it himself.

Taking care of me.

As I fight back tears, I remember I have an umbrella in the car and grab it to hold over Declan, hoping to keep some of the freezing rain off him. He was right, it only took him a few minutes to get the spare on.

Dec looks up at me as he starts tightening the lug nuts on the spare. "Did you hit something?"

"What?"

"It looks like there's a puncture on the side of the tire." He finishes tightening the spare and then stands.

Just when he straightens with the spare on the car and the flat tire in his greasy hands, the wind catches the umbrella, blowing it inside out before it grabs hold and carries it away. The thunder booms, the lightning cracks, and the rain, so cold it's nearly sleet, pounds down on us. Staring into those inky blue eyes of his, I decide I don't have the strength to fight this . . . to fight him anymore. I place my shivering hands on his beautifully soaked face, lean up on my toes and kiss the corner of his mouth before meeting his lips.

It's pouring rain and freezing cold, and I couldn't care less about any of it. My entire body sighs in relief as he reaches down and lifts me so my legs wrap around his waist. Declan carries us to the back door of the studio, his lips never leaving mine. He holds me with one arm anchored around my waist and his tongue tangling with mine while he fumbles with my keys. Finally giving up, he pulls his head back. "Can you please get us in this damn building?"

Taking the keys from his hand, I unlock the door while he wraps his other arm around me.

Walking through the hall, Declan stops us at the keypad

on the wall so I can unarm the alarm, then walks me straight into my office. He sits us down on my couch with me straddling his lap and pushes my dripping wet hair away from my face.

I pull back and study his face.

Those beautifully expressive eyes tell me everything I need to know.

I decide in that moment to let go of my fear.

21

DECLAN

"Belle, what's going on? Tell me what you're thinking?" I ask, cupping her shivering face in my hands.

She turns her head to kiss my palm, then closes her eyes. "Isn't it supposed to be the girl who wants to know what the guy is thinking?"

"Maybe, but I still want to know." I lean forward and gently kiss her lips. I hold her forehead to mine, leaving our lips only a breath apart. "You okay?"

She takes my ball cap off and wraps her hands around the back of my neck, running her fingers through my wet hair. "Why are you so patient with me, Declan? I keep pushing you away. Why do you keep coming back?" A tear drips down her rain-soaked face.

"Because you're worth it." I wipe the tear away with my thumb. "You're worth everything. I'll wait as long as you need me to because I know that this," I motion between the two of us, "is going to be the endgame, Annabelle. This is going to be the thing that changes my life. Nothing needs to happen right now. I didn't come here for that. I came here because you needed help, and I needed to be the one helping you. I know you can take care of yourself, but you don't have to do it all alone. You keep insisting that you don't have room in your life for anything else. But let me in. Let me show you what it can be like when you have someone to help carry the load. We can take this as slow as you need to. I'm not going anywhere."

"I don't know how to do this, Declan. I don't know how to let you in. I don't remember the last time I wasn't alone."

"Your pace, Belle." I run my hand over her wet hair and try to convince her, "Your pace."

She leans her head against my drenched shoulder, and I hear a sob catch on a laugh. "We're soaking wet, Dec. Your clothes are so cold."

"Yup." I pull her away from my body so I can see her face. "We're wet and cold. We should probably go home and get warm and dry. What do ya say?"

"Yeah. We can't have Philly's favorite quarterback catching a cold because of me." I hate that stupid nickname. "The city would never forgive me." She stands up and holds her hand out. "Come on. I've got to get Tommy. You want to come over for dinner? I could actually cook this time."

"You don't have to do that."

The smile that graces her delicate face could light up the entire Kings stadium. "It'd be nice to cook for another adult. I'm sick of nuggets and mac n' cheese. I've got some salmon and veggies I can roast. Super healthy, I promise."

"Annabelle, are you inviting me over for dinner?" I ask curiously.

She shoves me back. Well, she tries too. "Shut up. You've eaten at our house every week for the last month." When she moves to pull her hand away, I wrap my fingers around her wrist and pull her body against mine.

"I've eaten at your house, but Tommy's invited me. Not you." Those eyes roll, dimples pop deep in those cheeks, and my smile grows by the second. "I feel like I just got a first down, Hart. Let me enjoy it, would ya?"

"Watch it, Sinclair, or I'll take it back. Let's get out of here."

When we get back outside, the weather's gotten worse, if that's possible. We stop under the awning, and Belle turns to me. "Listen, I'm just going to grab Tommy and head to my house. Do you have a gym bag in your car? Because I don't have any dry clothes that would fit you at my house."

"I do keep a gym bag in my car. Somebody's been paying attention."

"Zip it, buster. All the guys do the same thing. It doesn't make sense for you to drive back into the city. Why don't you head to my house? There's a key under the front mat. Just let yourself in. We'll be a few minutes behind you."

"Annabelle, are you insane? That's not safe. What the hell?"

Her body stiffens, and she glares at me, annoyance written all over her face. "Can we argue about this when we're both warm and dry? Please?"

Grabbing her face in both hands, I kiss her until she turns soft and pliant. "Yeah, okay. But we *are* going to talk about this later. See you soon."

I don't leave the parking lot until I see her car pull away. Belle heads to pick up Tommy, and I go to her house. Her damn key was exactly where she said it would be. When I walk inside, I notice the keypad to the alarm next to the door, but it wasn't armed. She's not going to be happy with me when I also get on her case about that later. What the hell? She needs to be safer than this. If she's so good about arming the studio's alarm, why would she be so careless at home?

I go upstairs, searching for a linen closet and a towel and use what I'm guessing is Tommy's bathroom, judging by the dinosaur decals on the walls and the shower curtain. Even the giant green rug on the white tile floor is shaped like a triceratops. I decide to quickly jump in the shower to warm up and stand under the hot spray. The lavender vanilla body wash in here smells like Annabelle and makes me smile. It also makes me hard as hell, remembering what it was like to smell that scent while I licked my way up her beautiful body.

Christ, is it wrong to jerk off in a kid's shower? I pump my cock in my hand and get lost in the smell and memory until I hear the door slam open and the lid on the toilet seat get thrown back.

Oh, shit.

Have I mentioned the vinyl shower curtain is clear with only a few multicolored dinosaurs, not so strategically placed for a six-foot-six man? When Tommy flushes the toilet, the water turns ice cold, and I try to hold in the yelp that almost escapes. He must hear me move away from the showerhead because he turns around much more calmly than I was expecting and stares at me before yelling, "Belles . . ." He draws out her name. "Declan's in my shower, and his bird is way bigger than mine."

Oh, fuck.

22

ANNABELLE

Oh, dear God. "Tommy, get out of the bathroom." I knew Declan was in the shower. I heard it running as we walked through the front door. I didn't even think to tell Tommy not to go into his bathroom. He's not used to anybody else being in the house.

At least he didn't freak. That's something . . . right? I slip into warm white cable-knit knee socks, my cotton shorts and throw on the Philadelphia Kings hoodie Declan left here a few weeks ago. I'm not going for style right now, just comfort. Well, these socks make might my legs look great, so maybe it's fifty-fifty. After I towel-dry my hair and gather up my wet clothes, I open my door just as Declan's peeking his head out of Tommy's bathroom.

"Is the coast clear?" he asks, with the most adorably freaked-out look on his face.

"Yeah, Sinclair. I think you're safe from the scary ten-year-old."

He opens the door all the way, and my mouth waters at the sight of Declan Sinclair in a pair of black athletic shorts and a tight white t-shirt stretched across his broad chest and beautifully sculpted arms. Yum.

His shoulders relax, and he shakes his head. "So," he says uncomfortably. "I'm guessing Tommy was talking about the size of my... you know..." I love watching him get flustered.

"Yeah, Dec. He was talking about the size of your penis. We watched a show on Animal Planet last week, and they talked about the size of a horse's penis. This led to a very long, very uncomfortable conversation with my brother about different-sized penises. I may have told him his would get bigger when he gets older."

Declan chokes.

"In all fairness, he asked. I didn't just offer that up. And you were never mentioned. I'm guessing he noticed the size of yours, and it made him think of our conversation."

"Is that your way of telling me I'm hung like a horse, Belle?" Declan crosses his arms over his broad chest, a big shit-eating grin stretching across his face.

I take the wet clothes out of his hand and push him backward. "No. It's my way of telling you your dick is bigger than a ten-year-old's whose balls haven't dropped yet, Sinclair." I skip down the stairs, throw the wet clothes in the washer, and start to get dinner ready.

Declan follows behind, asking, "What can I do?"

I shake my head. "Nothing. I've got this. Why don't you go chill with Tommy? He's either watching ESPN or Animal Planet. Go talk football with your biggest fan."

He catches me off guard when he cups my cheeks, kisses my head and walks away. This man's touch does things to me that I'm not sure I'll ever be ready for, but I'm not strong enough to resist anymore.

If I add Declan to our lives, how will that change everything? I already walk a high wire every day. Will I be able to maintain my balance, or will I crash and fall to the ground below with no net in sight?

~

Tommy yawned all through dinner. I guess running around at Saturday sports camp tired him out. I generally try to put him to bed by eight-thirty, but today he put himself to bed an hour earlier.

When I come back downstairs after tucking Tommy in, I find Declan sitting comfortably on my couch with his feet up on the ottoman, fireplace turned on, and his phone in his hand. He looks good in my space.

When he hears me enter the room, he offers me his phone. "Kroydon University won. Looks like Brady and the guys are going to a bowl game this year."

I take the phone out of his hand and read the text chain. I love seeing the guys so happy. "Good. They deserve it. It's been a rough season for them." I hand him back the phone, drop down next to him on the couch, and lean my head on his shoulder. "Thanks for coming to my rescue today, Dec."

He pockets his phone and wraps an arm around me. "Belle, we need to talk about you leaving a key under the mat. And while we're at it, why don't you arm your security system at home?"

I shift to face him. His arm slides down to my waist, and I try to decide the best way to answer. "I didn't know what my parent's code was. After the accident, when I finally walked through those doors, I set off the alarm. The alarm company called, and I knew the password. It had been the same since I was a little girl, but I didn't know the four-digit code. They turned the alarm off for me, and I just . . . I guess

I just never reset it. I've never used it since I've moved back in."

"Annabelle." Declan searches my face before speaking again. "I can't imagine what that must have been like. But baby, you've got to set the alarm. You and Tommy sleep in this house. You've got to be safe."

"You're not wrong, Dec. But it's not like this is a bad neighborhood. My neighbors are a surgeon and a stockbroker. We don't usually get someone looking for an easy score around here," I try to laugh it off, but the look Dec gives me tells me it's not working. "I'll think about it, okay?"

When he doesn't budge, I reach over and wrap my arms around his neck. "I'll try. That's the best I can do, Declan."

Declan pulls me onto his lap and runs his hands up my exposed thighs. "I should go home, Belle. The game's at one o'clock tomorrow. I'm kind of intense when it comes to my routine."

I tuck my knees under myself on either side of his lap and grip his shoulders. "Oh, yeah? I'm all too familiar with routines. What's your night before a game routine?"

Damn. His erection is growing harder beneath me.

My body has ached for this man for weeks.

Dec's calloused palms move under my hoodie, sliding up my ribs, stopping to rest under my breasts. He's making sure not to touch, but just the feel of those rough palms on my sensitive skin is heaven.

"I try to relax. If I'm going to watch TV or game tape, I make sure I turn it off at least thirty minutes before bed." His hands dance up and down my sides, making goosebumps break out along my skin as he continues, "I go to bed at nine, because my body has me up by six every morning, no matter what. So, the closer to nine I hit the sheets, the closer I am to the nine hours of sleep I should be getting."

When I shiver in response to his hands and voice, he adds, "It's almost eight now, Annabelle. I should be going home." The words spill from his lips, but he makes no attempt to move. His hands make another pass at my ribs, brushing the underside of my breasts, and I may whimper. When he does it again and smiles at the noise he elicits, I decide it's definitely a whimper.

His words from earlier echo through my mind.

It's now or never, I decide. "What about exercise, Dec?"

"What do you mean?"

"What do you think of exercise before bed?" Oh my God. I just felt his cock jump beneath me. If I had on panties, they'd be drenched.

"Oh, that." He leans in, his breath whispers in my ear, "I limit all taxing cardio to two to three hours before bed. I don't want it to interrupt my sleep cycle."

His warm breath on my ear is killing me before he licks around the lobe, causing me to wiggle in his lap.

I have no idea when I became this wanton woman. Before I give myself a moment to overthink, I ask, "So, if it's really slow exercise . . ." I grind down on him slowly and drop my voice to a whisper, "so slow and so quiet that you're barely moving, barely speaking, is that on the bad cardio list?"

Declan crashes his mouth to mine and stands without missing a beat.

I wrap my arms tightly around his neck and lock my legs behind his back.

His lips are soft and demanding. His arms wrap around me as he carries me up the stairs, only pulling his mouth away long enough to ask, "Which room?"

"End of the hall," I pant. "On the right."

He moves quickly and quietly past Tommy's room into

mine, shutting the door gently behind us and locking it without ever taking his lips off mine. He carries me to the bed and lays me down before standing up and reaching behind his neck to pull his shirt over his head. The insanely gorgeous man standing in front of me is every woman's fantasy, and he's mine.

For tonight, he's mine.

A smile stretches his face. "Yeah, baby. I'm yours."

Oh God. Did I say that out loud?

"I'll never be anyone else's. Not tonight. Not tomorrow. I'm yours, Belle."

Declan rids himself of his pants and stands gloriously naked in front of me. A lifetime of hard work on the field has carved his body as if from stone, every muscle on display. He doesn't ask me if I'm sure. He doesn't hesitate. He grips my shorts and pulls them down my legs before crawling up my body.

His hoodie is still covering a third of me when he sits on his knees between my splayed legs. He grips my wrists in one hand and holds them above my head, flat on the bed. Then he swiftly pushes the sweatshirt up my body. When he gets it shoved up to my wrists, he ties them together with the sleeves and slips it around the wrought iron spindles of my bed.

"Declan," I pout. "I want to be able to touch you." I pull at the ties, but they don't give.

Declan licks into my mouth before making his way down my body. He slowly pulls off my socks one at a time before whispering, "Slow and quiet, Annabelle. Those are the rules tonight." The gleam in his dark blue eyes sparkles like the ocean at night before he feasts on my pussy like no man ever has. When I moan loudly, he stops and looks up at me through those dark lashes from between my thighs, whispering, "Be quiet, baby, or this ends. We don't want to wake up Tommy." Then he winks and pushes his tongue inside me.

Holy shit. I hadn't even thought about waking Tommy.

"Stay with me, Belles," he whispers as his tongue circles my clit and his hands lift my hips, holding my pussy closer to him. His eyes hold mine as he licks and sucks, while I pull at my restraints and rock my hips helplessly in his hands. He builds me up over and over without letting me come, never pulling his eyes away. Finally, Dec swipes his flat tongue along my sex before curling a finger inside me. I orgasm on a soundless moan seconds before Declan climbs to his knees and sinks slowly into my wet heat.

He holds my body to him with one arm while he frees my wrists with his other.

Our words are whispered soft and slow and so fucking hot.

Our motions are the same. So slow. So powerful.

The silence in the room makes every push of our legs, every pull of our hands, every touch of our lips so much more intense.

He holds my mouth to his as his lips caress my skin and tells me, "I've never felt anything better than your body, Belle. So tight. So wet. So hot. So fucking mine."

Each word is a whisper in the air.

Each whisper hotter than the one before.

Each slow snap and deep push of his hips against me builds me higher.

My legs wrap around his hips, knees bent, toes pointed.

"Fuck, you feel incredible, baby."

My hands skim over his damp, hard body and grasp his tight ass as he thrusts deep inside me. Dec holds himself there and lets me ride him from below, taking what I need while he keeps a hand on my neck and his lips on my mouth.

"Take what you need, baby. Take my cock."

I'm surprised when Declan pulls me up and spins me around. He holds my back to his chest and slams into me from behind, over and over. That hand I love so much goes back to my face and angles my head so he can kiss me again. His lips are never far from mine. His other hand quickly finds my clit, and I'm completely at his mercy and ready to lose my mind.

"Declan," I pant, my chest rising and falling with each heavy breath. "I'm so close."

"Let go, Belle. I've got you."

Those words were exactly what my body needed to shatter.

I think I've been holding my breath my entire life, and I can finally breathe again.

23

ANNABELLE

Lying sated on Declan's chest, I try to calm my heart and my head.

With his hand tracing circles on the bare skin of my back, I try to shake away the crazy thoughts that are running through my mind.

That was so much more than sex.

I know I said I was ready for this, but am I?

My black swan is back, smoking a cigarette and sipping champagne. "*Stop overthinking. You're going to ruin the post-sex euphoria. Just enjoy the orgasms,*" she lazily tells me.

My white swan is straightening her tutu and fixing her bun. "*Guard your heart. Learning to fly took years. Crashing and burning only takes one wrong move. Are you sure you're ready to take that leap? Do you think he'll catch you if you fall?*"

My insane thoughts are interrupted by a beeping coming from Declan's phone. He reaches down to the floor and pulls it out of the pockets of his shorts, swipes something then places it on my nightstand.

I lean up on my elbow and soak him in. "Everything okay?"

"Yeah. It's my warning. Eight forty-five. I've got to get to bed. I'm sorry, Belle. I wish I didn't have to leave." Declan sits up, his beautifully sculpted back on full display.

God, I love a strong back.

My black swan sips her champagne. "*Just ask him to spend the night. Imagine all the orgasms.*"

My white swan grabs the champagne flute and pours it over the head of her nemesis. "*Time to make a decision, Annabelle. Are you ready to fly again?*"

"What time do you get up in the morning?" I ask quietly. Timidly. Unsure.

"Six. Why?" My heart stutters at the confused look on his face. This man goes from sex-god/athlete to clueless man so quickly, and I'm unwillingly falling for both versions of him. I'm falling for all the sides of Declan Sinclair.

I run my shimmery purple fingernails around his left nipple and watch his skin break out in goose-bumped flesh. "Because if you wanted to, you could just sleep here. God bless Tommy. One of the things that kid is exceptionally good at is sleeping in, and Sundays are the only day he gets to do it during the school year. He won't wake up tomorrow morning before eight."

When Declan doesn't answer right away, I begin to rethink my offer.

Fuck flying.

My heart was safer with both feet firmly planted on the ground.

But when those midnight blue eyes of his crinkle at the corners as he smiles at me, my head and my heart slow down.

"Are you sure, Annabelle?" He runs his fingers over my head and tugs the end of my hair.

"As long as it won't interfere with your routine, Dec, I'm sure. Only you know if it's going to throw you off."

He tugs the end of my hair again before leaning down, kissing me and whispering, "Think you can control yourself if I spend the night?"

His velvety smooth voice holds such a sarcastic tone that I reach behind me, grasp my pillow, and smack him with it. Then, completely naked, I stand up, slowly walk over to my vanity, and turn to face him before I slowly slip on my pink fuzzy robe.

He's already hard again, and I'm ready to permanently banish my damn swans when they high-five each other.

Declan leans his head back against the wrought iron headboard and groans, "That's not playing fair, Belles." He licks his lips, and I know I've won.

I wag my finger back and forth in front of him. "I don't see any refs here, Sinclair."

When I move toward the door, I hear the bed creak before those strong arms wrap around me from behind. I'm thrown down on the bed with a bounce and try hard not to laugh too loudly.

"No refs here, Hart, because we're on the same team." Dec puts a knee on the bed before his hands cage me in.

"Oh, yeah? You think we're gonna make a good team, Sinclair? You and me?"

"Nope." He kisses me quickly. "You, me, and Tommy." Then he leans in and claims my mouth slowly before getting up, grabbing his shorts, and walking into the bathroom.

I guess it's time to fly again.

∼

*D*eclan and I didn't talk about how we wanted to handle our new relationship status before he left this morning. Just like he said, he woke up at six a.m., kissed me, told me he'd lock up with the spare key he was planning on keeping, and then he was gone.

I stuffed my face in his pillow, inhaled his scent, and tried to fall back asleep, but my mind wouldn't let me. Instead, I kept replaying the night before, wondering if it was an epic mistake or if it was fate.

Can I do this?

Can I offer my heart to this man?

Can I add him to my delicate balancing act?

If I take the leap, will the fall take one more thing from me?

∽

*H*ours later, when Tommy, Amelia, and I show our lanyards to walk into Coach Sinclair's suite at the stadium, my fingers are crossed that nobody asks about Declan and me. But knowing this crazy crew, I know I'm fucking screwed.

Coach's suite is amazing. It's supposed to seat up to something silly, like thirty people, but it's only ever Coach's family and close friends, a group we're lucky to be included in. You can watch from inside the glass walls or sit in one of the three rows of outside seats the box has access to. A private bar, private bathroom, personal waiter, and a buffet of food make this the perfect way to watch a game in my opinion. But that's coming from someone who really could care less about football. Though, I've caught myself enjoying it more this year now that I get to watch Declan play.

Everyone's here today. Brady and Bash are standing next to the food, filling their plates with chicken wings. Murphy has his arm wrapped around Sabrina's waist while they talk to his mother and sister, Carys, about the upcoming wedding. Nattie and Chloe are the only ones who notice us when we walk in. Nat jumps up from her seat at the window and bounces over to us. "Hey, Tommy boy. You ready to watch our Kings crush the Sentinels today?" The Sentinels are the Kings biggest rivals and beat us out for the final playoff spot last year before going on to win the big championship at the end of the season. According to Declan, this game is always a bloodbath. Add in that the Sentinels were last year's team to beat, the Kings want it more than ever. Nat holds her hand up for a high five, and he smacks her palm, then makes his stuffed Rex do the same.

Tommy is wearing his black and gold number thirteen Sinclair jersey and his matching Kings hat today. Of course, Rex matches him because why wouldn't he? Even Amelia is wearing a Kings hoodie, and this is her first game.

I may have slipped the Kings hoodie I was wearing last night on over my Rolling Stones tee.

When the rest of our friends hear Nattie and Tommy, they all turn. All voices stop and stare. It's not often that a new person is in this box, and I can feel Amelia shrink next to me. "Hey, guys. This is my friend Amelia. She owns Sweet Temptations. The new coffee and sweets shop in Kroydon Hills."

Amelia gives a little wave.

"Yup. She's my new crack dealer." Katherine glares at Nattie, who just shrugs. "What? You know caffeine is my drug of choice."

"Mom's still refusing to let me drink coffee," Carys pouts.

Nattie's shocked face cracks me up. She spins on Katherine. "Pretty sure that's child abuse, Katherine."

"Yeah, Mom. You're abusing your child," Murphy adds sarcastically, wrapping his arm around his sister.

Katherine smacks the back of Murphy's head. "No, my love, *hitting* you is child abuse."

"I'll hit him for you, Ms. Murphy. Just say the word," Bash offers.

Nattie moves to stand between Bash and Murphy, then pushes them apart. "Dad said no hitting after the last time. Remember?"

Everyone turns their heads to look at Brady, who takes the wing out of his mouth, drops it on his plate, and moves to the outside seats before yelling back, "That wasn't my fault!"

Amelia's eyes bounce around the room, trying to keep up with everyone. "Your friends are insane, Belle." There's a touch of awe in her voice, before she adds, "I think I love them," a little quieter.

The game is a nail-biter. Even I'm holding my breath throughout. There are never more than two points separating the two teams until we're halfway through the fourth quarter, and the Sentinels score a field goal. With five minutes left on the clock, the Kings have to score a touchdown, or they'll lose the game and their chance at the division title.

Declan calls a time-out, and we're left waiting.

I'm watching from the inside window while everyone else sits outside.

"You doing okay, Annabelle? It's hard watching them battle it out." I look up and see Katherine standing next to me, sipping a soda.

"Yeah. I know how much he wants to show all the naysayers that he's worth it and that he didn't get the job because of his last name." I look out onto the field and see them lining back up. "I really want them to win."

Katherine places her hand on mine. "How long have you and Declan been together, Belle?"

"What?" My head snaps to hers, a denial on my lips until I see the knowing look in her eyes. "It's really new, Katherine. Would you mind not saying anything until Declan and I have a chance to talk about it?"

She pats my palm reassuringly. "That's completely up to you, and I'll follow your lead. But may I give you some advice?"

I nod.

"Don't wait too long to fill your friends in. Sneaking around feels awful and only hurts the people you care about when it comes out in the wash. Take it from someone who knows."

The crowd goes insane, and I hear the announcer over the sound system. "Sinclair's at the twenty, the ten. Touchdown Philadelphia. Declan Sinclair just ran it in for sixty-two yards. The Kings win. The Kings win! They beat the reigning champions."

Katherine and I scream as everyone jumps to their feet to celebrate.

An hour later, we were all still gathered in Coach's box waiting to congratulate him and Declan on the win. We'd watched the post-game press conference on the big screen TV on the wall and were thoroughly enjoying the rest of the afternoon. When the door opened and Coach stepped in, followed by Declan, we all stood to congratulate them.

Coach kissed Katherine on the cheek and hugged Natalie. It was sweet.

Declan, however, wasn't as sweet. With laser focus, he found me in our little crowd, crossed the room, picked me up off the floor, and crashed his lips to mine. My arms wrapped around his neck as my feet dangled off the floor before he whispered in my ear, "I think I found my favorite good luck charm."

"Shut the front door!" Nattie exclaimed.

Followed by, "I knew it!" from Chloe.

This was certainly one way to let everyone in on the status change in our relationship.

Eventually Declan placed me back on my feet just as I heard Tommy ask, "Why's Declan kissing Belles?"

Murphy cleared his throat to answer. "Well, little man —" Brina immediately covered his mouth with her hand.

In hindsight, we probably should have just let him finish whatever he was going to say because with Tommy's next breath, he announced, "Declan's bird is way bigger than mine."

24

DECLAN

Annabelle buries her face in my chest and laughs at Tommy, who'd already moved on. "Oh. My. God. Declan. I'm so sorry," she whispers.

I hear Carys ask Tommy if he wanted to see something on her phone and was immensely grateful for my soon-to-be stepsister.

Murphy slaps my shoulder. "Good to know you're packing more than the middle schoolers in the stadium, Dec."

Snickering, Sabrina shakes her head at Murphy but won't make eye contact with me.

"So," Nattie pipes up. "I thought you two were just really good friends." She looks at Belle and me with an eyebrow raised and a silly smile on her face.

"Natalie Grace, give your brother a break. He's a grown man and doesn't have to tell you every aspect of his life." I've got to remember to thank my father tomorrow. "Of course, I, on the other hand, see him every day of the damn week. Ya think ya might've given me a heads-up, son?"

Fuck the thank you.

Amelia catches me off guard when she jumps in, "Wow. You're a fun crowd, but damn, you're all up in each other's business." She chuckles, then glances around the room as if she's expecting a response or worried she said something wrong.

"Well, yeah," my sister tells her. "We're family. It's what we do."

Amelia points between Nattie and me. "You two are family." Then she points at Murphy and his mom. "And I think they're family."

She's cut off by Bash, who slings his arm around her shoulder before telling her, "Yeah, our definition of family is a little different. You'll get used to it if you stick around long enough." Bash is smiling. Amelia, not so much.

She pushes Bash's arm off her shoulder. "Nice try, little boy."

Bash steps back, hands going to his chest and feigning hurt.

"Burn. Looks like you got shot down, pretty boy." Brady doubles over laughing.

Bash shoves Brady back. "Fuck off, QB."

Dad clears his throat, trying to sound stern. "Kids." When everyone in the room looks up, he laughs too, "Fuck it. We beat the Sentinels today! Next step, division champs!"

Yeah, we are.

~

I'd wanted to ask Belle if I could follow her home after the game but second-guessed myself, not wanting to look clingy or needy. Oh, how the tables have turned. A year ago, I'd have been the one running from the first whiff of a needy, clingy relationship. Now, I'm worried about being that way myself.

I'm halfway home when my phone rings. "What's going on, Hunter?"

"Can't an agent check in on his number one player after he beats last year's championship team? Great game, man. I'll be there in Cali when you play next Sunday, cheering you on." Hunter offered to fly out for today's game, but it seemed pointless, knowing I'd be playing in his backyard next week when we play Oakland.

"Works for me, man. We going over the interview info then?" I've agreed to two different interviews. One is scheduled for mid-December, and the other for January. "I can't fucking believe that December is only a few days away."

"Well, believe it and be grateful you don't have a game on Thanksgiving." The fucker laughs then pauses. "Seriously, do you even remember the last time you got to sit down with your family on Thanksgiving Day? High school?"

"Yeah, man. Never got to go home for Thanksgiving while we were at Notre Dame." Hunter keeps talking, but I drift off, thinking about the holiday this week. We're not flying out until Friday, so Dad wants to do Thanksgiving at his house with everyone, and I'm the asshole who never thought to invite Belle and Tommy.

"Right, Dec?" he asks, but I have no clue what he just said.

"Sure, man. Listen, I gotta go. We'll catch up Sunday." I hit the button to end the call and turn left instead of heading home.

Kroydon Hills is an old town a few minutes outside of Center City, Philadelphia. I live in Center City. My understanding is that Kroydon Hills has always been a community of affluent families. Senators, business owners, CEOs and chairmen of the board live in this town. And for the last two years, Philly's pro-football coach has lived here too. Dad's house is less than ten minutes from Annabelle's, and that's only if you hit one of the few stoplights in town.

When I turn right onto Belle's street, I see Tommy and her walking up to their front door. She mentioned she needed to drop Amelia off before coming home, but I thought she'd have been home already.

When I pull into the driveway behind her cute little white SUV, I see her send Tommy in the red front door before she turns to look at me, hands on her hips and an annoyed expression on her face. As I hop out of the Bronco, she stomps to meet me.

"I told those guys it wasn't a big deal. I just left the light on." She's determined to be pissed at me over whatever she's currently got going on.

Holding her face in my hands, I kiss those lips I'm falling in love with and shut her up. "I have no idea what you're talking about."

When Belle raises those emerald-green eyes up at me, she looks a little more zen, which puts a goofy smile on my face.

Yup. I did that.

"I told Nattie not to call you," she huffs.

I tuck a lock of her caramel-colored hair behind her ear and breathe in her lavender scent. "Can we go inside before your neighbors decide it's fun to watch you yell at me? Or worse yet, post it on social media. Please?"

When the dimples pop in my girl's smile, I know I've calmed her down. I might not be the most versed in being in relationships, but I know enough to know not to tell a woman to calm down. My way worked much better.

Annabelle leads us inside before hollering up the stairs, "Tommy, it's time to get in the shower."

"Do I have to?" he whines from the top of the stairs. "I showered yesterday, Belles."

"Tommy," she says sternly, leaving no room for argument.

I force myself not to laugh.

Moments later, the shower turns on, and Belle walks into the kitchen. "Want something to drink?" I shake my head no and watch her turn a burner on before placing a kettle on it.

"So, what didn't you want Nattie to tell me?" I slip off my suit coat and hang it on the back of a kitchen chair. Coach insists we wear suits to and from the stadium on game or travel days.

Annabelle turns around as I roll up the arms of my starched white dress shirt and stares. "Hey," she pouts. "That's not fair. I'm annoyed with you. Put away the arm porn." She points at my forearms and the black leather Tag Heuer watch they sent over when they sent the contracts.

"Belles, seriously, I have no idea why you're annoyed." I cross my arms over my chest and lean against the table. I might flex a little. I can't help myself. I like seeing her smile, and I like it even more when it happens because she's looking at me. "I came over because I meant to ask you yesterday, and truth be told, the day before that too . . . I meant to ask if Tommy and you would come with me to my dad's for Thanksgiving?" Fuck, this woman can get me tongue-tied.

"Oh." She looks confused, then turns back to the tea

kettle and pours the water into a white mug with "NY Ballet" written in sparkly black lettering. When she turns back to me, she's dunking a teabag in her mug. "Sorry. I thought—" she cuts herself off. "Never mind." Forcing a smile, she asks. "Are you sure you want us to come with you Thursday? Isn't it just family?"

I hate the timidness in her voice. "You really don't get it yet, do you?" When she just stares at me, I soften my voice and continue, "My father, brother, and sister all already think of Tommy and you as family. It has nothing to do with you and me being together, considering they all suspected, but no one knew anything until a little over an hour ago." I reach out and pull her to me.

Belle slides her mug on the table and wraps her arms around my waist. "Declan . . . We only really got together last night. How can you be so sure of everything?"

I lift her hair off her shoulders, letting it spill down her back. "We might have started last night in your mind, but in mine . . . In mine, we started when we met."

She lifts up on her toes and grabs my face in her hands before kissing me. "You scare me, Declan Sinclair. You scare me so much. You're so damn sure of yourself."

I pull back, my hands moving to her hips. "I'm not, Belle. That might be what everyone else sees, but I get nervous the same as everyone. I question things. I question most things. What I don't question . . . what I am sure of . . . is us." I push her back before lifting and sitting her on the counter. I want her at eye level for this. "Everything happens for a reason, Annabelle. I believe that. We may never know what the reasons are, but they're there. I was brought here to play for Philly, and I used to tell myself that it was so I could be close to my family. I guess, in a way, it was. But the day I met you, the first day I saw you in my dad's yard, I knew that wasn't the real reason. You were."

She blinks wildly before her eyes meet mine. They're big and full of unshed tears. "I'm sure of us, Belle. And I was willing to wait for you to get there as long as I needed to. I thought we were finally on the same page."

She sniffles and runs her delicate hands up the sides of my neck into my hair. "I'm sure of you, Declan." Her legs lock around my thighs. "I'm sure you won't hurt me. Won't hurt us. I'm not sure about everything else." Those eyes show so much fucking anguish. "I feel like the universe has been conspiring against me for a while, and that scares me. I don't want to admit that I'm falling in love with you, and the life I can see myself living with you, only for it to be taken away." Her tears begin to fall, hard and heavy.

"I'm not going anywhere, Annabelle. I'm here. Tommy and you are my endgame, and I'm not letting anything get in the way of that."

She leans her forehead against mine. "Promise?"

"I'll always catch you, Belle."

⁓

Hours later, when I'm trying to fall asleep with this incredible woman in my arms, I start thinking about my life and taking stock. I've always been goal-oriented. Never been afraid of hard work and earning what I want. And right now, I see my goal more clearly than ever before.

I want this woman and the little boy asleep down the hall in my life and home forever. I want to come home to them every day.

I want to celebrate the big moments and the little

moments with them. I want to teach Tommy what being a man means and help him navigate this crazy world.

I want to hold Belle's hand and make sure she knows she's safe and loved, supported, and cherished.

I think Belle wants the same thing.

I just need to convince her we're worth it.

I want to marry Annabelle Hart.

Monday morning, I kiss Annabelle goodbye at six a.m. She barely opens her eyes before rolling back over and shoving her face into my pillow, making me smile. I grab my phone off the nightstand and my gym bag off the floor, lock the house up with the key I never returned and don't intend to, and jump in my Bronco. Once I turn the car on and the heat up, I sit for a minute, letting the engine warm up.

When I open my phone to check for messages, I see a text chain from the guys last night.

Group Text:

Brady: Dec, did Belles tell you about the studio?
Coop: Dude, it's 10 p.m. Dec's in bed, and his phone's off. No way he's seeing this. He's too fucking anal to be awake. His schedule is more regimented than the Navy's.
Murphy: Know who likes anal?
Coop: You're gonna die, Murph.
Murphy: Chill, Coop. I was gonna say Rocky.
Coop: The dog? Dude, you're sick.
Murphy: Fine. I was gonna say your sister.
Brady: You're gonna die, Murph.

Bash: Chill, guys. Dec, man. You need to talk to Belles. The light was on at the studio, and the door wasn't locked.
Coop: What are you guys talking about?
Bash: Belle had an issue with the alarm at the studio last week. It turned out to be nothing, but it was weird. Then yesterday, she noticed the light inside was on at the end of the day after she'd been gone for hours. She swore she turned the light off. It freaked her out. Then she realized the door wasn't locked.

Shit. I never found out what she was talking about last night. This must have been it.

Brady: Yeah. She was dropping Amelia off and saw it. Says she's never that forgetful. Just ask her about it. It could have been a coincidence.
Coop: So, does this text mean he finally claimed Belle as his?
Bash: Dumbass.
Bash: You think anybody claims Annabelle Hart? She's way too independent for that shit.
Murphy: Fuck you, Dr. Phil.
Brady: You'll see one day, Bash. It's gonna knock you on your ass.
Coop: Call me when you can, Dec.
Murphy: Ask him about the size of his dick and why Tommy's seen it.
Coop: WTF?
Brady: True story. Just ask.

These assholes dropped it after that.
Fuckers.

Declan: Thanks for the heads-up, guys. Coop was right, and my phone was off. Just seeing this now. I'll talk to Belle about it tonight. BTW—Tommy walked in while I was in the shower.

Declan: Don't be jealous your dicks aren't bigger than a fourth grader's.

25

ANNABELLE

I may have a little extra pep in my step Wednesday morning when I stop by the bakery before opening the studio. I'm not really a morning person. I loathe being woken up before six a.m. But that was before Declan Sinclair woke me up at five this morning with his mouth on my pussy.

Forget Folgers in my cup, I'll take Declan in my bed.

On second thought, why do I have to choose?

I want them both.

He spent the night again Sunday night and basically hasn't slept in his own bed since. It's only been a few nights, but I think he's moving in. Monday night, he came home after practice and helped me make dinner. I noticed he had an overnight bag with him and left some of his manly stuff in my bathroom. He's made sure he leaves before Tommy wakes up. Even yesterday, when he didn't have practice, he was out of bed and out of the house by six a.m.

I guess we should probably talk about it.

I need to talk to Tommy about it too. I need to know how much of it he understands.

Always Earned, Never Given

That should be fun.

When Amelia comes out from the kitchen, she looks more annoyed with life than usual. Her curly black hair is a mess, and what I think is powdered sugar covers her grey t-shirt and dark skinny jeans. "Hey, you okay?"

She blows her hair out of her face before answering me. "Yeah. I had a late night last night, working on Thanksgiving orders for pick up today. And now, my mixer's acting up on me. Whatever. It is what it is." With that, she turns around and starts on my usual coffee order. Guess I'm dismissed.

Plastic-domed pie tins line an entire side of the back counter. Pink bakery boxes with her minty green logo line the other. "Wow. You did all this last night?" That had to take hours.

"Yeah. I'm a new business, so I didn't want to turn away any orders. I've already got yours bagged up. Do you want it now, or do you want to grab it later?" She turns around and hands me my pumpkin spice coffee.

"I'll take it now. I've got a fridge at the studio. Hey, can I get some whip cream and cinnamon on this? I'm craving something sweet." I look at the cases while I hand her back my to-go cup. "Oh. I'll take two of those double-stuffed cream-filled donuts too, please."

When she hands me my bag, she's shaking her head. "How the hell do you stay as tiny as you do and eat like this? Not that I want you to stop. You're my best customer." She winks and sips from a bottle of water kept under the counter.

"Dancing all day will do it for you," I answer, slightly embarrassed.

"Yeah. We'll go with the dancing. I'm sure it has nothing to do with the hottie keeping your bed warm." She walks around the counter with my pink Sweet Temptations bag in her hand. I ordered a few pies and some chocolate chip cookies for tomorrow night.

"Nope. The hottie in my bed may be the reason I'm tired, but dance and good genetics are the reason I can eat whatever I want." Amelia looks shocked before we both laugh. "Oh, shoot. Can I add a few of those doggie cookies too? Just in case Rocky's at Coach's tomorrow?"

"Yup." She plucks three cookies out of the glass canister on top of the bakery case and adds them to my bag. "You sure you're gonna be able to carry all this, Belles?"

"I've got it. Thanks. Have a happy Thanksgiving, Amelia." I step forward and hug her. She doesn't reciprocate. Amelia's not exactly touchy-feely, so I'm not surprised.

"Happy Thanksgiving, Annabelle." She may not hug me, but she smiles and pats my shoulder. She's getting there. One day she'll open up. Until then, I'll take what I can get.

~

That night when I get a text from Declan, letting me know he's on his way over and asking if I need him to pick anything up, I decide it's time to have a conversation with Tommy. We've just locked up the studio for the day and gotten into my car when the text comes through, so I guess there's no time like the present.

Glancing back at him through the rearview mirror, I see him looking at his iPad. "Hey, Tommy . . ." I say to get his attention.

His eyes meet mine momentarily before going back to whatever has his attention on the screen.

What the hell am I supposed to say? Your sister's an idiot who's fallen in love with a professional football player? Wanna put your heart on the line next to mine?

Obviously, that won't do. "Tommy," I try again. "Do you like Declan coming over like he's been doing?"

I have no idea what's going to come out of his mouth and breathe a sigh of relief when he answers, "Yup. Yup. Declan's awesome." He starts laughing his loud, boisterous laugh, and I relax. "Can he sleep in my room tonight?"

So much for relaxing. "What?" Please, please, please let him not be talking about what I think he is.

"It's my turn to have Declan sleep in my room, Belles. He's my friend, not yours." His laughter gets louder, and he claps his hands. "Sharing is caring, Belles."

Well, shit. I'm the one who taught him "sharing is caring." What the hell am I supposed to say now? "I think he's too big for your bed, little man." Okay, that was pretty good. "And, since sharing is caring, what do you say about you sharing Declan with me?" I wait a moment before adding, "Please?" Not too bad.

I glance back at him again, seeing how happy he is, and I know I made the right move letting Declan in. Even this frenetic pace we're keeping seems to be the right fit for us. In one month, I've gone from not wanting a relationship to not being able to imagine this man anywhere but beside me.

It still scares me, but I'm trying to not let the fear win.

"Tommy . . ." I try getting his attention back on me as we pull into our driveway. "Will you share Declan with me?" Please let him not melt down.

Tommy opens his door and hops out. "I'll share you with Declan, Belles." He laughs again and runs to the front door. I don't think he realized the difference between what I asked and what he said, but my heart felt it.

When we walk into the house, it smells fantastic.

"What stinks?" my chicken nugget connoisseur asks before running to the kitchen. "Belles, Declan's here again," he calls out. Then I hear, "Belles and I are gonna share you. Can you sleep in my bed tonight?"

By the time I make it into the kitchen, it's to see Dec holding back his laughter. "I think I might be a little too big for your bed, buddy." He looks over Tommy's head, checking in with me.

I nod once.

"Fine," my brother pouts. "But you're gonna keep sleeping here, right? 'Cause I like it when you're here."

Oh, my heart.

I walk over and pull my brother into a reluctant hug. "I love you, munchkin."

When Declan wraps both of us up in his arms, I wait for Tommy to pull away, but he doesn't. Instead, his little arms go around each of us, and he squeezes with all his might.

"I'm not going anywhere, Tommy. I'll sleep here for as long as you both let me." I feel him squeeze Tommy and me a little tighter and know I'll remember this as the moment Declan won my heart.

26

DECLAN

The house is still blissfully quiet when the light starts to filter in through Belle's sheer white curtains. I've been awake and holding this beautiful woman in my arms for an hour already, not wanting to wake her early on her day off. I told myself I'd give her until the sun came up.

Time's up.

Belle has quickly become my favorite addiction. The high I get from being with her is better than any touchdown. Just when I let my hand start to travel down her soft skin, the door flies open and bangs against the wall behind it seconds before Tommy runs in and jumps on the bed. He's wearing flannel pajamas covered in dinosaurs. His brown hair is a mess, and his smile is the definition of innocence. "It's Thanksgiving! I want pancakes."

Belle cracks one eye open, looks at him, and then at me before shooting up, wrapping her arms around his waist and dragging him down between us.

He pulls her pale purple comforter up over the three of us and laughs loudly. "Thanksgiving means pancakes,

Belles. Pancakes and strawberries. You know the rules." He snuggles in close to her and closes his eyes.

"How about donuts instead? I picked up a dozen yesterday at Amelia's shop. Why don't you head downstairs and grab one, and we'll see if you still want pancakes after that, okay?" Belles pulls up his shirt and gives him a big raspberry on his stomach.

I'm not used to seeing Tommy this open to touch, but it's a fun thing to see. His giggle is infectious as he climbs out of bed, nearly kneeing me in the balls in the process.

When he pulls the door shut behind him and runs down the steps, Belle closes her eyes and lays her head back on the pillow. "Well, that's not how I thought this morning was going to start." She rolls to her side and lays her hand on my bare chest before it starts to slowly travel down.

"Oh yeah?" I whisper quietly, turning my head to hers. "How did you think it would start, Annabelle?" I move her hair away from her pink cheeks. "Do you want it hard and fast before Tommy comes back?" I lean in and lick up her neck. "Or do you want to lie down while I eat your pretty pussy for breakfast? Tell me how you want to come, Belles?" I suck the lobe of her ear, making her squirm.

She pushes me back, then shakes her finger. "Uh-uh. Not this morning." Her fingers scrape against my abs before gripping the waistband of my black boxer briefs and pulling them down. When she moves to kneel between my thighs, I grab her face with both hands and claim her mouth, my tongue licking her lips before she pulls away.

"Nope. It's my turn," she whispers before her hand tightens around my cock, and her tongue travels up from my balls to the head, taking special care to lick the pearl of precum off the tip before her soft lips wrap around me, taking me in her warm mouth. Then she works her way back down to the base of my cock, one hand moving to my balls while the other grabs my thigh to steady herself.

"Jesus, baby. Your mouth is so hot. It feels so good," I growl.

Belle moans with those vibrant green eyes looking up at me through dark fringed lashes, and every image I've ever stored in my spank bank is immediately replaced by the one in front of me. I can't stop my hips from lifting off the bed, trying to get deeper. It doesn't take long to feel the pressure begin to mount and the need to come imminent. But this is not how I want to start the day.

Jackknifing up, I wrap my hands around her hips and pull her to sit on my lap and on my dick. She slept in one of my soft, worn Notre Dame t-shirts last night, giving me easy access. Pushing her panties to the side, Belle slides down on my throbbing cock.

I wrap her soft hair around my fist, tugging back until her neck is bared to me. "Take what you need, baby. I'm not coming without you." My hand reaches under her shirt, cupping her breast while I suck on her neck.

Her legs wrap around my waist. "Declan . . . God, it's always so good." The bite of her nails digging into my scalp creates the perfect pain.

"I need you to get there, baby." Letting go of her hair, I reach down and run my finger around her clit until her walls start to pulse around me. One final thrust and the orgasm washes over both of us.

Belle drapes her arms over my shoulders, her body lying limply in my arms.

"Happy Thanksgiving, Annabelle." I run my fingers under her shirt and up her back until my hand kneads her neck.

"Belles . . . I still want pancakes," is yelled from somewhere downstairs, and we both laugh.

The beautiful woman in my arms sighs deeply before she starts to climb off me. "Time to make the pancakes."

My grip tightens before I gently kiss her lips. "At least he's got good timing."

I love the laughter I get in response. "Yeah. We've got to get better about locking the bedroom door. Could you imagine what he'd tell everyone then?"

∽

Group Text:

Murphy: Happy Turkey Day, bitches.
Murphy: Don't forget – We're playing football at Coach's at noon.
Declan: You're fucking crazy, Murph. If any of us get hurt, the consequences are huge.
Nattie: HUGE! Aww, Dec. It's so cute how you're scared of Dad.
Bash: I can only stay 'til two. Then I promised my pops I'd be at his house.
Brina: Murphy and I are doing early Thanksgiving at Coach's, then we have to go to the country club to sit down with my parents.
Brady: Nattie and I told my mom we'd be there for dessert.
Belle: You people better be hungry for dessert or plan on taking some home with you. I bought out Amelia's store.
Murphy: Got any of those cookies for Rocky? Apparently, pregnant dogs like cookies the same way pregnant women do.
Belle: She's pregnant?

Nattie: Yup. The Pug next door knocked her up. Rocky's a hussy!
Brina: You gotta google a Pug & Bull Dog mix. They're the cutest things.
Chloe: OMG! They're sooo cute! They call them BUGS. A Bulldog Pug mix is a BUG! I want one.
Chloe: Hey - How come you can get out of dinner with the folks, but I'm stuck with them?
Brady: Sucks to be you.
Coop: I miss you guys.
Nattie: Three more weeks until you're home, Coop! Counting down the days.
Coop: Happy Thanksgiving, guys.

~

When Tommy, Belle, and I walk into my father's house, we're greeted by complete chaos. Rocky's running in circles until she sees Tommy and makes a beeline directly for him. He drops to the floor, and Rocky falls into his lap. She lays her head on his leg and happily whines while Tommy scratches her ears.

Nattie's in the family room, yelling at Bash, "Put Brady down. If you break him, I'll be so mad at you, Sebastian Beneventi."

Bash has Brady raised over his head in a deadlift.

"Who's stronger, QB?" Bash taunts.

Luckily for Brady, Dad walks into the room. "Put him down, Sebastian. He's fragile."

"Dad," Nattie whines while everyone but Brady laughs.

Belle pulls on my arm, dragging me into the kitchen, causing me to miss what happens next.

These guys are better than reality TV some days.

Katherine is yelling at Murphy, who's checking the turkey in the oven. "Leave the oven closed. You're letting the moisture out every time you open it, Aiden."

"I know what I'm doing, Mom. I've been binging the Food Network all week," Murph answers as he pours a box of chicken stock over the biggest turkey I've ever seen.

"He really has. I swear I've gained ten pounds just watching TV with him." Brina flips a page in the bridal magazine she and Carys are looking at while they sit at the kitchen table, discussing wedding flowers.

Belle places her desserts on the island that's already covered in appetizers and cookies. She takes the bag from me and adds them to the growing array of snacks and sweets.

Complete chaos. Any other time in any other place with any other people, this would be my worst nightmare. But in this house with these people ... I love it.

When Katherine turns around, I wrap my arms around her. "Smells fantastic, Katherine. Thanks for having us."

"Don't tell her, tell me," Murphy yells indignantly. "I got here at the asscrack of dawn to stuff and cook a thirty-pound turkey. Mom likes to try to tell me what to do, but I'm the expert." When Murphy turns around, I do a double take.

"What the hell are you wearing, man?" His apron is brown with a colorful turkey on the front holding a whisk like a microphone and singing "Pour Some Gravy On Me."

"Back off, Dec. You're just jealous of my apron." He pulls it out for me to see it better as if that were the problem.

"Whatever you think, Murph." I turn to see Belle and Katherine talking just as Tommy runs into the room with Rocky behind him, but moving much less quickly, and Nattie hot on their heels.

Nat's got an *"Oh shit"* look on her face, and I'm bracing

for the worst when Tommy opens his mouth. "Belles, did you know Rocky is pregnant? And she's gonna be a mom in a couple of weeks? And guess what?" he asks as he bounces on his toes from all the excitement coursing through his body.

"I don't know. What?" Annabelle gives Tommy her full attention.

He sits down next to Rocky and pets her gently. "Rocky needs homes for her babies, and Nattie thought maybe we could give one of the puppies a good home. Wouldn't that be so cool? We could have our own dog. Please, Belles?"

Damn. The look Belle gives Nattie should have her shaking in her shoes. Instead, she smiles, shrugs her shoulders, and says, "Wait until you see how cute the puppies are gonna be, Belles." Nattie sits on the floor next to Tommy and tickles his side, making him giggle, but he doesn't pull away.

When Belle looks to me as if asking what I think, I lift my shoulders and smile. "Why not?"

"What am I going to do with you Sinclairs?" she asks, looking between Nattie and me.

"Love us," Nat responds.

I wrap my arms around Belle's waist and whisper in her ear, "Yup. Love us."

When Belle pulls her head back, a beautiful pink flush covers her cheeks.

Nattie covers Tommy's eyes. "Eww. No kissing in front of the K-I-D."

"It's okay. They kiss all the time." Tommy hops up and starts to rummage through the Sweet Temptations bag until he finds a cookie for Rocky. "I saw Declan put his tongue in Belle's mouth." As if that bomb wasn't bad enough, he turns to me. "Did she have food stuck in there or something?"

I rub my hand down my face and watch Nattie redeem

herself... a little. She holds her hand out to Tommy. "Come on, little man. Let's go decide where the best place for the touch football game is. You thinking front yard or backyard?"

As soon as Nattie is out of sight, Katherine leans into me and Belle whispering, "Whatever you do, do not eat the brownies. Natalie made them, and they are not good." Her nose scrunches, and her lips purse before she walks away.

Once the kitchen calms down, I see my opening and grab my dad. "Hey, Dad, can I talk to you?"

He leads me into his office, shocking me. "You finally unpacked?" My eyes roam the office, and I'm floored by the difference in here. There are no boxes anywhere. His jersey is finally hanging on the wall, along with a few different framed shots of him playing and coaching.

"Katherine is a force of nature. She didn't want me working in a room full of boxes. Something about it not being good for productivity. It was bugging her, so I unpacked." When I just stare at him, he adds, "Well, she may have helped. Happy wife, happy life. Remember that, son." He drops into his chair. "So, I see things are progressing with Annabelle. Might want to watch what happens in front of Tommy. Your mother and I got a call from your preschool teacher after you told her that Daddy likes to hug Mommy naked." He chuckles, "Not a call I recommend having to take."

"I love her, Dad. I'm not sure if she's ready to hear it yet, but it doesn't make it any less true." I sit across from him before continuing, "She feels like home. Tommy and her. Like this is the life I was supposed to find. Supposed to live. Fate. What's that saying you like?"

"Amor Fati. 'Love your fate.' It was one of my favorite things I learned in my philosophy class in college." Dad eyes me for a moment before asking, "Are you sure, Dec? It's awfully fast."

"You don't believe that any more than I do. What did you tell me after you proposed to Katherine?"

"When you know, you know," he responds immediately.

"Well, I know. I have no doubt she's it for me." I pause and look at the family pictures behind him that rest on the built-in shelves. Pictures of my brother, sister, and me throughout our lives. Pictures of his family. "Annabelle's it, Dad. I want to marry her. I want to raise a family with her." I'm relieved when he smiles because I don't know how he's going to react to my next question. "I want to know if I could have Nana's engagement ring."

Dad's parents, my Nana and Pop, had the happiest relationship I ever saw. They were a true partnership in every sense of the word. They always held hands and danced in the kitchen after dinner. We used to stay with them during the summer, and I always looked forward to it. You saw the love shining in both their eyes until the day Nana died. Pop was heartbroken, but I still remember him telling me that the love of a good woman was the greatest gift any man could ever ask for and you need to make sure you earned it every day.

They were married seventy years before we lost Nana, and Pop left us a few months later. I think he died of a broken heart.

"You're the oldest, Dec. The ring's yours if you want it." He pauses for a moment, then clears the emotion from his throat. "I think Nana would have loved Annabelle and Tommy. She'd have doted on them both. Pops would have made her eat more and helped you teach Tommy everything he doesn't already know about football. I think it's an extraordinary thing to give Annabelle your grandmother's ring, son."

He stands and walks around the desk and then wraps his arms around me in the kind of hug he used to give us when we were little. "It's in the safe in my bedroom. I'll get it for you as soon as I can slip away. Do you know how you're going to propose?"

I shake my head. "No, I just want to have it when the right moment hits. I'm not sure yet if that's going to be a grand gesture or a quiet one. Guess I've should tell her I love her first."

"Yeah, you may want to get on that."

27

DECLAN

"Would you stop fidgeting? You need to exude confidence, not nerves. It's just a reporter. Man up, quarterback." If Scarlet Kingston is attempting to give me her version of a pep talk, it's not working.

I met with Hunter last week to discuss all the questions that Chip Martin could possibly ask me today. Belle and I discussed how we wanted to handle the inevitable questions that will come up regarding my personal life, and we decided together that the truth was best, with as few additional details as possible.

Hunter walks into Dad's office, rubbing his hands together like he just pulled off the ultimate heist. "Dec, my man." He crosses the room and puts his hands on my shoulders. "We ready to dazzle?"

I shove his hands off. "I'm not a figure skater, man. I don't dazzle." I finally stand up and start pacing around the room, impatiently waiting to get this show on the damn road. They scheduled the interview for a Tuesday afternoon and are conducting it on the field. Go figure. I just want to get it over with.

When a phone beeps, I look around the room and see Scarlet checking hers. "It's time. Remember, Declan, you're representing the Philadelphia Kings today."

"I represent the Kings every day, Scarlet." I pull the door shut behind me a little harder than necessary and head downstairs. When I get down to the field, I see my dad talking to one of the assistants. He agreed to answer a few questions after I'm done.

He squeezes my shoulder as I pass by and nods, silently telling me, *"You've got this."*

Here's hoping I do. I fucking hate the press. They hounded me both years I was up for the Heisman. I couldn't take a goddamn shit without them knowing. Being a college athlete is hard. The pressures are hard, and the expectations you put on yourself are even harder. Add in something like the Heisman Trophy race, and it's a pressure cooker waiting to explode. And of course, the vultures were circling, just waiting to get a picture of the wreckage.

Standing on the field, I wait for a pretty red-headed assistant to get me mic'd up and then take my seat next to Chip. In his late sixties, he's an older man who's been interviewing athletes for the last thirty years. His salt and pepper hair is cut short, and his suit is perfectly tailored. He looks like he could be your wealthy grandpa until he opens his mouth. Then you know you're in the presence of a powerhouse journalist.

We wait for the light on the camera to turn red before Chip begins to speak into the lens. "Good evening, ladies and gentlemen. Tonight, we have a special guest with us— Declan Sinclair, the rookie phenom from the University of Notre Dame, who was picked up in the first round of the draft by none other than his own father to be the starting quarterback for the Philadelphia Kings."

Chip turns to me. "Thanks for taking the time to sit down with me today, Declan."

"Thanks for having me, Chip." I smile like Scarlet hammered into me earlier and try to relax. Chip goes through some basic questions that I've been asked over the years, warming me up for his heavy hitters.

"So, Declan, tell me what it was like to grow up playing football in the shadow of your father, Joe Sinclair. A football legend in his own right, Joe Sinclair has played professionally, won multiple bowl games as a college coach, and has a championship ring from his previous job as assistant coach for a pro team in California."

"Well, Chip, Joe Sinclair might be a football legend, but to me, he was always just Dad." I shift in my seat. "He made sure my brother and I knew we didn't have to play football if we didn't want to. He wanted us to play a sport, but he didn't care what it was. He's just always believed that being a part of a team would help prepare you for life. We both picked football, and the rest is history."

"And how did you feel when you were drafted in the first round to your father's team?"

I look over to where my dad is standing with Scarlet and Hunter before answering, "It was definitely a bit of a double-edged sword. I was so incredibly excited to get drafted by such a great franchise, but I knew the fact that my dad was the head coach would be the bigger news. I've worked my whole life to be where I am now. I knew from the time I was in fifth grade that this was what I wanted to do with my life, and I pushed myself harder every year to get here."

I make eye contact with my dad before I continue. "One of the things my dad made sure to instill in both my siblings and me is that if you're going to do something, do it well.

Give it your all. Joe Sinclair doesn't believe in half-assing anything. And he definitely passed that on to his kids. If I saw a player I thought was better than me, or if I played a team that beat mine, it never makes me want to quit. Instead, it always made me push harder. Be better. It was hard at first," I tell him, "listening to everyone talk about nepotism and how I didn't fairly earn my spot on the team, but I've had to live up to being Joe Sinclair's son my whole life. Having people talk about it isn't really anything new."

I look away from Chip and directly into the camera. "But my brother Cooper gave me some great advice that I took to heart."

Chip smiles. "Oh yeah? Can you share with us what he told you?"

"He told me to win. That would be the only thing to change the conversation." I smile back at him and remember that day at the beginning of the summer. The day I met Belle.

"And did it? Change the narrative?" Chip asks.

"Not exactly. But I think people will always talk about the fact I play for my dad because it hasn't been done professionally before." Okay, this isn't going too badly.

Chip leans toward me. "And what do you say to those people, Declan?"

I smirk. Scarlet warned me not to, but I can't help it. "I don't say anything. My job is to be a good quarterback and to win games. I hope those people love watching them and talking about them as much as I love playing them. Everyone's entitled to their own opinions, Chip."

I take a sip of water as Chip shifts topics. "So, Declan, new city, new team, new love?" He lifts a picture from the table set up next to him. It's of Annabelle and me from the night of Senator Cabot's fundraiser. "Tell me about your relationship with Annabelle Hart. I believe you've gone on record to say she's a good friend, but now sources are saying that you're living with her. Could there be wedding bells in your future, Declan?"

I smile and shake my head. "Sorry, Chip. I'm not commenting on anyone else's business."

Chip laughs. "But I'm asking you about your relationship, Declan. Come on . . . Your fans want to know if you're off the market."

"It's safe to say I am very much off the market."

~

After the interview, I sit down in Dad's office with Hunter and Scarlet. "How the hell did they know I was living with Annabelle? Seriously, it's only been a few weeks. I haven't even officially given up my apartment yet."

"You're not going to find that out, Declan. They won't give you that information," Hunter tells me before Scarlet skewers him with her eyes.

"I'll have my office do some digging and get back to you. If we've got a leak in the organization, we'll find it. It was a good interview today. Try to focus on that, Declan." She turns on her heels and leaves the room as my dad comes in.

Dad watches her leave. "What's got her upset? I thought it went well."

"Yeah . . . We'll see." I fucking hate the press.

~

When Annabelle gets home that night, Tommy and I have dinner ready and warming in the oven for her. Tuesdays have become our guy time. At least, that's what we call it. There wasn't really much to do cooking-wise. The personal chef I use to prepare and stock all my meals has increased her volume and even started adding new things each week just for Tommy. Belle was amazed last week when he actually ate the fresh chicken nuggets and mac and cheese that "Becca, the Chef," as Tommy likes to call her, made for him.

She walks into the kitchen, throws her arms around me and squeezes, releasing all my pent-up stress from this crazy fucking day. "Hey," she says softly as she kisses me. "How did the interview go?" Belle turns and drops her Mary Poppins bag on the kitchen chair, pulling out her empty lunch containers, empty coffee tumbler, a small bag from the grocery store, a bag from Sweet Temptations, and a hair clip.

"Seriously, woman. How do you fit all that junk in there?"

She glares, and I smile. "The interview went pretty well. He stuck mostly to some version of the questions they gave us last week. He did pull out a picture of us though. He knew we were living together. I didn't confirm or deny. Just told him I was very much off the market." I wait until she's done twirling her hair up into her clip and then pick her up and sit her on the counter. It's become our thing. It puts Belle at my height, and she wraps her legs around me as I kiss those pouty pink lips.

"Oh, yeah? Off the market, huh?" She cocks her brow, trying to play coy.

"Yeah. Permanently off the market. See, there's this gorgeous, smart, caring, and amazing ballerina I've fallen irrevocably in love with. And I plan to love her until the day I die." The teasing in my voice is now gone.

Belle gasps, "Declan."

"It's true. I love you, Belle. That's not going to change." I hope to God I'm not scaring her right now.

Her fingers play with the front of my long-sleeved Henley. "I love you too, Dec. Seriously, you're the greatest thing that ever happened to me. I didn't think I'd ever be able to let myself love someone again. And don't get me wrong, I'm scared every single day that something will take you away from me, but that doesn't change the fact that I am madly, deeply, hopelessly in love with you."

My hands grip either side of her face as my lips find hers. She tastes like cinnamon and sugar and all Belle.

She lets out a tiny moan just before Tommy marches into the room. "Dinner's ready, and I'm hungry, Belles. Eww. You're kissing again," he complains. "Yuck!"

I pull back and lean my forehead against hers. "I love you, Annabelle Hart."

~

Later that night, after I finish reading Tommy his nightly story and tuck him in bed, I come back downstairs looking for Belle, but she's nowhere to be found. I've noticed that when she's working through something, she's usually downstairs in the basement in the small soundproofed ballet studio her parents built for her when she was little. She told me they left it there in case she ever wanted to use it when she visited.

When I open the door to the basement, Rob Thomas's "Pieces" is playing on the sound system. Belle is dancing with her eyes closed, and her caramel-colored hair is flying wildly around her shoulders as she spins across the floor. She's barefoot with black leg warmers, tiny black shorts, and a white cropped sweatshirt hanging off her shoulder with a thick black lacy bra strap showing.

Jesus, she's fucking gorgeous.

I'm filled with admiration for this incredible woman who has no idea how strong she is.

I lean against the door frame, arms crossed, waiting for the song to end.

When Belle stops spinning and opens her eyes, she sees my reflection in the wall of mirrors. "Jesus, Dec. You scared me."

I don't move.

Can't move.

The sudden silence in the room is deafening.

"You take my breath away, Annabelle."

We stand there, eyes locked across the room. Neither of us moves for what feels like forever until my body catches up to my brain and my long legs cross the room in a few steps to bring me in front of this woman who's quickly become my whole world. I gently clasp her hands in mine and hold them over my heart that's beating loudly against the walls of my chest. "Marry me, Belle."

Her eyes fill with tears. "Declan..."

"I know it's fast, but I want to spend every day of the rest of my life with you. I want us to conquer this world together. I don't want to miss a single moment of it, and I want you there with me for all of it. You and Tommy. I promise you, Annabelle, I'll love you until my last breath, and I'll always put you and our family first."

I watch those lips I love tip up into the most beautiful smile I've ever seen before she speaks, "Of course, I'll marry you, Declan Sinclair. I love you with my whole heart and can't imagine a world where that would ever change." She leans up on her tiptoes and kisses me. I'm so relieved and so happy I can't kiss her back at first.

After a moment, my mind catches up to my body, and I wrap my arms around her and lift her off the floor. Her legs wrap around my waist, and I look around the barren basement. "Baby, I want to do this right and spread you out on the bed upstairs, not take you up against the mirror."

She rips her shirt off and throws it over our heads. "Declan," she pants. "I've wanted you to fuck me in my studio since that first time you caught me dancing. I've fantasized about it. We've got the rest of our lives for slow and sweet. I want it here. I want it hard. I want you so bad, I'm shaking." She pulls at my shirt until she gets it off and adds it to the growing pile of clothes on the floor.

I walk over to the mirror and let her body slide down against the barre until her feet touch the floor, then spin her around so she's facing the mirrors. I lift her black lacy bra up and over her head and release her wild hair to fall down around her shoulders and back before pulling her booty shorts down her legs.

The sight in front of me brings me to my knees. Annabelle Hart, soon to be Sinclair, standing there perfectly in black leg warmers and absolutely nothing else. Her tight body is shaking, and her face is beautifully flushed with need. "Declan ... Please."

"You never have to beg me for anything, Belles." I drag my tongue up the inside of her thigh to her soaking wet, beautifully pink pussy. With one hand, I push her shoulders forward so she's forced to lean down against the barre and pop her ass out toward me while I run the thumb of my other hand along her pussy and circle her clit before following it with my tongue. I eat her like she's my last meal and revel in making my girl fucking moan. The soundproofing down here is incredible, which is good because there's no whispering happening or fear of little ears catching us.

She screams as she comes hard and fast with my name on her lips.

I stand quickly and shuck off my jeans and smack her perfect ass, admiring my handprint on her delicate skin. Then I glide my hand over her perfectly round ass, running my finger along her puckered hole.

Belle backs up further into me as I dip my fingers in her slick heat before lining my cock up and pushing in. We both moan from the overwhelming sensations. "God, how is it better every time?" I growl in her ear.

Once we find our rhythm, I rub my hand over her delicious ass and trace my wet fingers back down the seam until she backs up against me harder. When I look up, her eyes are holding mine in the mirror.

"Do it, Dec," she moans as my thumb pushes against that sensitive ring of muscles and finally slips in. Annabelle backs up one more time before she calls out and shatters in my arms with me following closely behind.

I wrap my arms around her and move her damp hair away from her face. "I love you, Belle."

"Forever, Dec."

28

ANNABELLE

Declan flew out Friday night for his final away game of the regular season. They have one more home game after this at eight o'clock on Christmas night. They won the game they played the weekend after Thanksgiving and lost the week after that. With less than two weeks to go until Christmas, they've already secured their place in the playoffs and are now fighting for the division title which would give them a bye week their first week.

I've quickly realized I hate his away games because I've fallen in love with having this man in my life, my home, and my bed. When he's not here, it all feels empty.

Tommy and I are on our way to Coach and Katherine's house to watch today's game. She invited all of us to watch it there and go over last-minute schedules and wedding details. Declan and I have kept our big news to ourselves for the past week. He wants to wait until Cooper comes home in a few days, and then we'll tell everyone together. So, for now, my pretty engagement ring sits in my jewelry box at home.

I'm happily singing along to a cool, acoustic version of Bryan Adams's "Summer of 69" when I come to a stop at the red-light in front of the dance studio and see the damn light on again.

What the hell?

I pull into the parking lot and leave Tommy in the car to run inside quickly and turn it off. What I find inside the building makes the hair on the back of my neck stand up. I immediately turn and run back to the car, making sure Tommy is okay and then call Nattie.

"Hurry up, slowpoke. You're gonna miss kickoff." Nat's voice is playful, and I can hear the commentators in the background.

"Nattie, I'm at the studio. I need your help. Do you think you can come and pick up Tommy?" The trembling in my voice makes it hard to hide my fear.

"Annabelle?" The playfulness of a moment ago is gone. "What's going on?"

"I need you to come get Tommy. Please." I don't want to talk about this in front of him.

No more questions asked. "We'll be there in five minutes."

The call ends, and I look at my trembling hands. Fuck. I get out of the car and shut the door before making my next call.

"Nine-one-one, what is your emergency?" the responder asks.

"My name is Annabelle Hart. I own Hart & Soul Academy of Dance on Main Street in Kroydon Hills. Someone has broken into my studio."

She confirms the address and tells me an officer is on his way.

As I'm disconnecting the call, I see Brady's Range Rover and Bash's Hummer both pull into the parking lot. Turning around, I face Tommy and force a smile onto my face. "Hey, little man, Nattie is here, and she's going to take you to Coach and Katherine's. Okay?"

"You're coming too," Tommy tells me, eyes never drifting from the game he's engrossed in on his iPad.

"I'll be a few minutes behind you guys, but I'll meet you there. I promise." Shit. I have no idea how long this will actually take. I'm banking on him having fun and not noticing that I'm not there.

Nattie, Brady, and Bash all get out of their vehicles and rush toward my car. Once I've gotten Tommy out, I hand Nattie his bookbag and shake my head no. I need her not to question me in front of him.

She must pick up on my silent message because she turns to my brother. "Hey, Tommy boy. Let's go get in Brady's car. We don't want to miss kickoff."

"Yes! Let's go watch Declan!" I'm suddenly grateful this kid prefers to stay in his own world most of the time.

Bash watches Nattie get Tommy settled in the blue Range Rover before turning back to me. "Okay, they're in the car. Tommy can't hear anything. What the hell is going on, Belles?" He looks worried. Glancing next to him, I see Brady does too, and the composure I was barely grasping onto slips out of reach.

The tears start to fall, so I angle myself away from Brady's car and try to hold back the sobs. "We were on our way to Coach's house when I noticed the lights were on in the studio again. I didn't think anything of it. I felt sick when I was leaving yesterday and rushed out of here, so I figured I just left the lights on. I walked inside to turn them off and lock back up, but I was so wrong. Someone's been in my studio."

Sebastian wraps his arms around me, pulling me tight against his chest.

"Did you call the cops, Belles? Do you want me to go in and check it out?" Brady offers.

"No." I stand straighter. "No, thank you, Brady. Please just get Tommy out of here. I don't want to upset, or worse, scare him. I'll get to the house as soon as I can. I've already called the cops. They're on their way."

Brady hugs me tightly, then pulls back and looks at Bash. There's an unspoken conversation between the two before he walks away.

"I'm waiting here with you, Belles. Should we go inside, or do you want to wait for the police out here?"

I manage to contain my shaky breathing as I wipe the tears away. "Thanks, Bash. I appreciate it. Do you mind if we wait for the police out here? I really don't want to go back inside yet." I lean against my car.

Bash leans next to me, throws his arm over my shoulder and squeezes.

I lean my head against him momentarily until my stomach decides to revolt again, and I run for the trees that back up to the parking lot, tossing my cookies for the second damn time today. This stomach bug started Friday, and I haven't been able to shake it yet.

Just my luck, the cop pulls up while I'm vomiting.

Fuck my life.

~

When Bash and I enter the house nearly two hours later, all eyes turn to us. Well, all eyes except Tommy's. He's too busy loving on Rocky, who's sprawled out on her pink princess bed next to him, eating up the attention. Bash and I split as he walks into the family room, and I head into the kitchen. Nattie, Sabrina, Carys, and Katherine follow me as soon as they see me. "Katherine, do you have any ginger ale? My stomach is in knots right now."

"Of course, Belle." She comes back seconds later with my drink and a sleeve of Saltine crackers. "Here, honey. Eat some of these. It should help." She steals a cracker before sipping her own ginger ale.

"What happened, Belle?" Nat sits next to me at the island. Her blonde hair is in two long braids, and she's wearing a number thirteen Sinclair jersey that matches the one I now wear for each of the games.

Brina sits on my other side while Carys and Katherine lean against the beautiful granite island across from us.

"Someone broke into the studio after I left yesterday or early this morning. The cops don't know how they got around the alarm system because it was still armed."

Gasps are heard throughout the room before Carys asks, "Did they take anything?"

I nod my head. "The only thing missing is my laptop. They did a ton of damage, but it doesn't look like they took anything else."

Nat places her hand on mine. "Damage?"

"They spray-painted the floor in Studio One with the word 'whore.' They broke the wall of mirrors in studio two. The drawers in my office were open, and the papers that were in them are scattered throughout the building." I hiccup, trying to stifle my sob. "I don't understand why someone would do this."

"Oh, honey." Katherine reaches across the island and holds my hand.

"Did the police find any evidence? Did they mention whether there were any other break-ins last night?" Leave it to Brina to think like a future lawyer.

"No. They didn't mention it." I take a tissue from the box Carys just pushed across the island. "I'm going to have to close the studio at least until I get everything settled with the insurance company and get the repairs done." I look over at Nattie, my lip quivering. "We're going to lose our students."

"We're not losing anyone." Nattie straightens. "Are your files with the student information saved to the cloud?"

I nod.

"I'll call the parents and let them know we have to close for now but don't expect it to be long before we're up and running again. They can look at it like a hiatus for the holidays."

Sabrina laces her fingers with mine. "I'll help."

"Me too," is echoed from Chloe, Carys, and Katherine.

The damn bursts, and I can't contain my tears. "Thank you. Thank you so much. I don't know what I'd do without you, all of you."

"And you'll never have to." Nattie stands up and looks around. "Where's the Mary Poppins bag? I know that's where you've got your log-in information written down."

I point to the floor by the side door before I run to the bathroom to puke . . . again.

29

DECLAN

I fucking hate team breakfasts before an away game. I love being part of a team, I've always thrived off the brotherhood. But the morning before a game, I'd rather be alone and getting mentally prepared than in this noisy conference room with forty other guys talking non-stop. This morning especially. They put a rush on Chip Martin's interview and aired it last night, building the hype for today's game. If we win today, we win the division title along with a bye week and home-field advantage for our first playoff game.

The pressure's on.

Maybe if I cared about eating before a game, I'd enjoy it more.

There's a long buffet table set up with everything you can imagine, from waffles and eggs to yogurt and granola. I'm waiting in line to get a smoothie and a slice of toast with almond butter when Dean Watkins makes his way over.

"Hey, Dec. Nice interview last night. You looked good, man." He high-fives me. "Just ignore the shit they're saying. The fucking assholes will say anything to get ratings."

"The hell are you talking about?" My heart sinks as the words leave my mouth.

Curt Kenny is standing behind me in the buffet line. We've coexisted this season with as little interaction as possible, neither of us having gotten over what happened two years ago at Notre Dame. He leans into Dean and me. "Yeah, Dec. She's hot, but that pussy better be twenty-four karat gold to deal with the fucked up brother that comes with her."

My heart rate speeds up as my vision goes red. "What the fuck did you just say?"

His smile grows obnoxiously big. "I said she must be able to suck like a hoover or have a snappin' pussy to deal with that fucking re—"

I earn the hothead title today when I punch him in the face. He stumbles back, falling into the buffet table. Silver chafing dishes of eggs and bacon fly everywhere as the table breaks beneath him. I feel the entire team jump up to separate us as Dean tries to pull me back and out of the commotion.

Curt struggles to get up and lunges for me. "You hit me over a fucking jersey-chasing piece of ass? What the fuck is wrong with you?"

I rip myself out of Dean's hold on a roar, trying to get to Curt. "I'm gonna fucking kill you, you piece of shit."

Dad enters the fray with two other coaches and moves to stand between us. "Dec, go with Coach Scap. Curt, go with Coach Campbell." When neither of us moves, he yells, "NOW!"

Coach Scap pushes me into one of the break-out rooms we've been using for meetings before asking me what happened.

"I need to see your phone, Coach." Mine is in my room, and I need to know what Dean and Curt were talking about.

Thank God, Coach Scap unlocks it and hands it to me with no more questions.

When I start scrolling sports media, it's everywhere.

Fuck.

I didn't even watch the interview last night. I didn't want to. But I did speak to Hunter and Scarlet afterward. They both said it went well. That's all I cared about.

I talked to Belle this morning. She said she watched it, and I looked handsome. Apparently, it did go well because the analysts are all saying good things.

"First-round draft picks are high-risk gambles, but the Philadelphia Kings got themselves a franchise quarterback with Declan Sinclair."

"A born leader."

"Declan Sinclair had no problem stepping out of the shadow of his legendary father to show football fans what talent and determination can do."

But then they go downhill from there and start talking about Annabelle and Tommy.

Fuck me.

"Is Declan Sinclair too good to be true? With his new fling's tragic life, is she another burden he's taken on?"

Dad walks into the room, and I spin, holding up Coach Scap's phone. "Did you know? Did you see these?"

He looks to Coach Scap. "Can you give us the room, Scappy?"

"Yeah, Joe." Scap holds his hand out for his phone. "We all gotta deal with this shit at some point, kid. You'll get through it."

I watch as he walks out and wait for my dad's answer. "Did you fucking know?" I yell through gritted teeth.

"I'm gonna let that slide this time because I'm your father and your coach and because I love Annabelle and Tommy too. But don't ever forget who runs this team, Declan." The veins in his neck are popping out as he forces himself not to yell back. "Lower your fucking voice. Now."

"Come on, Dad. I looked for thirty seconds and got a page of hits. They're calling her a charity case and Tommy special-needs baggage." I choke on the words, "I don't know how to handle this."

"Scarlet Kingston is all over this, Declan. I've been in touch with her all morning. We were trying to keep it off your radar before the game. I realize now that was a mistake, and I'm sorry for that, son. But what you just did out there is another level of shit. Care to tell me what the hell just happened?"

I stare hard at my dad.

"Maybe I need to reword that. I need to know exactly what the hell happened out there." When I still don't answer, he crosses his arms and asks, "If you want to play today, you have to tell me, Dec."

Fuck.

"He said her pussy better be golden to have to deal with Tommy. Happy?" I've never been this angry in my life.

"My quarterback just punched my tight end the morning before the game. As a coach, no, I'm not happy. As a father, I wish you'd hit him harder."

"Thanks, Dad. What the hell am I gonna do? How am I gonna fix this?" How am I gonna face Belles?

"You're a leader, and it's game day. This is the price you pay. This is being a professional, Declan. Assholes are always gonna say something. They're everywhere, including on our team. He's half the man you are, on and off the field.

He'll never know the kind of love you have because of Annabelle and Tommy. But here's the thing. We need Curt Kenny. We need him for this game. He's had it out for you since your fight his senior year. His draft status plummeted after that game. The Kings got him in the sixth round instead of the first. That cost him millions, and I have no doubt that played a part in what happened today. If I'd have known at the time that I was going to draft you this year, I wouldn't have taken him. But he's a good tight end." Dad's eyes look calmer and clearer than I feel.

"It's not my fault he didn't train harder." I leave out the fucking entitled asshole part.

I see Dad getting frustrated with me. "You'll have your chance, Dec. But for now, you pull your shit together and lead your team like the goddamn professional you are, son. Then, you're gonna go home and talk to Annabelle. She'll be okay. She's made of tougher stuff than this."

I can only hope he's right.

~

*H*ours later, when I'm stretched out, suited, taped up, and trying to get into the headspace I need to be in for the game today, I realize how much my life has changed in the past few months. Nothing has ever come before football. It was always my first and only love and my top priority. The only thing I cared about. There's never been a time when I haven't been 100 percent focused before a game . . . until today.

I'm struggling to force thoughts of Belle and Tommy to the back of my mind for the next sixty minutes of football. The locker room is loud, and for the first time in my life, my headphones are making me claustrophobic. Everyone has given me a wide berth and stayed away, but it's not helping.

Coach walks into the room, and all talking stops. "Gather round, men." He's looking right at me but talking to the room. "Last away game of the season. We win this, and we walk out of here as division champions with a bye week and home-field advantage. You get an extra week to give your bodies a rest, and I know how much you need that at this point in the season."

He's holding his rolled-up laminated play sheet against his leg. "Do you realize that as a player in this room, you represent the top half of 1 percent of anyone who's ever picked up a football? The skill, strength, and determination it took to get you here are only gonna get you so far though. You've gotta have heart to win. You represent the towns you're from. The towns you live in now. The city of Philadelphia. You give them hope. You give them something to look forward to. This is the first time in a decade this team has been in this position."

His eyes scan the room. "Everyone in this room is part of one family, and families fight. It happens. But when we fight, we keep it in-house, and we move on. And while I might fight with my brother, no one else is allowed to. We don't let that happen."

All eyes turn to Curt and me, standing across from each other. Coach continues, "You're Kings. Kings take what they want. We're gonna walk into that stadium today and take it from them. We're gonna march down that field and shove that ball down their throats. Because Kings don't ask for permission. They don't care what people think or say. They do what's best for their kingdom. Because Kings don't just win games. Kings build legacies."

The team starts to get noisy again.

Dad clears his throat and raises his voice, "Memento Mori, gentlemen. All men die. Leave it out there on that field and walk off it, knowing that you lived." His eyes meet mine before he growls, "We're fucking Kings. Now act like it!" and marches out of the room.

30

ANNABELLE

I put Tommy to bed when we got home tonight and promptly threw up again. When Katherine hugged me before we left her house earlier, she slid the number of her ob-gyn into my hand, and I almost choked. She couldn't possibly be thinking... No.

No way.

I have an IUD.

Jesus. Would that even be safe?

But now in the security of my own home, as I lean my cheek against my folded arms resting on the closed lid of the toilet, I start to consider it.

Because really... do I need to deal with one more thing today?

I'm just getting out of the shower and attempting to towel dry my hair, when I hear the alarm being disarmed and Declan's heavy footsteps walking up the stairs. When he walks into our bedroom in his fitted black suit and light blue dress shirt, I drink him in momentarily before reality comes crashing back down.

He drops his bag on the floor and leans against the

frame of the open bathroom door. "You doing okay, baby?" he asks so sweetly I wish I was able to say yes.

Instead, I walk into his arms and give up any final ounce of strength I had left that was holding me together. "It's ruined, Dec," I sob uncontrollably. "I've worked so hard for the past few years on the studio, and it's ruined." Ugly tears track down my face. "And who's going to even want to come back now to a studio whose owner the media has dubbed a charity case?"

"Annabelle..."

I pull out of his arms and walk into the bedroom, shaking my head. "Don't 'Annabelle' me, Declan Sinclair. I love you. I know that dealing with the media comes with loving you. But how am I supposed to ignore this? How do I ignore the things they said about my brother? About me? About us?" I grab my cardigan from the back of my chair and slip it over my tank before turning around and taking in the gutted expression on Declan's beautiful face.

"I know it's not your fault. I'm not upset with you. But how am I supposed to handle this? What am I supposed to do? To say?" I cross my arms and take a shaky breath as sobs wrack my chest. "Tell me, Dec. Please tell me what I'm supposed to do because I don't think I can handle anything else today."

Declan approaches me like he would a scared animal.

Slowly.

Carefully.

He lifts his hands tentatively before wrapping his arms around me. "I've been on the phone with Scarlet, Becket, and Max. They're going to get this handled. I promise we'll take care of it. I'll do whatever I have to, baby. Whatever we need. I promise you, Tommy and you are my only priority."

I back away again, my stomach rolling with nausea. "I

just need a little space tonight. Can you please give me some space?"

"What?"

My eyes meet his, and I feel worse than I knew was possible. "Just give me the night. Please?"

"But Belle . . ." Dec reaches out for me, but I take a step back.

"Declan, in the last twenty-four hours, I've been dubbed a charity case, seen the media write horrible things about my brother, had a stranger destroy my studio and call me a whore. I need some space. Please just give me that."

He nods. "Okay. I'll sleep in the guest room." He picks up his bag and walks through the door without looking back.

I know right away asking him to leave was a stupid thing to do. Letting him go is definitely the wrong move. But instead of going after him, I take the coward's route and drop to the bed so I can cry myself to sleep alone.

31

ANNABELLE

When Declan came into our room to kiss me goodbye Monday morning, the smell of his body wash made me need to jump out of bed and pray I made it to the toilet in time to vomit. And even after the way I treated him last night, he still held my hair and got me a damp wash cloth before asking me to go to the doctor today to see if I had the flu.

I managed to wait until after he left to have the complete freak-out I knew was coming and decided maybe I needed to see the gynecologist after all.

By the time I got Tommy to school, I'd calmed down enough to pick up a pregnancy test before heading back home. Being a whorish charity case apparently isn't enough for me. No, I'm an overachiever.

I need to be a pregnant whorish charity case.

Three pink boxes, two plus signs, two sets of pink lines, and two damn sticks that read "pregnant" later, I cried my way through begging Katherine's ob-gyn's office to fit me in today. Fortunately, when I dropped her name, they were able to squeeze me in before noon.

Now, here I sit, in a waiting room full of pregnant women, *waiting*.

God, I fucking hate waiting.

My eyes close as I tip my head back against the wall and try not to cry. But at least this explains why everything has been making me emotional lately.

I have no clue how I'm going to tell Declan.

I have even less of a clue how he's going to respond.

After the way I treated him last night, I don't even know how I deserve for him to respond.

Just as my thoughts start to spiral out of control, my name is called, and it's time to pull up my big girl panties.

I hold back more tears when I think about *how big* my panties will be soon.

~

Huge.

My panties are going to be huge.

Like circus-tent huge!

Twins.

Goddamn Sinclair genes.

I'm nearly ten-weeks pregnant with twins.

He knocked me up the very first night we were together.

Their beautiful little heartbeats were fast and strong and loud as they bounced off the walls in the tiny exam room. My doctor checked me over thoroughly and told me my IUD must have fallen out at some point. He reassured me that it's not common, but it does happen, and it has no effect on the babies.

Babies. Plural.

I'm going to have babies.

We're going to have babies.

Two.

When my SUV passes by Hart & Soul, I want to cry again at my once-beautiful dance studio that's now a crime scene, yellow police tape and all. Instead, I pull into Sweet Temptations for my daily caffein fix. A Pumpkin Spice coffee is just what the doctor ordered. And maybe a donut... or ten.

When I walk through the door, I thank God that the smell of double-stuffed, vanilla cream-filled donuts makes my mouth water instead of gag. I take in the room, seeing an older woman sitting alone in a Queen Anne electric-blue chair. I'm guessing she's with the gentleman ahead of me in line who's ordering two coffees and two muffins. Other than that, the place is empty.

When the older gentleman gets his coffees and bag of sweets, he turns and smiles at me on his way back to his companion. Good grief, that coffee smells good. Yes. Give me a big old cup of... FUCK!

"Hey, Annabelle. The regular?" Amelia smiles at me while she turns to make my coffee.

"Wait," I tell her. My next words pain me more than I knew was possible. "Can you make it a decaf?" Oh, sweet baby Jesus in a manger. How am I supposed to give up caffeine?

Side note: Sabrina's right, and her favorite saying is rather satisfying.

Amelia turns to me, a suspicious look on her face. "Decaf?" she asks, knowing something's up.

Shit. Think fast. "Yeah. With everything that's happened in the last twenty-four hours, I've inhaled a ton of caffeine. I think it's throwing my stomach off. I might need to cut back a little today." I'm a terrible liar, and I know it, but Amelia doesn't push me on it if she suspects anything.

"You doing okay with all the press stuff?"

"I'm okay."

Amelia lifts an eyebrow as if she doesn't believe me before turning back to make my wannabe coffee.

"Fine. So maybe I'm not okay yet, but I'm working on it. Safe to say, yesterday sucked, but I really don't want to talk about it."

She holds up the whipped cream, and I nod. "So, what the hell's going on with the studio? Your text yesterday was pretty vague, sister."

I made sure to give her a heads-up in case whoever hit my studio was looking at other places along Main Street, especially since Amelia lives above her shop. "I haven't heard anything else yet. I might swing by the police department after I leave here just to see if they have any updates."

The chimes ring above the door, and I turn to see Leah stroll in, looking as pretty as ever. Her long brown hair is curled today and hanging down around her shoulders. A tight pink puffer jacket and matching hat cover her up with another pair of killer knee-high leather boots making her legs look miles long.

Damn. And I'm gonna be as big as a house soon.

"Hey, Amelia. Hey, Annabelle." She waves a hand at the two of us before pulling off what looks like a cashmere glove. "What's going on, ladies?" She's bouncy and cheerful and everything I'm not feeling right now.

"Hi, Leah. What can I get you today?" Amelia motions toward the coffees.

Leah stands next to me and sniffs my coffee. What the hell? "I'll take whatever Annabelle has. It smells delish."

"Yeah. If it wasn't decaf," I mutter.

"Decaf doesn't taste any different, Belles. Get over it. I'll

Always Earned, Never Given

make sure to add a shot of espresso next time you come in to make up for it." She hands Leah her drink.

"Cheers." Leah holds her cup up to toast mine.

This chick is goofy, but I go with it. "Cheers."

Lightning fast, she grabs my hand and screams. Actually screams. "Oh. My. God. Is that an engagement ring?"

I didn't think about it when I put my ring on today.

Actually, yes I did. I wanted that ring on my finger when I went to the ob-gyn. I wanted Declan with me but instead, had to settle for his ring because I couldn't take him from football practice without being sure I was pregnant. And after the way I treated him last night, I really didn't deserve to have him with me.

"Umm, yes?" I haven't even told Amelia yet. Dec and I were enjoying keeping it to ourselves for now. We weren't in a rush for the media to catch wind of it. I lock eyes with Amelia, who's glaring at me.

"I guess I don't rank, huh? When did you get engaged?" she asks, a hurt look flashing across her face.

Damn it.

I have to remember to somehow fix this later.

Let's see how many relationships I can fuck up in a day.

I glance from her back to Leah. "We got engaged last week. But ladies, please don't say anything. We were waiting for Declan's brother to come home from Navy bootcamp this week before we tell his family. He wanted them all together when we broke the news." My phone rings, and I see it's Dec. "I'm sorry, ladies, I've got to go. See you later, Amelia." I wave at the two of them and hurry out of the shop before answering the phone.

"Hi, Dec."

"Hey, baby. How are you feeling?"

I burst into tears. "Why are you so good to me when I'm such an asshole?"

"Because I love you, Belle. It'll be my turn to be the asshole next time." Dec's voice is calm and soothing. "I've been worried about you. Did you make a doctor's appointment?" The concern in his voice breaks my heart.

"I did. It's all good. I'm gonna head home soon. Practice hard, babe. Love you." I don't wait for him to answer before I disconnect the call. I don't want to lie to him about the doctor's appointment, but I would never tell him something like this over the phone.

Pulling out of my parking space, I decide to skip the police department and call them instead. No update yet. They said the police report should be available by Friday if I need it for insurance purposes and that they'll keep in touch. Great. That just reminded me that I completely forgot about calling my insurance company.

When I walk in my front door, exhaustion takes hold, and I decide to call the insurance company after I lay down on the couch for a few minutes. I kick off my brown leather riding boots and get comfy on the couch. My pretty knee-high socks with the ruffle at the top are pulled up over my black leggings, and I'm wearing one of Declan's black Philadelphia Kings hoodies, keeping me nice and toasty. Once I lay my head down, my eyes close as I drift off to sleep in the pale afternoon sunlight.

"Baby, wake up."

I hear the words. At least I think I do. But I don't want to open my eyes.

"Belle, what time do we need to get Tommy? You've got to wake up."

I feel a warm hand caress my face and force myself to open an eye. "Hmm?"

"Babe, it's three o'clock. What time does his social skills group end today?" Declan's smooth voice is so soothing, I want to pull him down with me and go back to sleep. That is, until what he said finally registers, and I shoot up to a sitting position. Something I immediately regret doing when my stomach revolts, and I'm forced to run to the bathroom.

Declan follows me in and holds my hair while I vomit up bile since I'm a moron who didn't eat anything today, leaving me to dry heave until the nausea subsides. When I finally stop, Dec wets the hand towel from the towel rack and wipes my face before he picks me up and carries me back to the couch.

"Belle, you should have told me you were still sick. I would have come home." He sits me down gently and pulls the cream-colored Sherpa-lined blanket off the back of the couch to wrap me in, then squats down in front of me.

"Cracker. Please." My throat hurts so badly from vomiting up nothing that my words come out scratchy. "I think there's ginger ale in the pantry. Could I have some of that too?"

I close my eyes until he makes it back with my soda and crackers and pray this helps.

Declan sits on the ottoman in front of me and hands me my drink before he opens a sleeve of saltines. Thank goodness these are Tommy's favorite crackers when he doesn't feel well and I always keep a box or two in our pantry. I sip slowly and force down a few crackers before I look at the man in front of me whose entire life is about to change.

He tries one of my crackers. "These are disgusting. How do you eat these?" Dec moves next to me on the couch, gently wraps his arm around me, and leans me against him. "Baby, what time do we need to get Tommy? I'll pick him up.

You just rest." His fingers are running through my hair, and it feels so nice. It's the only thing that's felt nice today.

I slowly turn my head. "The late bus is bringing him home today. I spoke to someone this morning, and they said he should be here between four-thirty and five." I lean my head against his shoulder for a minute, soaking up his warmth. "I talked to them about the media and made sure they knew not to give out any information or let anyone in. I also verified the people who are allowed to sign him out. They promised me we're safe."

"Okay, good. Why don't you let me help you upstairs and get changed into pajamas then?" He kisses the top of my head gently.

I lift my head to look at this man I don't deserve. "I love you, Declan. I'm sorry I pushed you away. I was scared and took it out on you. It wasn't fair, and I shouldn't have done it."

Dec pulls me off the couch. "I'm so sorry this happened, Belle."

"It wasn't your fault. You can't control everything."

We head up to our room where I change into my softest pale-blue lounge pants and shirt and wrap myself up in my favorite white sweater. I step into the bathroom to brush my teeth before coming back out to Dec, who's sitting on the bed, his head hung low.

"I hate this, Belle. I hate that you had to deal with what happened at the studio without me. I hate that you and Tommy have been dragged into this media circus and it's my fault. I fucking hate it."

I walk to him, place my arms around his neck and stand between his legs. "Declan Sinclair, you listen to me, and you listen good." My fingers grip his head and force his eyes up to me. "You're the strongest man I know, but you cannot control everything. You've gotta let go of that idea. I promise to never shut you out again. I shut down when I get scared. And everything about yesterday scared me. Please be patient with me."

I move my hands to trace his strong jaw. "You and I will make sure Tommy is protected . . ." Oh God, Tommy and the babies.

"I would never let anything happen to either of you, Belle." His strong arms wrap around my back.

I turn and sit down on his lap. When I see the love shining in his eyes, I know we'll be okay. "What if there were more of us to protect?"

"What are you talking about, Belles?" His arm tightens around my waist while the other one absently twirls my hair.

I love when he plays with my hair.

"I love you, Declan." I feel my chest rise and fall with my deep inhale and exhale.

His inky-blue eyes glisten back at me. "I love you too, Belle."

I reach into the pocket of my sweater and pull out the sonogram image the doctor gave me. "Declan, I went to the doctor this morning. But not my primary. I went to my ob-gyn."

This incredible man looks confused, so I hand him the picture before telling him, "I needed a gynecologist to confirm that the six pregnancy tests I took were all correct."

A million emotions flash across those indigo-blue eyes before settling on fear.

He leans back, eyes shining with tears. "Is your IUD going to hurt the baby?" This man . . .

I shake my head, and my own tears start to fall. It might as well be my theme for the day. "No, my doctor said it looks like the IUD came loose and fell out before I got pregnant."

"So, the baby's okay? You're okay?" he asks, his voice unsteady.

I nod. "Yes. I'm fine. It's just morning sickness. Both babies are fine too." I point to the two little dots on the image.

Declan's hands frame my face. "We're having twins?"

"Yes. We're having twins. I heard their heartbeats today, and they were so strong, Dec. I wished you were there." I hold his face in my hands, mirroring him, and pray my kids get their father's eyes.

"I'll never miss another appointment, Belle." He holds me tightly in his arms, and I let myself believe for the first time today that everything is going to be okay. "I love you, Belle. You and Tommy and this family we're creating. You're my entire world." He lightly brushes his lips over mine.

I can't help but be relieved that I didn't destroy the best thing that ever happened to me last night.

Dec moves me off his lap and stands. "Let's get married this weekend."

Wait . . . what?

32

ANNABELLE

*D*eclan was serious when he said, "Let's get married this weekend", and after a long conversation later that night, I realized how right he was. We love each other. We already live together. He knows me well enough that he knew I wouldn't want anything big. But when he said, "I've waited my whole life to find you. Why should we wait longer to make it official?" I just knew he was right and kinda wished we could have flown to Vegas right then.

No way that was happening, but it was tempting.

Instead, we went to City Hall the following day and applied for our marriage license. We were told there's a three-day waiting period in Pennsylvania, and we could pick it up on Friday.

And that was that.

Dec insisted that I let him pay for the repairs the studio needed so we could get it up and running faster. He wouldn't take no for an answer, saying it was our money. I agreed only if he promised to let me pay him back when the insurance money came in. When I brought up the idea of a prenup, he shot me down right away, telling me, "Baby, you're never getting rid of me. I'll love you until I take my last breath. I don't need a piece of paper to protect anything. I just need you."

I mean, seriously, this man . . . They broke the mold when they made Declan Sinclair.

Now, here I am, Friday afternoon, trying to figure out what looks nice but will be easy on my knees if I get sick during the family dinner at Coach and Katherine's house tonight. Whoever called it morning sickness was an asshole. It's all day and night sickness. I hear my phone buzz from across the room and stop to look at it.

Group Text:

Nattie: How freaking long am I going to have to wait at this dang airport?
Nattie: I WANT TO SEE MY BROTHER!
Annabelle: Take a breath, Nat. Cooper's flight will land soon.
Sabrina: What are we wearing tonight, ladies? Do I need to shave?
Chloe: Ummm. Are you planning on getting laid?
Sabrina: Well, probably.
Chloe: Then shave your snatch, woman! WTF?
Sabrina: I meant my legs, crackhead.
Sabrina: As in - am I putting on a dress?
Nattie: I wanted to wear my new jeans. They make my ass look great.
Annabelle: Shut up, brat. Your ass always looks great!
Chloe: Yeah. Like you've got room to talk, Belles. I wanna look like you when I grow up.
Annabelle: Zip it, Chloe. I'm not that much older than you.

Sabrina: Whatever. I've got a cute new green plaid skirt I've been dying to wear.
Chloe: Seriously? When you actually were a Catholic schoolgirl, does the fetish get worse?
Chloe: Ten bucks says Murphy bends you over the bed before you get to Coach's house.
Nattie: Totally!
Annabelle: Oh, yeah. I'd be more surprised if he didn't.
Sabrina: Whatever . . .
Annabelle: I'll wear a dress. I've got a cute winter-white cowl-neck sweater dress.
Nattie: With your brown boots and those socks with the ruffle trim?
Annabelle: Yup!
Nattie: Damnit. I'm gonna have to find something cuter to wear.
Chloe: You guys are all little lemmings. Wear what you want.
Nattie: GTG. I see Coop.

Might as well wear this dress tonight. I don't know how much longer it's going to fit. Once my outfit is sorted, I walk into Tommy's room and lay out his jeans and a "Declan shirt." He started calling his Henleys "Declan shirts" because he wears them so often. I was just impressed that he was aware enough to notice that. I mean, come on, it's not like it has dinosaurs on it. Of course, I lay out a flannel shirt with dinosaurs on it to go over the Henley and tell him to get dressed.

I'm zipping up my brown leather riding boots when I hear the alarm disengage. We started arming it as soon as Declan started spending the night. He insisted. So now, as soon as we walk in the door, the alarm gets armed to "Stay." No getting in or out without turning it off.

I hear Declan drop his bag moments before I hear, "Belles, baby? Where are you?"

"I'm in the bedroom, babe." I smile to myself. I've been trying out the nickname thing on him. He's called me "baby" for a while, and even though I didn't love it at first, it's grown on me now. Something about the way he says it, and the way he looks at me when he does, just melts my insides.

When he steps into the bedroom, carrying a bouquet of daisies, I may actually swoon. "Declan . . . What are these for?"

He hands me the pretty pale-purple vase before his hands cup my jaw and his lips brush over mine. "I finally get to tell our family tonight that you're gonna marry me. I wanted to celebrate, and you've mentioned daisies are your favorite."

I place the vase on my vanity and wrap my arms around his waist. "I love you, Dec."

He squeezes me tight as Tommy bounces into the room. "Do you think Rocky will have the babies tonight?"

He hasn't stopped talking about this all week. Rocky is due December twenty-seventh, and I swear Tommy is going to make me drive over there every day during the entire two months that his new puppy has to stay with its momma.

"Little man, the puppies are coming soon. I promise. But you have to be patient. We've got to wait two whole months after they're born before they can leave their mommy."

His face falls like it's the first time he's hearing this instead of the fiftieth.

~

When we pull into Coach and Katherine's driveway a little later, there are cars and SUVs scattered everywhere. The beautiful brick house looks so pretty with white Christmas lights dotting the roof and lovely, red-ribboned wreaths hanging in each window. There's landscape lighting illuminating the whole house, and it looks so festive, I want to cry.

Jesus. If my hormones are this bad at just over two months, what will they be like a few months from now?

We follow Declan in the side door and hear Christmas carols playing through the speaker and laughter echoing throughout the house. The smell of fresh bread and Christmas wafts through the air. At one time, I loved this time of year, but that was a long time ago. Thanks to Dec, I'm starting to get some of that back.

When we enter the kitchen, it looks like we're the last ones to arrive. The whole gang's here, and all conversation comes to a halt when Cooper sees us.

It's only been three months since we've seen him, but he looks so different. His beach-blonde hair that he always wore a little too long and a little too shaggy was shaved off for boot camp and is currently a buzz-cut close to his head. It grew in darker than it used to be and is now closer to Declan's brown than Nattie's blonde. He's filled out too. He was a muscular kid before he left. Now he's a muscular man in his jeans and button-down black shirt.

He and Dec meet each other in the middle of the room and hug. Dec actually bear-hugs Coop and picks him right up off his feet. He drops him back down, saying, "Missed you, little brother." They do the back-pound thing, and Coop hits Dec's arm.

"Missed you too, man." Then he turns to Tommy and

me. "Tommy boy!" He raises his arms for a high-five, and Tommy surprises the whole room by running over to Cooper and throwing his arms around his waist. Coop looks at me, bewildered, and I know I look the same.

"You came back," Tommy exclaims.

This giant of a man bends his knees a little to get eye level with Tommy. "I promised you I would."

Tommy's arms circle his waist again. "Not everyone comes back."

Oh my God. I quickly cross the room and wrap my arms around my brother and Cooper. And cry. Because seriously, how could anyone not cry now? Luckily, Rocky comes over and rubs her body up against Tommy's leg, and that quickly diverts his attention.

Cooper gives me a gentle hug and whispers, "I think my brother just growled, Belles. Should we fuck with him?"

"No, asshole, you shouldn't. We've had enough of that this week," Declan answers him.

These are my favorite nights. Everyone is together and happy. Laughing and telling stories. Cooper brought his battle buddy, Linc, home with him for the next two weeks. He's a little shorter than Cooper, closer to Murphy's height, maybe six-foot-two or three, with close-cut blonde hair and eyes the color of a blue summer's sky. Not to mention that sexy Georgia twang. This southern gentleman has had a lot of fun, listening to all our stories and filling us in with a few of his own.

Coach and Katherine pass out flutes of champagne. Coach holds his glass up high before saying, "A toast to my son and Lincoln. We are so proud of you for choosing this path and—"

Coach is cut off by Nattie, "SHUT. THE. FRONT. DOOR!"

"What is it this time, Natalie?" Coach sounds like his patience is running thin.

Nattie points at me. "She's wearing Nana's ring!"

Everyone turns to stare at me, but it's the smile coming from Cooper that makes me smile back. Declan wraps one arm around me and one around Tommy. "What were we going to tell everyone tonight, Tommy?"

"Belles has been puking every day, but it's okay because my babies are in there, making her sick. She's gonna be fine."

Declan's hand covers Tommy's mouth as I scream, "NO!"

"SHUT. THE. FRONT. DOOR," comes from a shocked Coach.

Well, that wasn't exactly what I had planned.

33

DECLAN

*Y*eah... that was so not what we practiced on the ride over here. Pretty sure the squealing in the room is coming from Nattie, but when it gets louder, and I get shoved out of the way as the girls circle Belles, it starts to sound like every female in the room is making the same noise. And there are a whole lot of females in that room.

Even Rocky leaves the room.

Cooper wraps an arm around me. "Congrats, man. I'm guessing Nana's ring means there's a wedding coming with that baby?" He's trying to hold back his laughter, but when I start to laugh, he does too. Then Brady, Murphy, Bash, and Linc follow us over the edge.

Murphy slaps my back. "Dude, I was sure I was gonna be the first one of us to knock somebody up. So fucking glad it was you. So, shot-gun wedding? Really?"

I punch his shoulder. Hard.

"Fuck off, Murph. I asked her to marry me before we found out she was pregnant." But even that doesn't wipe the smile off my face. Belle is literally glowing across the room as she stands in front of the kitchen's big brick fireplace.

Bash shoves Murphy out of the way and shakes my hand. "Congrats, Dec. You're a lucky man."

"The luckiest," I tell them.

Brady smiles as he steps in front of Murphy. "When's the baby due?"

"Babies," I answer.

Cooper spits out his water. "I'm sorry. What?"

"He said babies, son. As in two." Dad joins the group of guys, wraps an arm over my shoulder and smiles. "Congratulations, Dec. Annabelle just told me the good news."

"Thanks, old man. You ready to be a grandpa?" I ask, goading him. My dad is in his mid-forties, but he doesn't look much older than me. I can't wait for our kids to call him "Grandpa."

"I don't know, Dec. When's the due date?" Dad cocks his eyebrow.

I smile and tell the group, "July seventeenth." Then I turn back to Dad. "We're not even messing with your training camp, old man."

Dad hollers over the noise, "Katie, where will we be on July seventeenth?"

Our group slowly moves to converge back into one big crowd with the women, instead of two small groups, and my hand finds Belle's back. I kiss her head, and she leans in against me.

"We'll probably be home from the hospital by then, Joe." Katherine smiles big and bright. "My due date is July third." She wraps an arm around Dad's waist, and he kisses her lips.

Carys squeals.

"What?" Murphy asks with a bewildered look on his face.

Sabrina grasps his hand and smiles up at Murphy. "I think your mom is pregnant, Murph."

"Ah hell, Coach. Seriously?" He wipes his hand down his face, and then looks at his mom. "Was it like . . . an Immaculate Conception?" Murph is seriously struggling.

"She's not a virgin, dude," Bash tells him.

Murphy shoves him. "Fuck off, Bash."

"Aiden James Murphy." Katherine glares at her son. "Language."

Carys laughs and elbows her brother. "You got middle-named by Mom."

"Sorry, Mom." Murphy glares at Carys before adding, "Shut the front door." He smiles at Nattie, then looks at his mother. "Is that better, Mom?"

"Much." She smiles happily.

"Seriously . . . You're pregnant? You guys really . . ." Murph doesn't finish the sentence because Dad smacks the back of his head.

"Watch it, Murph," Dad tells him.

Poor Linc stares in shock or maybe awe. I can't tell. "Damn, Cooper said you guys are crazy, but seriously, I feel like I'm in an episode of the Kardashians."

Nat laughs, "The Kardashians have nothing on us."

~

Once dinner's done and everything's gotten somewhat back to normal, talk circles back to our engagement. "We really don't want to wait. We don't want anything big. We picked up our license today and are just going to go to City Hall one day this week," I tell the table.

"Fuck that," Murphy says as Katherine glares. He pulls out his phone then looks back up. "I can get certified online right now. I'll marry you right here." Murph looks around the table and rubs his hands together. "Let's do this."

Belle squeezes my leg under the table. "Everyone we love is here, Dec."

"Your mother's not here, Declan," Dad reminds me.

My mom and I barely talk these days. She's living the life of a retired model in Italy with a boyfriend a few months younger than Nattie and Cooper. "Somehow, I think she'd be okay with missing it," I tell my dad. Nattie and Cooper agree, and I turn to Belle. "What do you say, Belle? Wanna marry me tonight?"

She smiles at me and then turns to Murphy. "Murphy, I swear to God, if you utter one single, solitary cuss word during my wedding, I will projectile-vomit on you. Go ahead and try me. It's my new superpower."

His lips tighten as he makes a face that's a mixture of fear and disgust.

"Give me your phone, Murphy." Dad reaches for Murphy's phone and then turns to us. "If anybody here is going to marry the two of you, it's going to be me."

Belle laces her fingers with mine. "I'd love that, Coach."

"Annabelle, I think it's high time you started calling me Joe, sweetheart." Yeah, I love my dad.

A few minutes later, Katherine has the formal living room in the front of the house set up perfectly for us. The lights are off in the massive open space. Vaulted ceilings with old wooden beams arching across the room frame a two-story brick fireplace that Dad and I are standing in front of. The mantle is covered in tapered red and white candles arranged within an evergreen garland. More candles are lit and scattered throughout the room, giving it a golden glow.

A beautiful twelve-foot-tall blue spruce Christmas tree, dotted with hundreds of tiny white lights and red velvet bows is lit behind us. The girls grabbed all the poinsettia plants wrapped in red velvet from around the house and arranged them in two rows to make an aisle for Belle to walk down.

"You ready for this, son?" my father asks me as I wait for my bride to enter the room.

I look around the room at our friends and family. Sabrina's standing next to Murphy, Carys is with Katherine. Bash and Chloe are on the other side of the room with Linc and Brady.

And then I see Nattie enter the room with a few red and white flowers that I think were in the arrangement that sat at the center of the dining room table during dinner. They're tied together by a small red velvet ribbon. My sister is smiling at me the way she used to when she was little and thought I could do anything.

Nattie nods toward Carys, who surprises me when she starts to sing an *a cappella* version of "Forever Young." It's gorgeous and haunting and so perfectly Annabelle.

My next breath is stolen from my lungs when my kid brother helps the kid I've come to love like my own walk Annabelle Hart down the makeshift aisle to me. Her beautiful creamy-white sweaterdress clings to her curves and stops mid-thigh. Her brown boots stop below her knee with a cute little white ruffle popping out of the top. Her wild caramel-colored hair is down around her shoulders, and I think Katherine wrapped up the rest of her dinner-table arrangement and gave it to Belle to carry.

Cooper hugs my girl and whispers something in her ear that makes her smile, then moves to stand next to me. I step forward and offer Tommy my hand. He smacks it before running over to sit on the floor with Rocky.

When the beautiful woman in front of me graces me with her smile, I know I've won my last inch. She laces her fingers through mine. "I love you, Declan Sinclair."

When I kiss her lips, Dad clears his throat. "I didn't have much time to put anything together to say tonight, but watching the two of you, it looks like my job is pretty easy." He looks between us. "Have you thought about vows?"

I smile and take both of Belles hands in mine as we turn to face each other. "Annabelle Hart, I feel like I've been waiting my entire life to find you. And now that I have, I promise to earn your love and your heart every single day. You, Tommy, and these babies will always come first. I promise to love you, support you, protect you, and dance with you for the rest of our lives. You're the love of my life, Belle."

She lets go of one hand to wipe away the tears streaming down her cheeks. "Oh, wow." She sniffs. "That was really good," she laughs lightly. "Declan Sinclair, I promise to always give you my love freely. We've earned each other. I think somehow, my parents led me to you so you could love me enough for me to realize I was safe enough to love you back. So you could give me you and your family and make me feel secure enough to not lose my mind when I found out we were starting our own family so soon. Thank you for bringing the magic back to my life. I promise to love you with my whole heart and soul."

I raise my hand and cup her face, my thumbs wiping away her tears.

Out of the corner of my eye, I see my dad wipe away his own tear before speaking, "By the power vested in me by whatever website Murphy found, I now pronounce you Mr.

and Mrs. Declan Sinclair." He turns to me with complete delight on his face. "You may kiss your bride."

We step toward each other. My hands cradle her face as my mouth claims hers. After a moment, I hear shouts and clapping. We pull apart and turn to face everyone. Nattie is crying harder than Belle was, wrapped up in Brady's arms, and she's the first one to step forward and hug us. She's followed seconds later by Cooper, who wraps his arms around the three of us.

"Oh my God, you're my sister now!" Natalie proclaims.

Dad joins our group hug, telling Belles, "Welcome to the family, Annabelle."

34

ANNABELLE

Nattie and Katherine both offered to keep Tommy for us for the night, but the invitation to Nattie's house meant he got to go home with Rocky, so Nattie won. I don't know who was more tired by the time everyone started to head home, me or Rocky.

I spoke to Katherine a lot tonight about being pregnant. She said she was tired and nauseous the entire time she was pregnant with Carys, but with this pregnancy, she hasn't had any morning sickness and has energy to spare. Apparently it was the same way when she was pregnant with Murphy. The doctor warned me with two babies, my body was doing twice the work, and my HCG levels were higher and throwing my hormones off even more than normal. All of this combined means that it's ten p.m., and I'm falling asleep during the ten-minute drive across town to our house.

When we pull into the driveway, I force myself to function and reach for the door, but Dec frowns. "Stay right there, Mrs. Sinclair. Don't move." He gets out of the Bronco and rounds the front of the SUV before pulling open my door and lifting me in his arms.

My arms circle his neck, and I don't even think about fighting him. Why would I when I'm safe in my husband's arms?

Wow. That's going to take some time getting used to.

I lay my head against his shoulder and close my eyes. "You know how sexy your strength is?" I ask, when my football God of a husband unlocks the door, disarms and then re-arms the alarm, and carries me up the stairs without ever putting me down or breaking a sweat.

He walks into our bedroom and sits down on the bed with me still in his arms. "It's not a hard thing to do when your wife weighs nothing, baby."

"It's not just your physical strength I find sexy, husband." I stand and cross the room, looking for the wedding band I picked up this morning while he was at work and Tommy was in school. I also grab my phone out of my Mary Poppins bag and pull up my favorite sexy playlist before pressing play. An acoustic version of "Wicked Games" by Stone Sour starts to play throughout the room. When I move back and am standing between is spread legs, I place the black velvet box in his hand and tell him, "It's your inner strength I find the sexiest, husband. You don't bend for anything." I pull off one boot. "You stick to your beliefs." The other boot goes next. "Money doesn't sway you. Your bosses don't sway you. Your loud family doesn't sway you."

I pull my dress up slightly and straddle Declan's lap. "Thank God, you didn't let my scared, stubborn heart sway you." When I brush my lips over his, he tries to take control to get more, but I pull back. "Open the box, Dec."

Those inky-blue eyes bore into me before he finally cracks the box open and then looks back up at me. "Two rings?"

"Yup. One is rubber. In case you want to wear it at practice." I pull the other out of the box and hold it in my open palm. "This is your real wedding band though. It's brushed black tungsten. It's the strongest metal wedding bands are made of. Kinda like you, hubby."

Dec takes the band from me, examining it. Then he tips it on its side and reads the inscription.

"My whole heart and soul."

"Annabelle, I love it." He brushes my hair away from my face and hands it back to me. "Now, put it on me so I can be the groomzilla I didn't get the chance to be."

When this man smiles, my soul is at peace. I place the ring on his finger and pray it fits when I slide it down.

Oh, thank God.

Dec's lips touch mine, and I back off his lap as the song switches to Sam Smith's "Stay With Me." I pull the hem of my dress up as I slowly sway my hips to the beat of the song. When his calloused covered palms slide up my legs and under my dress, I let him take control. He pushes the dress up and over my head and sucks in his breath.

"I can't imagine I'll ever stop being thankful that you give yourself so freely to me, Belle." His hands caress the underside of my breasts that are encased in a nude lace demi-cup bra before he leans in and sucks a nipple through the lace, sending a thrill down my spine. "Oh baby, they're so sensitive," he hums as he unhooks my bra.

When I move to put a knee on the bed to get closer to him, I'm lifted and seated next to him as he stands up. "Dec, I wanted you closer, not farther away." There's no hiding the neediness in my voice.

He reaches one arm behind his head and pulls his navy blue Henley off before unbuckling his belt and jeans, and then he drops to his knees. He pulls my nude lace thong off, leaving me in nothing but my white lacey knee-high socks, and just stares at me. "Jesus, you're perfect," he tells me before his tongue licks a line up my center and back down, purposely missing my clit. He parts my folds with the pad of his thumb, teasingly dipping it in and out of me before licking again and sucking my clit into his mouth.

I bend my knees and rest my feet on the edge of the mattress on either side of Dec's head, leaning up on my elbows so I can see this magnificent man between my spread thighs. Moments later, I'm nearing orgasm when he presses a finger in my pussy and another in my ass just as he nips my clit, and I scream out. I have to push his head away when the sensations become too much before falling back on the bed, my heart thundering wildly in my chest.

Declan stands next to the bed and kicks off his jeans and boxers. "We've got the house to ourselves tonight, baby, and I want to try something. You trust me?"

"Unquestioningly," I answer. I don't know when it happened, but this man, my husband, is the other half of my heart. He's my world. My soul. The overwhelming emotions rush over me before Declan pulls me from my thoughts.

I hear him open my bedside drawer and then ask, "Where's your vibrator, Belle?"

"What?" I sit up. "Why would I need my vibrator when I've got you?"

"Trust me, Annabelle. We aren't going to get many nights where I can make you scream, and I want the whole fucking street to hear you tonight." He reaches down, drags his middle finger through my slick, wet pussy, and then raises that same finger to his mouth and sucks it. And yeah ... I might have just orgasmed again.

"It's in the top drawer of my dresser under my panties. I didn't want little hands to find it," I admit.

Dec pulls it out of my drawer and stalks to me with my

purple vibrator in one hand and a bottle of lube in the other. I bite down on my bottom lip, excited for whatever he has planned.

Dec drops his newfound prizes next to me on the bed, grips my waist, flips me over and pulls me up onto my knees. He smacks my ass and then licks it. "You ready for round two, baby?"

I look over my shoulder and watch him as he rubs lube over his thick cock then runs his hand over the vibrator with the leftover lube. "Oh yeah, I am."

He licks up my spine and bites down on the soft spot where my neck meets my shoulder.

"Declan . . ." I beg. "I need you." My core aches.

He turns the vibrator on and runs it over my clit and down my pussy before pushing it in just the slightest bit. "You're gonna get me, baby. And I'm gonna get all of you." He repeats the motion a few times before I feel him trace a lotioned finger along my ass before pushing against the ring of nerves.

And oh my God, it feels insane. Too much, too soon and yet, not enough. "Dec," I pant, "I need more."

He smacks my other ass cheek, and it stings but also sends a thrill through my body. "Whose greedy pussy is this, baby?"

I look over my shoulder and smile. "It's yours, husband. Now take care of it."

"Oh, I plan to, wife." The hand that was gripping my hip moves.

Then, I feel it. He has the vibrator thrumming against my clit as he starts to push his thick cock into my ass. I tense, not realizing at first that I'm holding my breath.

"Relax, Belles. Breathe out and push back." He clicks the

button, sending the vibrations up a notch, and I inch back on him slowly.

"Oh, God," I cry out with the exquisite combination of pleasure and pain invading my body.

"That's it, baby. Take my dick." He pushes the vibrator all the way in my pussy. "Take what's yours, Belle. Only yours." He finally works himself into my ass, and I scream out.

"Too much. Oh God." I grip the sheets in both hands.

Declan stills immediately. "You want me to stop, Belle?"

"God, no. Just go really slow, Dec," I tell him as I feel him start to move.

After a moment, the pleasure-pain combination turns to only an exquisite pleasure, and we find the rhythm only Dec and I know.

When he wraps his arm around my chest and pulls me up to him, changing the angle, I lose all control. A kaleidoscope of colors explodes in my eyes as I experience the most intense orgasm I've ever felt in my life. When I collapse, I don't even know if Declan has come. My limbs just give way beneath me.

I lay there, entirely spent, and vaguely hear him leave the room. When he comes back in, I feel a warm washcloth move between my thighs. "Dec?"

"Yeah, baby?" He cleans me up then throws the washcloth back into the bathroom.

"Good shot," I tell him. Then add, "I wanna do that again when I can feel my toes."

He kisses my neck and then climbs into bed and pulls the blanket up around us. His arms gather me against his chest, and I'm cocooned in the warmth of Declan Sinclair.

"We've got the rest of our lives, Belle."

Before I drift off to sleep, my last thought is that the rest of our lives doesn't sound like nearly enough.

35

DECLAN

The next day, news of Belle and me picking up our marriage license is all over the city of Philadelphia with speculation on when we're getting married and whether it's a shot-gun wedding. That's the part I hate the most.

Dad, Cooper, Murphy, and I are getting fitted for our tuxes for Dad and Katherine's wedding when a journalist and his crew have the nerve to come inside the door and try to get a picture. "Can we get a statement, Declan?"

It's almost comical to see Murphy and Cooper close ranks so that they can't get the picture of me they want. Dad walks out of the dressing room and over to the reporter. "Here's your statement, guys. My son is happily married to an amazing woman I'm proud to be able to call my daughter. Now, if you ever want access to my pressroom again, get the hell out of here and let me enjoy my day off with all my sons." Dad holds the door open for the reporter and photographer to leave, then turns to the shop owner. "I'll give you a thousand dollars if you'll close the shop for the next hour while we're here."

"Done," the older gentleman tells my father as he flips his sign to "Closed" and locks the front door.

While Murphy checks out ties, Cooper and I sit down in the two leather chairs set up outside the dressing room. "So, you thinking about moving yet?" Coop asks, leaning back and crossing his leg.

I blow out a breath. "We haven't talked about it yet, but we need to. I need them safer than where we are now, but it's their home. It's the only home Tommy has ever known, and it has all Belle's memories of her parents. I don't know how she's gonna feel about leaving it."

"She's probably not gonna be thrilled about the idea of leaving it, but Belles is a momma bear. She knows the best thing for Tommy and my future nieces—"

I cut him off, "They could be nephews, asshat."

"Nah. It would be so much more fun to watch you deal with two girls." He lifts his eyebrows and grins an evil grin. "Anyway, she's gonna want to keep the kids safe, and you need more privacy and more security for that. I'm not saying lock yourselves behind a wall, but you need what Brady's parents have. You need land between you and your neighbors that you can fence in. You need a kick-ass security system. You know I'm right, man." Cooper looks over at Murphy, who's holding up a navy blue tie with green shamrocks on it and shakes his head. "It's New Year's, Murph, not St. Patrick's Day."

"Whatever. I like it, I'm getting it," Murphy grumbles.

We spend the next hour with each of us getting our tuxes fitted before Murphy steps away to take a call. When he comes back, he announces, "Rocky's having her babies. I need cigars."

Murphy and Cooper leave in Murph's car, and I drop my

dad off at his house before I head over to find Belles. She'd gone over to the home that Murphy shares with Brady, Nattie, and Bash this morning to pick up Tommy. Brady and Bash were giving Linc a tour of Philadelphia, so Belle texted me earlier that she was going to hang out at the house with the girls for a little while. I can only imagine what's going to come out of Tommy's mouth if he sees Rocky giving birth.

When my phone rings, I see Hunter's name flash across the screen and hit the speaker. "What's up, man?"

"They know, Dec. I'm so sorry," Hunter answers, frustration lacing his voice.

"Dude, they've been following me all morning. Dad just gave a statement an hour ago. We knew once we filed for the license, it would only be a matter of time," I tell him. "There's nothing we could have done differently."

"Dec, man . . . They know Annabelle's pregnant. They know it's twins. According to the article that just ran, it came from a source within her doctor's office."

"Fuck!" I hit the steering wheel. "How am I supposed to tell her this? What the hell am I supposed to do now?"

"Scarlet wants to meet as soon as you can. She and Becket will meet you at the stadium, and they'll conference me in." He waits a beat. "You still there, Dec?"

I pound the wheel again. "Yeah, I'm fucking here. Fuck! Tell them I'll meet them in twenty minutes." I disconnect the call and turn the car around.

~

Thirty minutes later, I'm sitting in Scarlet Kingston's office, pissed off with my hands fucking tied. Scarlet sits behind her sleek white desk. Her hair is pulled back in a low bun at the back of her head. She's got on jeans that are so tight, they should be cutting off her circulation with a black cashmere sweater and bright red heels, making her look as intimidating in her day-off clothes as she looks in her skirt suits. Becket leans against her desk, listening to Hunter's voice through the speaker phone. In his worn jeans and faded Foo Fighters t-shirt, he seems relaxed and not at all concerned.

The first thing I thought when I saw him was that Belle would love that shirt. "Listen, Hunter. My office is in the process of sending a cease and desist letter that should help going forward, but it's not gonna touch the damage that's been done."

"No, you idiot," Scarlet says to her brother. "That's my office's job. I've pulled everyone in, and we're working on getting a statement out. Once I'm satisfied with the statement, I'll send it to Declan and Annabelle for approval, and we'll release it. This statement should be the only time it's discussed publicly." She looks across the desk at me. "Do not answer any questions. Tell your wife the same thing. This is it. You're not some tabloid whore, and I'm going to destroy everyone who ran this story."

I glare at Scarlet. "Oh. I thought that's what you wanted. Me talking to the press and public, I mean."

The door swings open, and Max Kingston walks in. "No, Declan. We wanted you to step up and become the face of the organization. And you've done that. You've done your interviews. You've answered the questions in the press room and the locker room after games. The public gets Declan the quarterback. They get Declan out in public. They have no right to this. If I have to personally shut this shit down myself, I will."

When Max stops next to my chair, I stand and shake his hand.

"Please tell your wife I'm sorry she has to go through this. And hey, congratulations." He grins. "She's a lucky lady."

"Yeah, we'll see how lucky she feels after she hears this."

36

ANNABELLE

Tommy begged me to stop by Amelia's on the way home from Nattie's house today. He said we needed to buy Rocky cookies for when we see her tomorrow. This kid really thinks we're going to visit his new puppy every day until Goober can come home to live with us.

God help me, it's going to be a very long two months.

We manage to sneak in the door ten minutes before she's ready to close.

"Tommy boy. How ya doing, kiddo?" She winks at him before turning to me. "And how are you feeling, little momma?" Her eyebrow quirks, and she looks at me like she wants to kill someone on my behalf.

I'm not entirely sure she wouldn't.

Amelia hands Tommy a vanilla cupcake and a carton of chocolate milk. "Hey, Tommy, why don't you go sit on the couch so Belle and I can catch up for a minute?"

He grabs the goodies and starts to walk away when I call after him, "What do you say?"

"Thank you, Amelia," Tommy grumbles and then does as he was told.

"How you holding up, Belle? I saw the articles earlier. Those fucking assholes." She turns back to the coffees. "I'm out of your pumpkin. Wanna try my new creation? I'm calling it 'Christmas Cookie.'"

"Sure," I say excitedly before adding, "but decaf, please."

Amelia shakes her head. "I should have known when you asked for decaf last week."

"Yeah, well—" I'm cut off by the sound of knocking. Amelia and I turn to see Leah knocking on the door. She doesn't look quite as put together as usual. Her hair is up in a messy bun, and she's wearing sweatpants and Uggs. Glad to know she doesn't always look perfect.

"Sorry, we're closed," Amelia shouts through the door. Then looks back at me. "Ignore her."

Leah knocks again but gives up after a minute and walks off in a huff.

"That girl is a hot mess. Do you know she lives across the street above the children's boutique?" she asks as she hands me my dessert in a cup. It smells heavenly and is covered in whipped cream and red and green sprinkles and has a tiny candy cane sticking out of it. "I noticed her going up there last week and have paid closer attention since. She's definitely living there."

"It's odd that she's never mentioned it before." I sip my coffee. "Wow, Amelia. This is delicious. Thank you." I glance over, making sure Tommy's okay. "Before I forget, can I get a box of dog cookies, please? Rocky had her babies today, so I think we're going to be visiting her often."

Amelia grabs a pink bakery box and starts filling it up. "Oh, yeah? Did he pick his puppy out?" She looks sweetly over at Tommy.

"He did. The runt of the litter. He's the cutest little brown-and-white thing. And so tiny," I tell her.

"Did he name it yet?" she asks as she tapes the box closed and hands it to me.

I add it to my Mary Poppins bag. "He did. Goober Hart will be joining our family in two months." I smile, remembering it. "Nattie called the puppy a little goober when he tried to walk over his brothers and sisters to nurse, and that was it. Goober Hart was named. It was adorable. I started researching how to get him certified as a therapy dog for Tommy. I hope it works out."

"So, are you okay? I mean, about the articles? Talk about an invasion of privacy." She's pissed for me, and I appreciate it.

"I'm fine. Does it suck? It sucks big old hairy balls. But there's nothing we can do. Dec's losing his mind over this. I swear, I'm more worried about him. Everybody around here forgets that I grew up in the world of professional ballet in New York City. I've grown up watching this happen to people I know and dealt with this to some degree myself already. You have to be willing to give up part of yourself and your privacy to dance at the level I did before coming home. It's no different for Declan. He just refuses to give up his privacy. And I get it. But I don't want him trying to protect us to screw with his career."

Amelia walks around the counter with a big box of cupcakes. "You're pretty level-headed for someone who's supposed to be pregnant with alien quadruplets."

"Shut up," I tell her.

"Is it really twins?" She hands me the box.

"Yup. The Sinclair genes are strong."

Her hard eyes soften. "Lucky kids."

Group Text:

Brina: Belles, Tommy wants the runt, right?
Annabelle: Yes. Goober Hart Sinclair will be coming home with us.
Chloe: I want the all-tan little girl!
Nattie: Do you have a name?
Chloe: No. She needs to have eyes before I name her.
Brina: She has eyes. They're just closed.
Chloe: Potato. Po-tah-to.
Brina: Whatever. Bash is taking the dark one. The boy.
Nattie: That leaves one more. Who's gonna take the last one?
Brina: I don't know. Carys wanted her, but Katherine is so no way.
Annabelle: Smart woman.

37

DECLAN

We spent Christmas Eve at my dad's house. It was loud and crazy, just like our family. I'm fairly sure Tommy was given every dinosaur that ever sat on a store shelf. My dad and Katherine gave Annabelle and me a weekend away in a private hut over the ocean in Jamaica and said they'd happily take care of Tommy while we were there. Nattie got the babies matching onesies that say "Little Sinclair" on them. They're both white with black lettering. There were also tiny pink tutus and little pink socks that look like ballet slippers in a box next to two miniature stuffed footballs. She says she's happily passing on that nickname to her future nieces or nephews.

Apparently, everyone's convinced karma's gonna be a bitch and give me girls. The joke's on them because I would love nothing more than to have two beautiful baby ballerinas who are the spitting image of their mother. Boys, girls, or one of each, I don't care.

Belle and I didn't stay too late, knowing I had a game on Christmas Day. After being told that Santa wouldn't be coming until he was fast asleep, Tommy finally went to bed.

He wasn't happy about it, and I'm pretty sure he was on a massive sugar high. He kept talking about trapping one of Santa's elves like they did in a Christmas show called *Prep and Landing*. This kid has been obsessively flipping back and forth between that and the *Toy Story Christmas Special*. I never thought I'd be able to recite an animated movie word-for-word at my age, but I can.

Every single word.

I'll be happy to give him his new noise-canceling headphones tomorrow. His broke a few weeks ago, and it's been driving Belle nuts ever since.

She drops down next to me on the couch after tucking Tommy in and lays her head on my shoulder. "We've got to wait a little while before bringing all the presents out. Last year, he almost caught me. I don't want a repeat."

I grab her feet off the ottoman and place them in my lap to rub them. Within minutes, my wife is sound asleep, and I'm left sitting on the couch, thinking how good my life is.

~

Christmas morning, we're woken up by a happy squeal, followed by Tommy running in and jumping on the bed. "He came. He came. He came." He pulls the blanket off Belle. "Belles! Santa came. We need to go downstairs." He jumps off the bed and heads for the door.

"Tommy, if you go downstairs, you cannot open anything until we get there, and we need five minutes. Go sit on the couch. We'll be right behind you, bud." He races out of the room, and Belle stands up, stretches, and then races to the bathroom. She's still sick all the time. She's coming up on twelve weeks in her pregnancy, and our fingers are crossed that the morning sickness will stop then.

She comes back out of the bathroom a minute later with a toothbrush in her mouth. "You better get moving, hot stuff. He's not going to wait forever."

She walks back into the bathroom, and I follow. Standing behind her, I lean my hands on the white marble countertop and cage her in. "Thank you, Annabelle."

Belle spits out the toothpaste. "For what? We said no presents."

"For giving me a family." I kiss the top of her head.

"Pretty sure that was your gift to me, Dec." She twists and kisses my lips. "Now brush your teeth and get downstairs. We'll be lucky if he hasn't opened everything already at this rate."

I watch my wife walk away and stare after her. Belle has on cable knit white socks pulled up over her knees, tiny white cotton shorts with little red and white candy canes scattered all over them, a red tank top, and a long white sweater thrown over it. Her hair is in a messy bun, and her face is fresh and glowing.

She looks pure.

She looks beautiful.

She looks like every fucking fantasy I've ever had come to life, and all I can think about is how I want to get her dirty later tonight.

Watching Tommy open his presents is like watching the living embodiment of pure joy. He's as excited about the ninety-nine cent dinosaurs that Belle attached to each tag as he is about the three-foot-tall, animatronic T-Rex.

Not gonna lie, that thing's cool as hell and surprisingly solid.

When he's finished opening his gifts and exploring his

stocking and is happily stuffing his face full of Amelia's double-stuffed vanilla cream donuts, I hand Belle the bag I got for her, and she gives me her mean mom look.

I'm becoming familiar with it.

"'No presents' means no presents, Dec." Then her dimples pop deep as she reaches down on the other side of the couch and hands me a big red box with an elaborate plaid ribbon. "But somehow, I knew you weren't going to stick to our deal. So, this is for you, my love."

"Okay, babe. You go first," I tell her.

I watch as she opens her gift and her eyes start to tear up. "Declan . . . I love it!" She slips off her white sweater and pulls down her new black Philadelphia Kings hoodie, then stands and turns so I can see the back. "Mrs. Sinclair" stretches across her shoulders in a glittering gold script with my number thirteen sparkling beneath it. "It's perfect, Dec."

When she sits back down, she orders, "Now, open yours."

I pull off the plaid ribbon and then rip off the red foil paper. It's a large, framed picture of the moment right after our wedding. Belle and I are in the center with Cooper and Tommy on Belle's left and Nattie and Dad on my right. She's had it matted and framed in a beautiful platinum frame and the date is engraved at the bottom. I put it down and carefully lean it against the ottoman before I cradle her face in my hands. "I love it. Thank you." My lips brush over hers.

"I thought we could hang it when we find a new house."

"Really? I wasn't expecting that." We discussed the idea of moving a few days ago, but I didn't want to push it yet.

Belle shrugs her shoulder. "I know we agreed not to discuss moving," she whispers, not wanting Tommy to hear, "until after Christmas. But I think it's the right move for us.

We need to make sure we're safe. The safest place for us isn't here."

"I'm sorry, baby. I'm so sorry."

Belle shakes her head. "Don't be sorry, Declan. It's not your fault. It's just a fact. I already started looking online, and I don't think we even have to leave Kroydon Hills. We'll just have to move to your dad's side of it." She smiles. "You know, where the giant houses are."

"I love you, Annabelle Sinclair." I pull her into my lap and kiss her again. "Hey, Tommy," I call out.

His curly head turns to me. "What?" He looks confused.

"I love you, little man."

Without thinking, he responds, "Love you too, Declan."

With my hand resting on my wife's stomach, I close my eyes and take it all in.

Life is good.

38

ANNABELLE

Declan had to leave the house hours ago to get to the stadium, and he had no problem getting himself together. I, on the other hand, have had all day and still barely feel like moving. I've forced myself to do it, but man, a cup of coffee would have gone a long way today. I tried to clean up the insanity that is currently my living room, but I don't know why I bothered. Tommy keeps hopping from one toy to the next, so I'm not sure what the point of putting any of them away actually is.

So, instead of fighting it, I gave in. While Tommy happily played in front of the pretty Christmas tree, I laid down on the couch for a few minutes and closed my eyes. Well, I intended for it to only be a few minutes, but when my phone chimes with an incoming text and I see the time, I realize it was more like an hour.

I quickly look over to where I left Tommy, and he's still contentedly playing with all his dinosaur figurines. They've formed an army to try to fight off the three-foot-tall animatronic dinosaur he got from Santa.

Amelia is coming with Tommy and me to the game

today. She doesn't have any family in the area to celebrate the holiday with, so she jumped at the chance to join us. I know she likes watching football, but I like to think it's because she liked the idea of spending Christmas with us too.

Amelia: Merry Christmas, Belle. What time should I meet you today?
Annabelle: You don't have to meet me. Tommy and I will pick you up.
Amelia: Just tell me what time to be at your house, Annabelle.
Annabelle: I can hear your eyes rolling, Amelia. You're a pain in my ass. You know that, right?
Amelia: Good thing your ass is small. What time?
Annabelle: Three-thirty
Amelia: See you then!

Little does she know I told her thirty minutes later than when I want to leave today. It only takes fifteen minutes to walk from Mail Street to our house, so that leaves me plenty of time to drive over and get her before she decides to walk over in the freezing cold temperatures we're seeing today.

Guess I better get a move on.

Before long, I've got Tommy and Rex both dressed in matching Kings jerseys and Santa hats. I've got on my best skinny jeans, black knee-high chunky-heeled leather boots, and my new Mrs. Sinclair jersey. My hair is down, and I paid a little extra attention to it and my makeup. If I'm going to get bombarded by reporters today, I might as well look good while they do it.

I don't know that I'll ever get used to this aspect of loving Declan Sinclair.

I talk a good game, but it's still a little unnerving.

Declan's worth it though.

He's worth everything.

"Come on, Tommy. Get your coat on, please. It's cold outside," I holler into the family room as I fill up my Mary Poppins bag with today's essentials. "Tommy," I call out again when there's no answer.

Where is this kid?

When I walk into the family room, I find him on the couch with his new headphones on, watching *Toy Story That Time Forgot*. It's basically a *Toy Story* Christmas movie. His favorite movie but with extra dinosaurs. The kid is in heaven.

I pull his headphones off and put them around his neck. "Come on, kiddo. We need to go get Amelia."

With a nod of agreement, he grabs his iPad and Rex and follows me to the kitchen. Once I've grabbed my bag and keys, I shove my phone into the pocket of my jeans and lock up.

Once Tommy is buckled up in the back, I turn around to get myself in the car but see Leah strolling up my driveway. She's a mess. Flannel pajama bottoms and Ugg boots are showing beneath her open puffer jacket. Her blonde hair looks stringy and tangled like it hasn't been washed for days. And her mascara is smeared and looks like it ran down her face when she was crying . . . two days ago. Everything about her screams take a shower and sleep it off.

She looks like a Harley Quinn reject, not at all like her typically high-end put-together self.

As she gets closer to the car, I hear her singing, "Santa Baby."

Quickly closing Tommy's door, I force a smile. "Merry

Christmas, Leah." Now that she's closer, I see her hair extensions are also coming out.

Damn. This girl is a hot mess.

"Is it really a Merry Christmas? I mean, I guess for you, it's a perfect Christmas." She gets uncomfortably close, and I smell the alcohol on her breath. "You've got everything you want this Christmas, and I've got nothing."

Okay, this isn't good. "Leah, honey, I'm sorry you're having a bad day. Is there somewhere I can drop you off?"

"That's it. Just get rid of me. That's what people do. That's what he did." She raises her voice, before turning away from me and muttering, but I can't quite hear what she's saying.

"Leah, I'm sorry, but Tommy and I have to go." My instincts are telling me to get the hell out of here. I put one leg in the car, but she grabs my arm.

"I don't think so, Annabelle," she says my name in a cold sneer.

Then she brutally yanks, and I hear the pop of my shoulder dislocating as intense pain washes over me.

This bitch just dislocated my shoulder.

But that doesn't stop her from pulling me out of the car. When I try to push her away, she pulls a small silver gun out of her pocket. "Don't scream, Annabelle. Don't say a word, and I won't hurt him." Then she nods toward Tommy, who's blessedly engrossed in his video and headphones. "You're coming in the house with me right now, and so's the brat in the back. Get moving."

"Why don't we just leave Tommy out here?" I try to convince her. But the gun gets shoved into my side.

"Get him out now," she slowly instructs, and I suddenly realize the very real danger we're in.

I grab my bag with my right arm, holding my left arm

close to me and get out. When I open Tommy's door, I gently pull down his headphones. "Hey, bud. I need to take care of something. I want you to go right to your room when we get inside. Okay? Right to your room and watch your video. Got it?"

My blessedly oblivious little brother smiles big as he nods his head and pops his headphones back on his ears.

I kiss his head. "Love you."

Once we're both out of the car, Leah yanks my bag off my shoulder. "This stays here. God only knows what you carry around in that monstrosity."

I drop the bag on the ground near the car and continue to walk in front of Leah with Tommy in front of me.

"Disarm the alarm. No funny business, Annabelle. I'm watching."

My hands shake as I punch the code into the keypad.

Luckily, she isn't paying any attention to Tommy, and he does as he's told and goes to his room.

"You, sit over there." Leah motions to a couch in the family room.

Once I sit down, I start trying to strategize how the hell I'm getting us out of here.

Shit.

Did I do the right thing sending Tommy upstairs? I wanted him safe, but did I just make this more complicated?

Fuck.

Leah walks into the kitchen, talking to herself about how it's supposed to be her.

She still has a direct view of me from the waist up, but the couch is blocking the rest of me. I slip my phone out of my jeans and shove it in my hoodie in one quick move. Inside the hoodie, I keep my thumb on the bottom button to unlock it and thank God I never upgraded to the newest iPhone.

When she walks back out into the family room, she has a butcher knife in her hand.

My mind whirls, looking for something to use as a weapon when I catch sight of what she's wearing. "Why are you wearing Declan's Notre Dame jersey?" My heart plummets. "Oh God, did you do something to Declan?"

"Uh-uh-uh. No questions from you. I tried to be your friend. It's not easy, ya know? You're a closed-off little thing. Had to stake out the damn coffee shop just to finally meet you. It wasn't hard to do once I moved in across the street. Gave me total access to the studio too."

"You?" I gasp. "You broke into my studio?"

"Jesus Christ, Annabelle," venom spews from her lips. "Yes. Your studio. I had to figure out what it was that made you so damn special. Why he was willing to give you the chance he never gave me. How else was I supposed to change his mind? Hmm? How else was he ever going to realize what a mistake it was throwing me away? Besides, the studio wasn't as easy to get access to as the house."

"You were in my house? How?"

"How? she asks." She spins on me. "Like it was hard. I've had cameras in here and your precious little studio. I've been watching you for weeks. What I can't figure out is what you have that I don't? When Declan told you about me, did he happen to mention that I graduated from Notre Dame in four years with a master's in computer engineering?"

"Declan never talked about you," I answer before good sense kicks in, getting me backhanded across the face. Thank God, she didn't cut me.

When her eyes catch sight of the open box with the onesies Nattie gave us, a guttural scream rips from her curled lips. She picks one up with the tip of the knife, then slices it in half.

"You really are having fucking twins. When you told him that, I'd hoped you were lying to trap him. But not Little Miss Goody-Two-shoes. Of course, you had to go and get pregnant with twins. What a fucking fairy-tale ending for you." She's pacing my family room with a knife in one hand, and I think she has the gun in the back of her jeans. "Do you know most fairy tales have tragic endings? That's going to be the ending you get today. If I can't have him, you can't have him either. Now, let's see. Do you think this knife is too big to cut those babies out of you?"

I hear a car door shut outside and then feel a heavy weight come down on the back of my head before Leah's voice starts to sound like it's in a distant tunnel. "Do you think this is the job of a paring knife or a butcher knife?"

It's the last thing I hear before my eyes start to close.

39

SEBASTIAN

"Come on, Sammy. We've gotta get going." It's Christmas Day, and I'm amazed I convinced my brother to come with me today to the Kings game. We just finished lunch with our pops, and I wanted to get moving, but the two of them are in Dad's office, talking business.

Business I'm happy to not be a part of.

Mafia business.

It's the life Sammy and I both grew up in and the worst kept secret in Kroydon Hills. Dad runs the Philadelphia mob. Has my whole life. It's all Sammy ever wanted to do. Be like the old man. I've gotten as far away from it as I can. With Sammy's help, I even managed to get Dad's blessing to go to college and eventually to medical school.

"Stop whining like a bitch, little brother. I'm coming." Sam opens Dad's door and smiles a shit-eating grin. "See ya, Pops." He salutes our dad.

"Yeah," is my father's response, and we finally get the fuck out of here.

As we both pile into my black H3, I remind my brother,

"You're not carrying, right? You know you can't get into the stadium with a gun."

"Just worry about yourself, Bash. We're good. I'm not a fucking amateur." He ruffles my hair like he's done since we were little. Sammy's ten years older than me, but I'm three inches taller than him.

It evens us out.

"Come on, man. I told you if you wanted to sit in Coach's box, you had to leave the gun at home." I glare at him, refusing to pull out of the driveway.

He lifts his leather jacket up so I can see there's nothing there. "Don't be a dick, Bash. I'm not carrying. Now, let's go watch the Kings kick some ass. Your boy's won me a whole lotta money this season."

"Declan?" I smile at Sam.

Sam nods. "Yeah. He's a good bet."

Sam and I try to get together once a week for dinner, but his schedule's been getting more complicated as Dad loads more on his plate. I'm actually kinda psyched to get to spend today with him.

Kroydon Hills is a small town, and Annabelle Hart—now Sinclair—doesn't live that far from Dad's house. But when I drive by her corner property, something looks off. I turn the corner and pull the car over.

"What the fuck are you doing, Bash? I thought we were in a rush." Sam looks up from his phone. "Why are we stopped at the ballet teacher's house?"

I turn to him. "Do I want to know why you know who lives here?"

"You asked me to look into the break-in at the dance school. Part of that is looking into the owner." He looks back down at his phone and ignores me.

"Listen, I'll be back in a minute," I tell him. Something feels off.

"Whatever. Make it fast."

"Yeah. Let me get right on that." I get out and slam the Hummer door. Belle's front and back car doors are open. That's what got my attention when I was driving by. But when I get close to the car, I spot Belle's Mary Poppins bag lying on the ground, its contents spilling out.

When I check out the car, I see Rex in the back seat and get a bad feeling. Tommy never leaves Rex anywhere. Maybe Belle got sick again. I shut the car doors and shove her stuff back in the bag before picking it up and walking up to the front door.

I raise my fist to knock but hear a woman yelling.

That's not Annabelle.

I crouch down to look in the picture window to the left of the front door.

Fuck.

The air is knocked from my lungs when I see a woman standing in the living room with a big fucking knife and Belles lying unmoving on the floor.

Tommy is nowhere to be seen.

I duck back down and run back to the passenger side of the Hummer, hoping that if the chick looks out the window, she won't see me.

Sammy rolls the window down. "What the fuck are you doing?"

"There's a woman in the house with a knife, and Belles is on the floor," I tell him, trying to suck the air back into my lungs.

"The kid?" Sammy asks.

I shake my head no. "I couldn't see him. What the fuck do we do, man? We need to call the cops."

Sam exits the car quietly, and a switch flips in his eyes. People have talked about my brother for years. I heard someone once say that my brother was a cold-blooded killer. The smiling, laughing big brother I've been around all day is gone. Philly's next mafia boss is in front of me now. "We don't call the cops, Bash. Follow me. Do what I say or stay in the car. Got it?"

"Yeah, man." I shake my head and follow him around the side of the house.

When we hop the fence, he turns to me. "Seriously, your friends have white picket fences? Did we even grow up in the same fucking world?"

I look at him with wide eyes, not believing he's joking right now. He smiles back at me like it's no big deal.

This is so fucked up.

When we get to the back of the house, we have a better view of the room. Sam sticks his head up and tries to assess the situation and then crouches back down. "Okay, some chick who looks like a cheerleader having a bad day is walking around with a kitchen knife in one hand and a tiny pink dance skirt thing in the other. The dance teacher looks like she's knocked out, but I don't see any blood. So, that could be a good thing."

"Thank fucking God." I bless myself with the sign of the cross—something I haven't done in years.

"I've done everything in my power to keep you out of my world your whole fucking life, Bash. What the hell are these people messed up in?"

Sam is pissed, and I don't have an answer for him.

"You're killing me here, Sebastian," he growls.

"What's the plan, Sam?" I don't really care if I'm killing him so long as Tommy and Belle are still breathing and Sammy and I walk out of here.

Sam takes out a lock-picking kit from his jacket and shakes it in my face. "Never leave home without it." He smiles again, and his eyebrows shoot up as he starts to work on the lock.

I hear the moment the lock disengages.

"Listen, little brother. Leave the knife-wielding psychopath to me. You just get the dance teacher and the kid out of the house."

I take a breath. "They have names, you know."

"It's better if I don't know." Sam pops the door open, and the damn alarm dings that a censor's been breached.

Shit.

40

DECLAN

There's an hour left before kickoff. I'm sitting at my locker with my Bluetooth headphones on and my gameday playlist blaring in my ears.

This is what I do.

This is what works for me.

When a call cuts through the music, I turn and reach for my phone on the top shelf of the locker to see who the hell would call me an hour before the game. I see Belle's name and picture flashing across the screen. "Hey, baby. Everything okay?"

No answer.

"Annabelle?"

Still no answer.

I'm about to disconnect the call, assuming she must have butt-dialed me when I hear a voice I haven't heard in years.

"Uh-uh-uh. No questions from you. I tried to be your friend. It's not easy, ya know? You're a closed-off little thing. Had to stake out the damn coffee shop just to finally meet you. It wasn't hard to do once I moved in across the street. Gave me total access to the studio too."

"You broke into my studio?"

"Jesus Christ, Annabelle. Yes. Your studio. I had to figure out what it was that made you so damn special. The studio wasn't as easy to get access to as the house."

I turn to Dean Watkins and grab the front of his compression shirt in my fist. "I need you to get my dad."

"I'm right here, Declan. What do you need?" He walks over with Max Kingston, Beckett Kingston, the team fixer, Dino Morano, and a few off-duty Philly cops who moonlight as security guards. He must see the alarm on my face. "Everything okay?"

I start to answer my dad but hear the voice again.

"Do you know most fairy tales have tragic endings? That's going to be the ending you get today. Now, let's see. Do you think this knife is too big to cut those babies out of you?"

"She's got Annabelle. She's got Belle, and she's talking about cutting the babies out." I look around, not knowing what to do, then turn back to Dean. "Call the cops. Call the cops and tell them to get to my house. My ex-girlfriend, Leighton Devlin, is at my house holding a knife on my wife."

Before Dean can reach for his phone, one of the cops at Dad's back holds his phone to his ear and makes the call.

Dad turns to Max. "Max . . ."

"Go, Coach. Scappy will take over for you. Keep us in the loop and take Dino with you." He slaps Dino on the back and then grabs one of the cops. "Can you get them the hell out of here quickly?"

"Yeah. We got it covered." The cop turns to me. "Come on, Sinclair. I've got a car with me. Come with me, it'll be faster."

I look to my dad, who puts his arm on my back, and we walk out of the room. All the while, I hear my ex-girlfriend in the background ranting about how Annabelle stole what's hers.

The cop and Dino sit in the front of a squad car while Dad and I sit in the back. Dino stays on the phone with his contact at the police station, relaying what I'm telling him.

"I can't hear her anymore. She must have moved away from Belle. Fuck!" I scream, wanting to throw my phone but needing to keep it close. Then there's a click, and the line goes dead. "The phone disconnected," I yell to the car. "I lost her. I lost the fucking call. Can't you go fucking faster?"

Dad grabs my arm that's waving the phone around. "Take a breath, Dec. The cops are going to be there any second. It's going to be okay. We'll be there soon."

41

ANNABELLE

The first thing I realize as I start to wake up is that my head is throbbing.

Why is my head throbbing?

Who is talking?

Why am I on the floor of the family room?

It starts to come back to me in flashes. Leah walking up the driveway. Me telling Tommy to stay in his room . . . Oh, God. Did he listen to me? I try to look around to find him but don't see him anywhere.

I hear a voice say, "I mean, I know he fucks like a beast. It's easy to fall for him, but you deluded yourself into thinking it was real. That was your first mistake. The second was when you thought you were going to be the mother of his children."

Leah walks over and kicks my side. "Like I was ever going to let that happen."

I try to get up, but when I try to put pressure on my arms, I'm reminded that she dislocated my shoulder.

Jesus, how am I going to get out of this?

"He was mine," she continues. "Mine first. I laid claim to

him my freshman year of college. He never dated anyone after me. He waited for me, for the timing to be right."

Leah paces around the room. I'm pretty sure she's talking to herself as much as she's talking to me.

"Guess it's time to force the timing to be right." She spins back to me just as I hear the alarm that sounds whenever a sensor opens.

She quickly looks at the front door before turning to the kitchen.

I try to scramble to my feet and see . . . Bash and his brother push through the door.

What are they doing here?

Bash runs for me, and his brother tries to talk Leah down, who's pulled the gun out of the back of her pants and is now waving both it and the knife wildly in the air.

Bash wraps an arm around my waist and hits my dislocated arm in the process, causing me to stifle a yelp.

When Leah waves the gun our way, he steps in front of me.

"You're aiming a gun at my brother. You don't want to do that," Sam tells Leah in a tone that gives me chills.

She laughs. This fucking nut job actually laughs. Hysterically.

"Oh, yeah? And who exactly are you supposed to be? The cavalry? It doesn't look like you're in any position to tell me what to do, now does it?" She swings her gun between Sam and us. "One of us has a gun in this room, and it's not any of you."

"You have no idea who I am, lady, or the slow, painful ways I can make you beg for death before I finally give in and kill you."

Everything that happens next feels like slow motion.

Leah lunges for Sammy.

Bash tries to intercept Leah, who manages to slash his side with the knife.

Blood shoots everywhere.

Sam lunges to take Leah down, but I get to her first when I swing Tommy's three-foot animatronic T-Rex at her head, causing her to stumble but not fall. That is, until a single shot is fired, hitting Leah dead center between her eyes.

Sammy and I look toward the door, and I think Leah may have hit my head harder than I thought because I see Amelia holding a gun.

Then I throw up.

~

Amelia runs into the room, completely ignoring the very dead body on the hardwood floor. Dropping to her knees in front of me, she tries to help me up. "Jesus, Annabelle. Are you alright?"

"I'm fine. Help Bash."

"You're not fine, Belles," Bash growls at me. "Where the hell is Tommy?"

"I'm up here," he yells as he starts down the steps. "I heard something."

"Amelia?" I ask, and she nods.

"Got it." She gets up and moves to meet Tommy on the stairs. "Hey, Tommy boy. Let's go wait outside, okay?"

How is she this calm?

How is this happening?

"What's wrong with Bash?" Tommy asks innocently from the bottom of the stairs.

Bash groans. "I'm okay now that I know you are too, Tommy boy."

"Yeah," Amelia adds. "He got a boo-boo." She angles Tommy away from where Sam is blocking Leah's body.

Sam waits for Amelia to get Tommy out of the room. "What the fuck happened to listen to me and follow my lead, asshole? At no point did I tell you to lunge for the psychopath with the knife." He check's Leah's pulse, then grabs the blanket off the back of the couch and drapes it over her.

"I was more worried about the gun she'd pulled on you," Bash groans and stands up, his hand covering his bleeding wound.

"Well, next time, listen to me. That was a toy gun." Sam kicks the gun away.

"What?" I ask in a half-scream. "She got me in here with a toy gun?" I stare at the blanket on my living room floor, and wonder when I entered the twilight zone.

"Don't worry about it, dance teacher. That would have fooled most people." He looks around the room. "I'm guessing the cops are gonna be here any second. Wanna get outside so we can get our stories straight with Snow White out there?"

We make our way out front to where Amelia and Tommy are sitting on the steps. My poor brother has no clue how close we came to losing everything today. Maybe I should say my fortunate brother got to stay oblivious to it all.

Amelia stands and eyes Bash's brother. "Who are you?"

"Sam Beneventi. Who are you?" He cocks a brow.

She looks him up and down, unimpressed. "The girl who saved your ass."

"Yeah . . . right. So, what's the story?" Sam looks around at the three of us.

"The story is, I was coming to meet my friend to go to a

football game, knocked on the front door, and nobody answered." Wow. I didn't even hear her knock. "I thought I heard shouting, so I went to the side door. It was wide open. I looked inside, and saw her slash Bash across the stomach, then aim a gun at tall, dark hitman over there."

We all wait for Amelia to continue, but she stares at us first. "Well, you all know the rest. She aimed it at him, and I'm faster and have better aim." She looks at me. "It was self-defense."

"Why did you have a gun?" I ask.

"Where did you learn to shoot like that?" Bash seconds.

"Self-defense" is all she gets to say before the police invade my ordinarily quiet street, and my brother shoots off the steps and wraps his arms around me.

42

DECLAN

"Seriously, man. Can't this goddamn car move any faster?" We're two fucking streets away from the house when we pull up to an orange barrier that's been set up, and the off-duty cop who's driving huffs out his annoyance.

"I'm gonna run the rest of the way," I tell my dad and the other guys before I get out and slam the door behind me.

When I round the corner, there are black-and-white police cars everywhere. Red and blue lights whirl in the dusky sky. Two red ambulances are parked in our driveway, and the police are swarming our yard. The neighbors are all standing out on their porches, staring in disbelief.

It looks like a scene out of a horror movie.

I don't even know which way to move or who to ask for help. I take a step toward the house, and I see men exiting the front door. They're wheeling out a gurney with a body bag on it, and I nearly drop to my knees.

"Annabelle!" Her name is ripped from my lungs.

That can't be her.

It can't.

I'd know.

I'd feel something.

Tommy peaks his head around an open police car door and screams, "Declan!" His headphones are hanging around his neck, his iPad is in one hand, and Rex is firmly clutched to his chest. His puffy black jacket and Philadelphia Kings hat are on and in one piece.

He doesn't look hurt, not physically at least.

I sprint across the yard and pull him away from the car before wrapping him in my arms and lifting him off his feet. "Tommy. Are you okay? Where's Annabelle?"

He squirms to be put down, but I need this more than him right now.

A young police officer approaches us. "Mr. Sinclair?"

"Where's my wife? Where's Annabelle?" I hold Tommy tighter while I wait for the answer.

The cop points to one of the two ambulances. "Mrs. Sinclair is over there."

I don't wait for him to say anything else. I cross the lawn to the ambulance with Tommy still in my arms and say a silent prayer that she's okay.

As I walk up the driveway, one of the ambulances starts backing out, and I yell for them to stop. They don't listen and continue backing out and taking off, but a tall guy with dark hair in a leather jacket walks away from the moving vehicle and over to me as I stop. He looks familiar, but my brain is moving in slow-motion, trying to process everything.

"She's in this one, man." He points to the other ambulance and then follows me to the back where the doors are open. My wife is crying as they wrap her arm in a sling and secure it close to her body.

"Declan," she sobs when she sees me. "Oh my God, Declan." Tears stream down her beautiful face.

I climb in next to her on the opposite side of the EMT. I wipe the hair away from her face, scared to touch her anywhere. "Belle, what happened?"

She leans her head against me and closes her frightened emerald-green eyes.

"Are you okay?" I need to hear it from her. "Where are you hurt, Belle?"

Once the EMT gets her arm positioned the way he wants it, he steps back and looks between us. "We're going to head to the hospital now, Annabelle. I'll give you a minute, but we've gotta go."

"I'm coming with you," I tell them both.

Belle grabs me with her good hand. "No." She shakes her head. "You stay with Tommy. Don't let him out of your sight. Follow me there, but stay with him, Declan."

"Baby." I kiss her head. "My dad's here somewhere. I'll find him. He can take Tommy to the hospital. I don't want to leave you."

"No." She shakes her head. "He stays with you," she insists. "Please."

I look over to the EMT. "Can you give us a minute?"

"Yeah." He nods reluctantly. "Five minutes, then we need to leave. You need to get scanned, Mrs. Sinclair."

When he hops out, the guy from moments ago knocks on the open door. "I don't want to interrupt, but I wanted to tell you they took Bash to the hospital and I'm gonna head over there soon."

"What happened to Bash?" I ask, having no fucking idea what's going on.

"I'm Sam Beneventi, Bash's brother. I'm sure Annabelle can fill you in. But if you want to find me, I'll be at the hospital. I'd say nice to meet you, but not really, considering . . ." He looks around the yard, then back at Belle. "Have you seen Snow White?"

"Who the fuck is Snow White?" I ask the two of them.

Tommy answers from the foot of the ambulance. "That's what Sam calls Amelia," then goes right back to his game, like they're all old friends.

I look between Belle and Sam. "What the hell is Amelia doing here?"

"Excuse me," the EMT walks back over and interrupts, "but we really need to get to the hospital. If you're coming with us, hop in. But only one person can come. If not, you've gotta get out."

I look at Belle, who shakes her head no. "Please stay with Tommy. I love you."

"I love you too." I brush my lips over hers but have a hard time forcing myself to move. I glare at the EMT who won't let me just bring Tommy with us. "Keep her safe," I growl before I get out.

Tommy tucks Rex under his arm and holds my hand. He looks between Sam and me. "Is Bash okay?"

"He's gonna be fine, kid. Chicks dig scars," Sam tells him.

Tommy puts his headphones back on, hits play on his iPad, and then his hand goes right back to mine.

"What the hell happened?" I ask Sam as my dad and Dino make their way over to me.

Sam glances from me to the two of them. "Uncle Dino. What the hell are you doing here?"

Dino smirks. "We'll talk later. Where's the girl?"

"The dead girl or the one who shot her?" Sam asks matter-of-factly.

"Who shot who? Can somebody tell me who's dead?" I spin when a hand comes down on my shoulder.

A detective dressed in khakis and a sports coat with a badge hanging around his neck is standing behind me. "Mr. Sinclair, I'm Detective Schultz. I'm sorry to do this now, but we need to ask you a few questions."

"No," Dino tells him. "He's going to the hospital to be with his wife. He'll come down to the station tomorrow." He places himself between the detective and me.

Detective Schultz acquiesces and gives me his card. "If you think of anything or want to talk before then, give me a call. My number's on the card."

I look around at the people surrounding me. "I need to get to Annabelle."

Sam motions to Bash's black Hummer. "I'm leaving now if you want a lift."

"Yeah, man. Thanks," I tell him.

"I can take Tommy with me," my dad offers.

"No. I've got him. I just want to get to the hospital." I shift toward Sam. "Can we leave now?" I ask, impatient to get to my wife.

Sam nods and walks away.

Dad watches Sam leave, then turns to me. "Call if you need anything. Katherine is going to pick me up here, and I'll find you at the hospital as soon as I can."

"Thanks, Dad." He hugs me quickly, and then Tommy and I get into Bash's car.

~

"So wait, let me get this straight." I glance in the rearview of the Hummer to make sure Tommy still has his headphones on. Once I'm confident he can't hear me, I continue, "She had a knife pulled on Belle when you and Bash got there? Bash got in the way, stepping in front of Belle and was stabbed in his side? You rushed her, and Amelia fucking shot her from the kitchen door?"

"That about sums it up." He glances my way, then shrugs. "Annabelle's shoulder is definitely dislocated. But it could have been a whole hell of a lot worse."

"And they think Bash is gonna be fine too?" I'm having a hard time wrapping my head around this shit storm.

Sam pulls the big black-on-black Hummer into a parking spot in front of the Kroydon Hills Hospital's Emergency Department. "Yeah. The cut is superficial. He should get a few stitches out of it."

"I owe you, man. I can't even think about what would have happened if you and Bash hadn't gotten there when you did. If there's ever anything you need..." I offer Sam my hand.

He smiles at me and turns the car off.

"Win us the big trophy some season soon, and we'll call it even."

43

ANNABELLE

I feel Declan's hand holding mine before I even open my eyes to see him. The room is dark and quiet, and my mind is flooded with memories of the night my parents died when I rushed home to sit by Tommy's side in this same hospital. I have to suppress the shiver that runs down my spine. Once the adrenaline wore off earlier, everything hurt. The EMT was right, my shoulder was dislocated, and I have a severe concussion.

Because I'm pregnant, I can't have anything stronger than acetaminophen to help with the pain. They were able to x-ray my shoulder with extra lead aprons to protect the babies. They also insisted on an MRI to make sure there was no internal bleeding but were able to do what they called a fast scan which only took a few minutes. The machine's humming vibrations managed to put me to sleep but I don't know for how long.

I squeeze Dec's fingers, and he jolts up.

"Hey," he whispers. "You're awake." He leans over the hospital bed and kisses my lips gently. "Want me to get the nurse?"

"No." I look around the room for a clock but don't see one. "How long was I out?"

Dec glances down at his phone. "About a half an hour."

"Where's Tommy?" I can't imagine how he's handling all this.

Declan brings my hand up to his face and presses his lips against my fingers. "He's with Nattie in the cafeteria. He was hungry. Once Dad got here, he called the crew. Everyone is here. How do you feel, baby?"

I close my eyes, and sit for a second before telling him, "Like someone put my brain in a blender." I'd laugh if I weren't scared it would hurt. "Thank you."

"For what? This was my fault. You'd never have been on Leighton's radar if it weren't for me." His eyes drift away from me.

"Declan, look at me." Those inky-blue eyes are holding on to so much anguish, it's heartbreaking. "Leah's actions were her own. Not yours. You had no way of knowing that someone you dated five years ago would go crazy now. She lied about her name. She lied about what she was doing here. She was completely delusional. She thought once she got me out of the way, you'd be all hers. There was no way you could have known." I try to pull our joined hands back to my face, but he won't let me.

"When you called me . . ." He leans forward against the bed. "Jesus, Belle. When you called me, and I heard what she was saying . . ." A single tear falls down his cheek. "You always say that I can't leave you. Well, it goes both ways, baby. Please don't ever leave me."

"I didn't even know the call went through. I was trying to call the police before she knocked me out." I manage to pull my hand away and cup his face. "I'm sorry if I scared you."

He covers my hand with his and leans his face into it.

"Sam told me what happened once he and Bash got there. Are you ready to talk about what happened before that?"

"I was so scared I'd never see you again. She caught us when we were getting in the car, held a gun to my side and forced us into the house. I sent Tommy upstairs, and she didn't stop him, so I don't think he saw anything. Is he okay? Does he seem upset?" I ask, knowing I may never forgive myself for the answer.

"He's fine, Belle. His only questions have been about when he can see you and whether Bash's boo-boo is fixed," Dec laughs a small, pitiful sound.

"Oh, God. How's Bash?" I try to sit up, but pain shoots behind my eyes, knocking me backward.

Declan stands to move my pillow behind my head before sitting next to me on the edge of the bed. "According to Sam, Bash is hitting on the nurses. He got twelve stitches, but it didn't hit anything internally. He's gonna be out of here today. You, on the other hand, have to spend the night."

There's a quiet knock at the door before Bash's head pokes in. "How's the patient?" He looks between Declan and me and then takes in all the machines. "I can come back later."

"No," I tell him quickly. "Please. Come in here and show me you're okay." I feel the tears I've been trying to hold back since I woke up finally break free.

Bash walks to stand next to Dec, followed by Sam, who shuts the door before leaning against it.

Declan gets up and hugs Bash. "I can't thank you enough, man." Then he looks over to Sam. "Both of you. You saved my family."

The flood gates open, and there's no holding back my tears. All three guys look at me, worried, as I hiccup between heavy sobs that make my head hurt worse. "Bash, I don't know how to thank you."

"Then don't." Sebastian runs a hand through his dark hair, followed by a painful wince. He's going to have to be careful about the way he moves for a while. "Are the babies okay?"

"Yes. Both babies are perfect. I had an ultrasound as soon as I got here." I point to one of the machines monitoring me. "See that?"

Sam pushes off the door to look closer.

I smile at two of my three heroes. "That's the babies' heartbeats." I lay my hand back down, and Declan laces his fingers with mine. "They're safe because of the two of you and Amelia."

Sammy smirks. "So, if they're boys, you'll name them Sammy and Sebastian, right?" He winks.

"I thought I was winning a trophy for you," Declan taunts.

Bash gently shoves his brother. "Don't listen to him. Have you seen Amelia?"

"No." My eyes meet Declan's, and he shakes his head no. "Would you let me know if you hear from her? I've got to stay overnight but should be out tomorrow."

Bash agrees, then leans down and kisses my forehead. "Do you want me to tell the horde of people I'm assuming are in the waiting room that you're awake?"

I exchange a look with Declan and then agree. As Bash straightens to leave, I grasp his hand and look from him to Sam. "Thank you. Thank you for everything. You're my heroes."

"Don't go ruining my reputation, ballerina." Sam's lips tip up into a crooked smile before he looks at Declan. "I want that trophy, quarterback." He quietly exits the room, and Bash follows him out.

A few minutes later, Nattie and Cooper knock on the door, and Tommy runs through. "Slow down, Tommy boy. Belles doesn't feel great," Nattie gently warns him.

Declan moves so Tommy can sit in the chair next to the bed. Nat sits on the bed by my feet, and Cooper stands behind her before speaking, "They're only letting two of us in at a time, but they made an exception for the little man."

"Are you hurt, Belles? Did they give you band-aids?" Tommy asks innocently.

"I'm fine, bud. I just have to wear this sling for two weeks, and then I'll be good as new." Not totally accurate, but he doesn't need to know about the concussion or bruised ribs.

Tommy eyes all the tubes and wires connecting me to the machines. "What's that?" he asks, pointing at the babies' heart monitor.

"That's the babies' heartbeats. See?" I point up. "Baby A Sinclair is red, and Baby B Sinclair is blue."

Tommy thinks about that for a minute. "Belles, are you a Sinclair now?"

"I guess I am," I tell him, looking around at Declan, Nattie, and Cooper.

Tommy's eyes do the same before he says, "You're all Sinclairs. And the babies are gonna be Sinclairs too?"

Declan sits on the arm of the chair and squeezes Tommy's shoulder. "That's what happens when you get married, bud."

"But I'm not a Sinclair. Can I be a Sinclair too?" There's a gasp in the room before those eyes that look so much like mine beg me to say yes.

I look at Declan, not knowing what to say.

"You wanna change your name, bud? You want to be Tommy Sinclair instead of Tommy Hart?" Dec asks him gently.

"I want both," he tells us with the innocence only a child can possess.

Cooper moves closer to Tommy. "I think that sounds perfect, little man. Tommy David Hart Sinclair. It has a nice ring to it." He moves behind Tommy, who's smiling as proud as a peacock right now.

"Tommy Hart Sinclair." Nattie kisses his cheek. "Perfect!"

Tommy grimaces and wipes away the kiss.

"We'll get it done as soon as we can, bud," Declan tells him.

"The Sinclairs are gonna have a lot of Harts," my little brother adds, having no idea how right he is.

44

ANNABELLE

Two days later, I'm at Coach and Katherine's house, losing my mind a little. My house is a crime scene, and we aren't allowed back in yet. I'm okay with that because I don't know how I'm going to feel walking back into the place that used to hold some of my happiest memories but now also holds my worst nightmare. I've been waited on hand and foot since I got out of the hospital yesterday, and it's driving me a little crazy. For someone like me who's not used to that, it's not easy.

I'm sore, not dying.

But I have to remind myself that it's coming out of a place of love. At the moment, I'm sitting on the couch with Cooper and Linc, watching an *Avengers* marathon while Declan is at practice. This room is the epitome of comfort, with an oversized, buttery-soft brown leather sectional sofa in the center and a big-screen television over the fireplace. The guys started a fire when we turned on the first *Captain America* movie, and it's been roaring since. I'm warm and as comfortable as I'm going to get right now. "So, are you guys excited about the next phase of your training? Still glad you're pushing to be SEALS?"

Linc is sitting at the far end of the couch in one of the built-in recliners, looking pretty comfy himself in a Navy hoodie and sweats, his buzz cut already starting to grow in. He shrugs. "I'll miss the home-cooked meals again, but I'm ready. It's going to be harder to get back to the rigidity of training after spending two weeks with y'all."

I love his southern accent.

Coop doesn't look as excited. "I hate that I won't be able to fly home when the babies are born. I'm still happy with my decision, but missing everything definitely makes it harder."

"We'll fly out, Coop. You'll get weekend leave, and we'll fly out to you. We'll make it work. I promise." I pull the throw blanket up a little higher and feel ready to cry for the ten millionth time today. Fucking hormones. "Now pass me some damn popcorn. The twins are hungry."

Popcorn immediately hits my face. "Did you just throw popcorn at me?" I ask, astonished.

"Welcome to the family, Belles." Cooper's smile grows right before he gets beaned in the head with a peanut M&M. "What the fuck?" he yells at Murphy and Bash, who've just entered the room.

"We don't throw food at ladies, Coop. You're never gonna get a girl that way. Do we need to work on what you need to do to get laid?" Murphy's laughing so hard at his own joke he doesn't see the slap coming to the back of his head from Carys, who walked in behind the guys.

"Cooper doesn't have time for girls. He's in training, you moron." She walks around the couch and sits down between Coop and me. Carys grabs the bowl of popcorn from Coop's lap and places it in mine. "Please tell me guys get smarter as they get older, Annabelle?"

"The right guys do," I chuckle.

Everyone finds a spot to sit down as we watch Captain America and Iron Man battle it out against each other. Just as I pop a piece of popcorn in my mouth, the doorbell rings. Carys checks an app on her phone. "Amelia's at the door."

"Oh, thank God." I get up gingerly from the couch and rush as much as my body will let me. Once I open the front door, I see Amelia standing on the porch in her jeans and hoodie. Her black hair is held back by a red bandana, and her hands are shoved in her pockets. "You're here. Are you okay? You've got to be freezing," I say, my breath visible in the cold air as I step aside for her to come in.

We hear the groans coming from the family room as I guide us into the formal living room to give us some privacy. "Wow. Sounds like the whole team's here." Amelia sits down on the couch across from the giant Christmas tree, then turns to face me. "Are you okay? I mean, I read your texts. So I know you're going to be okay. But are you really okay?"

"That's a whole lot of okays." She stares at me, unblinking. I guess making light of the situation isn't going to work. "How about I'm doing pretty well, and the babies are fine? How are you? You've gotten my texts, but you haven't answered a single one." I sit down next to her, careful to not jostle my slinged arm.

"I'm alright. The cops agreed it was self-defense and won't be pressing charges." She looks uncomfortable. Not nervous, but something's up.

"Is there more?" I ask, worried for her.

Amelia cocks her head to the side and thinks about it before answering. "There is, but I'm not ready to talk about it yet. I don't know if I ever will be."

"I'll be here when you are," I tell her honestly.

"Yeah. I guess saving someone's life means you're stuck with them, right? Are you like my bitch now or something? Oh, I know. Can I name one of the babies?" A smile is plastered on her face, but it's not genuine.

I guess I'll have to wait her out until she's ready to talk. "Nope. No naming babies. Bash and Sammy already tried that."

"Oh yeah? How is the tall, dark, and handsome hitman and his kid brother?" There's a glimmer in her eye. That's interesting.

"Bash is good. He's already coming up with stories to tell when someone asks about his new scar. And I guess Sam's good. We haven't seen him since the day it happened." I don't think any of us want to relive that day.

Amelia nods in agreement. "Scars are cool."

"That's what I said!" is yelled from the other room.

The two of us laugh. "No privacy in this house, huh?" she asks.

"Nope. Declan has a realtor lined up for us later this week. We're gonna check out a few houses." Not much of a choice now.

"Wow. Is Kroydon Hills losing its favorite *it* couple?" she asks.

Declan walks into the room, his gym bag in his hand and a compression shirt on, showcasing every single one of his delicious muscles. He leans down and kisses my head. "Kroydon Hills hasn't seen the last of the Sinclairs."

We hear groaning coming from the other room. "So cheesy," hollers Murphy, I think.

Coach enters the room. "How come when I ask one of them to do something, they can't hear me, but when they're eavesdropping, they can hear every word?" He kisses my head in the same spot Dec just did and smiles at Amelia. "You staying for dinner, Amelia? We're ordering out tonight, and Katherine ordered more than we could possibly eat."

"Thanks, Mr. Sinclair—" She's interrupted by Coach, who's ignoring the fact she was obviously about to decline his invitation.

"Perfect. We'll put out more plates." He looks around at the three of us. "One piece of advice when you go house hunting. Make sure there's plenty of room for a big table. The best days of your life will be the days that table is full."

I watch him as he walks into the kitchen and mentally move a big dining room up my list of wants for the new house.

~

*S*omehow, the girls ended up hearing about dinner, and it turned into a madhouse with Nattie, Sabrina, and Chloe coming over too. Everyone was here, and Coach was right. It was a great night. Fifteen of us fit around Coach's big reclaimed wooden table that's fit for a king. Well, for quite a few kings. Once everyone left or went to bed, Declan and I curled up in the white princess bed in Nattie's old room. It's comfortable, but I feel like we're going to dirty it up. Everything in this room is white or grey. Soft white bedding and gauzy white material hang down the canopy covering the bed. Sheer white curtains frame the windows and brush against a plush grey rug. Even the furniture is white.

"You know there's no way your sister picked this stuff out, right?" I soak it all in. "Nattie loves color."

"Yeah. Dad had a hard time letting her grow up." Dec climbs into the bed next to me, then pulls the blanket up.

"Do you think I'll be the same way? Not wanting to let Tommy and the babies grow up?"

Declan made sure to start sleeping on my left side since my right arm is the one that's recovering. I lean my head against his chest and tell him with complete sincerity, "I think Tommy and our babies are going to be the luckiest kids in the world to have you on their team, loving them. I love you, Declan. Thank you for never giving up on me."

His lips brush over mine. "I'm the lucky one, baby." He settles himself in the bed, before whispering, "Love you, Belle."

"Forever, Dec."

EPILOGUE
DECLAN

One Year Later

It's surreal. Standing here for the second year in a row, watching as the confetti floats down on the screaming stadium. Someone just dumped an entire cooler of Gatorade over Dad's head on the sidelines. The whole thing is so intense. We were the underdogs when we won the big game last year. No one expected us to win. In some ways, it's easier to go into a game where you're expected to lose because you can only go up from there. The Philadelphia Kings do well when we're the underdogs. In the locker room before last year's big game, Dad called it fate.

Amor Fati.

We won that day.

I kept my promise to Sam Beneventi last year, and I bet he's fucking ecstatic to see us do it again today.

Two days after the win, Belle and I closed on a house a few minutes away from my dad and Katherine's. It's a five bedroom and now has a fully finished basement with a home gym on one side and a dance studio area on the other. We also made sure it was soundproofed.

I got my tattoos a few days later. Everyone's been talking about them this season. One bicep says "Amor Fati" with the Sinclair family crest beneath it. The other bicep has an olive branch wreath with "Memento Mori" written inside. I like to think fate brought me to Belle, and I want to cherish every fucking minute of the life we have because it can all end too soon.

Nothing's promised. It's earned.

"Declan. Declan." One of the female sideline reporters grabs me. "How does it feel to win two championships in a row?"

"It feels amazing, Cindy." I look around at the crowds starting to make their way onto the field.

"When you were first drafted to Philadelphia, there was a lot of talk about you playing for your dad and whether you earned your spot. What do you want to say to the people who questioned you now?" she asks as she shoves the microphone back in my face.

"I say, I hope they enjoyed the game." I see Belle running toward me. "I'm sorry. I see my wife."

Reporter forgotten, I open my arms as Belle walks into my embrace. She's wearing a new Mrs. Sinclair hoodie since the one I gave her last Christmas had to be cut off when she was in the hospital. Her long hair is up in a ponytail. One hand is holding Tommy's hand. He's totally decked out in his Sinclair jersey and Kings hat with Rex clutched close to him in matching gear. Belle's other arm is wrapped around the older of my two baby girls. Everly has on a mini-Sinclair jersey with black leggings covering her chunky legs, pinks socks, and a pink tutu because . . . well, that's how my wife dresses the girls. Nattie is next to her, holding

Gracie, who puts her arms out to me, immediately wanting her daddy.

Yeah. They've got me wrapped around every single one of their fat little fingers.

Gracie is younger by two minutes and much quieter than Everly. They're like night and day—two gorgeous little baby girls with their momma's emerald-green eyes and blonde Sinclair curls. Coop likes to joke and say they look more like him and Nattie than me, but I don't care. As long as they look like Belle, I'm thrilled. The girls have special-ordered noise-canceling headphones on their little heads and are looking around with wide eyes at this spectacle.

Annabelle stretches up on her toes and kisses me. "Nice job, number thirteen. I got a little nervous for a hot minute there. Way to bring it home." She leans into my ear and whispers, "You know what you get tonight?"

I wrap my hand around her neck and hold her face to mine. "What do I get tonight, baby?"

"Anything you want." She bites my ear and smiles that smile I love more than life.

The guys walk out onto the field, offering their congratulations. My brother pounds my back. "Thanks for making it to the big game this year. It was really nice of you to play it in Cali this time." He hugs me. "Seriously. Great game, man." Cooper being stationed in California has been challenging. He just qualified for the SEALS and now has another year-plus of training to undergo.

The quarterback from the other team walks over to me. "Good game." He shakes my hand. "You're a lucky man, Sinclair."

"Thanks."

It's nice to win.

It's great to be able to play football professionally.

And he's right, I am one of the lucky ones.

But what makes me truly fortunate is in my arms right now.

It's the people who are standing here with us.

It's my family.

It's this woman whose love I'll never take for granted.

Whose love I earned one inch at a time.

THE END

WHAT'S NEXT?

Sebastian's book, Under Pressure will be releasing in September, 2021.
Want to see what everyone's favorite broody, football player is up to?

Preorder here - https://books2read.com/KKH4

Prologue
Sebastian

Superstition is a funny thing. Very few people would admit to believing in superstition, yet most of us abide by the laws of it, at least on some level. This is especially true when you grow up in an Italian family, like mine. I've had red wine in my glass at dinner since long before I turned twenty-one because it's bad luck to toast with water. I'd never throw my hat down on my bed because that's what's done when you die. Rain on your wedding day or the day of your funeral is considered good luck—God's blessing. My Pops was full of this shit. My Nonna, my dad's mother, still believes in every last superstition she grew up with in Calabria before she and Pappa moved to Philadelphia over sixty years ago.

Growing up, my dad would randomly spout off about it.

I don't know if he actually believed it, but he respected it.

I wonder what he'd think about the snowstorm of the century that's going on for his funeral today. They actually called it thundersnow on the news this morning. They're calling for nearly a foot of it before the end of the day, but that's not slowing the mourners down. When the Don of Philadelphia dies, everyone shows up. My family. THE family. My friends. The FBI. You name it, they're here. And here I sit, under a canopy across from his black and gold casket. Nonna is sitting between my brother, Sammy, and me, and, on my other side, sits Emma. My friends not so affectionately nicknamed her Trainwreck a few years ago. She's holding tightly to my right hand as if her life depended on it.

Up until today, it might have.

My friends stand off to the left at the back of the crowd. I can feel their eyes burning into Emma right now. They don't get it. They've always been free. Free to choose the life they want to live. Free to choose who they want to love. We all moved out at eighteen, and for them, that was the epitome of freedom. For me, it was just a holding zone for the life that was being forced down my throat the same way they are lowering my father into the ground today.

Today is a day for mourning, but what does it say about me that I hope that today's mourning leads to tomorrow's freedom?

When I glance over at my friends, I see her, and I know what I have to do.

I know what freedom means.

I know what choice I have to make.

Bash's brother, **Sam Beneventi**'s book, Rise Of The King, will be releasing on December 9, 2021.
Stayed tuned for the blurb and cover reveal.

Preorder - https://books2read.com/RotKing

WANT TO READ MORE ABOUT THE KINGS OF KROYDON HILLS?

They are all available to read FREE in Kindle Unlimited.

Go back and see where it all began with Brady & Nattie, in All In.
1-Click: https://books2read.com/KKH1

Nothing prepared me for meeting Brady Ryan.

I've been called football royalty my entire life.

Born into a family that has experienced the highs and lows of the game.

Constantly surrounded by football players. Professional players. College Players. Coaches.

I'm supposed to be spending this year finding myself, but can I do that with him by my side or is he just another player?

Natalie Sinclair came into my world and changed my life.

Her father was the new professional coach in town, and her twin brother played on my team.

This tiny dancer fit into our circle of friends like she was the missing piece.

Neither of us might have been looking for something serious, but that changed the day we met.

Now nothing can keep her from me. Not her twin brother. Not the threats of a jealous ex. Not even myself. Now I just need to convince her.

She's it for me. She's the end game.
I'm all in.

Watch our favorite ginger giant fall in love, in More Than A Game.
1-Click: https://books2read.com/KKH2

Aiden Murphy has always made me nervous.
He's larger than life. Always the center of attention.
I'm the opposite.
I hate to have everyone's eyes on me.
He lives his life in public, and I like to live behind the scenes.
I had never been on his radar one single day in his very loud life, and then I was...

What is it about Sabrina Cabot that throws me off my game?
This uptight senator's daughter is the exact opposite of the type of woman I'm typically attracted to... and maybe that's a good thing.

She makes me want to be a better man.
To get more serious about life.
To slow down.
To give more.
But will she be willing to give me her heart?

At some point, life has to be more than a game.

ACKNOWLEDGMENTS

M ~ Always.

Kelly & Dena ~ The two of you keep me sane. Love you both.

Deana ~ There has never been a better big sister. .

Mom ~ Every Momma-bear instinct Annbelle had was based on the way you fought for us.

To my PA, Savannah ~ Three down. Thank you for keeping me organized and for having all the answers. Thank you for making my crazy ideas a reality. I'm so lucky to have found you when I did. I hope you know you are stuck with me.

To my one and only Alpha, Tammy ~ You are the best! Thank you so much for every time you pushed to dig deeper. Thank you for every tweak. For every comma. For every funny note.

Brianna ~ Our brainstorming sessions are LIFE! Thank goodness for voice memos, and thank goodness for our mutual forced friendship. I'm lucky to have you in my corner.

My Betas, Brianna, Brittany, Vicki, Kelly & Heather ~ I cannot thank you enough. Thank you for taking the time out of your own crazy schedules to read Belles & Dec. I cannot express how grateful I am, or how much your notes fuel me.

My Street Team, Kelly, Shawna, Vicki, Ashley, Heather, Oriana, Shannon, Nichole, Tash, Nicole, Hannah, Meghan, Amy, Christy, and Emma ~ Thank you, ladies, for loving these characters and this world.

Golden, you are so talented! The cover you created for Annabelle & Declan is beautiful. Thank you for taking my idea and walking me through what we needed to do to make it a reality.

Kiki and all of the amazing ladies at The Next Step PR. Thank you so much for all of your guidance. I'm so lucky to have the opportunity to work with you.

To all of the Indie authors out there who have helped me along the way – you are amazing! This community is so incredibly supportive, and I am so lucky to be a part of it!

Thank you to all of the bloggers who took the time to read, review, and promote Always Earned, Never Given.

And finally, the biggest thank you to you, the reader. I hope you enjoyed reading Belles and Declan's love story as much as I enjoyed writing it.

ABOUT THE AUTHOR

Bella Matthews is a Jersey girl at heart. She is married to her very own Alpha Male and raising three little ones. You can typically find her running from one sporting event to another. When she is home, she is usually hiding in her home office with the only other female in her house, her rescue dog Tinker Bell by her side. She likes to write swoon-worthy heroes and sassy, smart heroines with a healthy dose of laughter thrown and all the feels.

STAY CONNECTED WITH BELLA

Amazon Author Page: https://amzn.to/2UWU7Xs

Facebook Page: https://bit.ly/2Pjd734

Reader Group: https://bit.ly/34tirVE

Instagram: https://bit.ly/3wJxm9Z

Bookbub: https://www.bookbub.com/authors/bella-matthews

Goodreads: https://bit.ly/3yW83Um

Newsletter: https://bit.ly/38eBKVF

Made in the USA
Middletown, DE
02 July 2021